FLOOD TIDE

FLOOD TIDE
Ana Schnabl

**Translated from the Slovenian
by Rawley Grau**

DIVIDED

Published in the United Kingdom by Divided in 2025.

Divided Publishing
Rue de Manchesterstraat 5
1080 Brussels
Belgium

Divided Publishing
Deborah House
Retreat Place
London E9 6RJ
United Kingdom

https://divided.online

First published in Ljubljana, Slovenia in 2020 by Beletrina Academic Press as
Plima. Translation made with the support of the Slovenian Book Agency.
Copyright © Beletrina Academic Press 2020
Copyright © Ana Schnabl 2025
Translation copyright © Rawley Grau 2025

Cover image: Richard Kern, *Alisa Smokes*
Designed by Alex Walker
Printed by PBtisk, Příbram

ISBN 978-1-7395161-5-4

August, *August,* is the cruellest month. —Dunja Anko

1

Branches from the old pine tree were leaning over the white balcony wall. Long, heavy branches, with the cones barely holding on. At the first gust of wind the branches would strike the metal railing and a cone would fall off. If it fell onto the balcony, it would roll across the tiles; if below, then across the paving stones of the walkway to the building. And not just cones, clumps of pine needles, too, would succumb. The male cones sprinkled granules of yellow pollen across the orange balcony tiles, pollen that had missed its chance to find a scale on a female cone, and when wind blew again, more gently, it collected into beads. Everywhere was the smell of trees, and something else too, but what, exactly? Spring soil, worms, grass (sodden at first, then dry), exhaust fumes, seafood risotto? All that of course, definitely, but also his lavishly applied deodorant, an overemphatic blend of eucalyptus and grapefruit and juniper.

It was an unpleasant, terribly unpleasant, smell, and more than once her mother and father and she herself would have headaches from the fumes, but there was no talking to him about it. So don't smell it, he would always say. Just hold your nose, he would snarl, and look daggers at them.

The poorly sealed glass pane in the balcony door, which spring after spring let the damp into the living room, rattled as he stepped onto the balcony and slid in his slippers across the ceramic tiles. Again the pollen swirled behind him. Rearranging itself. Tilting his head, he studied the design spilling across the floor. It was not to his liking, so he angrily smeared it with his heel into one of his own: he aimed for symmetry, always and everywhere, although by then he must have known that symmetry could not last, that something – life, fate, nature – soon spoiled it. And sure enough, the wind blew in like a bullet. At once the picture turned a creepy yellow and some of the pollen returned to its source, back to the tree. With any luck, to the female cones.

He waved his slender hand in front of his nose, the fingers spread but loose, in an exaggerated fan-like gesture, exactly as his idol did, that outrageously notorious singer, whenever he performed on a high stage overlooking a sea of people. Under those circumstances, theatricality was a necessity, the only way for any gesture to be seen. But on a nameless balcony . . . well, dreams and passions were beyond his skills of mimicry.

He also tried to dress like the singer. He *tried*, but all he could manage was a cheap and rather eclectic approximation. Those narrow black trousers of leather or silk became his father's too-wide ash-grey jeans cut off above the ankles; instead of the white, collarless shirt, also silk, he had to make do with a T-shirt promoting Primorska Meats or Kraš Chocolates, tucked deep below his belt, while the substitute for the leather jacket with a few hundred platinum studs and chains was a dark-brown corduroy coat with a gold zipper. The socks were indeed white (a great success) but, sadly, so were the trainers. Black trainers were not to be found so far from America, so far from prosperity. And if he expected his parents to buy him a pair of elegant black leather shoes, of which there were plenty in the shops, he would have to behave more like an adult, they chided; on a teenager's feet such shoes would look like a bad joke, they teased. The most superstar thing on him, therefore, was a long silver-plated chain, on which he had hung a dog tag engraved with a fictional soldier's name, blood type and Rh factor, which he had purchased at a stand by the beach.

He reached for a branch that was pressing against the shutters of his bedroom window – wood scraping wood, which had been rasping its own slow, irksome rhythm ever since he'd got home from school – and pushed it down, anchoring it for the thousandth time beneath the window ledge. This Sisyphus should be thought lucky, at least happy: his mother had forbidden him to cut back the branch, which to her seemed charming, even atmospheric – she *so enjoyed looking at it* from her armchair in the living room – and his mother's whims had to be respected.

Before leaning on the railing with his elbows, he first twisted back distrustfully one last time: the trapped branch had swayed slightly – *if that damn fucker gets loose again . . .* – yes, this or something similar her irritated brother must have muttered.

Resting on the cool metal, he then raised his sharp shoulders and crossed his right leg in front of his left. Licking his lips, he touched his left trouser pocket, where he kept a metal case containing cigarettes from a variety of sources, begged, pilfered or extorted, including one that was Italian and another French. He felt like a smoke, of course he did, but he needed to be careful. If his father caught him, he'd give his son a conspiratorial smoker-to-smoker grin and maybe even compliment his style, but if his mother caught him, oh God, there'd be hell to pay for sure. So he rubbed his face, dug his hand into his black curls and chose three, which he straightened and smoothed between his index and middle fingers. He kept checking the car park and the access road up to it, anxiously craning and contorting his neck, hopping left and right along the wall, standing on tiptoe, bending his knees, in the hope of finding a clear sightline between the trees and rhododendrons, a narrow tunnel with none of those damn branches, through which he would be able to observe her and her mother approaching, but there was no good angle. At least not for him, not for his poor eyesight, to which, out of vanity, he had denied the use of glasses for two years now, ever since the optician issued the prescription. She, on the other hand, from the patch of green next to the access road, concealed behind an enormous metal bin for recycling paper, had a good view of him. A very good view.

She could even see him shake his left pocket to make sure his lighter was in the case, and the relish, the criminal dexterity, with which he finally lit up, never mind the consequences. He was flicking the ash as far as he could from the balcony, but in vain; the wind blew it back at the building every time, flakes sticking stubbornly to his clothes. Every so often he would plant the arm he was smoking with in his other hand and crook his elbow, straighten his back like a peacock and click his slippered heels. She giggled, partly because he looked funny, posing like a prince, but mostly because she envied him: he could have been an excellent dancer – she was sure of it; he would have been brilliant, just like Michael. He had a rare gift – he had already penetrated the choreography of smoking, of keeping things neat and of walking, at times visible simply in the way he sliced a pizza. She often watched him from behind the door, open just a crack, of their shared room: there, he allowed his gift to blossom into improvised but captivating variations of hip-hop, jazz dance, vogueing, and whatever else was *it*. His economy and precision, his suppleness and determination, but also his softness and strictness, speed and clarity, his presence and magnetism, and her, well, stiff legs and arms that had a tendency, as their aunt had once determined, *to flail* and, as far as dance lessons went – *which your family can't afford anyway* – were simply too unwieldy. Too *angular*.

His cigarette glowed red, burnt right down to the filter – how very French, but also how Hollywood, how manly – and he stubbed it out on a rusty part of the railing where a mark would hardly be noticed, blending in, as it did, with the overall scenery of decay. But just when he was about to toss the butt towards the patch of green with the bins (and directly at her), he flinched. More precisely, *they both* flinched.

Ciao, Jovanka! The shout came from the little walkway hidden behind the cypress trees, which connected the car park of their building to the car park of the building next door. It was their mother. *Let's get together tomorrow. I'm really sorry I can't talk longer, but I have lunch to make*, she continued even after Jovanka, probably in resignation, had turned away from her. *I'll call you and we'll arrange something*, she added raspily as she entered the yard in front of their building, by which time Jovanka had most likely vanished into her own tower block. Dražen, on the first floor, went pale, gritted his teeth, shoved the cigarette butt into his trouser pocket, rolled his eyes (he must have remembered that the cotton would stink to high heaven), pressed his pelvis to the balcony wall and gripped the railing with both hands. He then peered up the curving road to the school as if a thousand white horses were coming down it in magnificent procession — this was the last thing she managed to catch before she dashed out to her mother, who was carrying two big bags of shopping.

Thanks for waiting, Kitten, her mother said with a gentle smile. *Time got away from me a little when we were chatting; she's had no luck finding a job; she used to work down in Lucija, in one of the shops by the canal — you remember, don't you, where they sell stockings and leggings and such, but she got laid off two months ago*, she explained, forgetting as always that she was talking to a child. She stopped abruptly below their balcony and, with a somewhat irritated sigh, set the bags on the ground. Her daughter, a few steps ahead, now leapt to her aid, staggering a bit as her unwieldy arms lifted the bags. *They might be too heavy for you*, her mother frowned, then wearily shrugged her shoulders and, looking up at her pensive son on the balcony, at once started shouting — yes, she was shouting again, not angrily but with definite sarcasm: *Just look at him pretending I'm not here! Did you at least sweep up there, since you're already outside? If not, then do it, why don't you? I can hardly wait for spring to be over! That awful pollen makes it look like terminally ill people have been weeing all over our balcony!*

Brother and sister exchanged glances. At first, they were merely embarrassed because their mother always had to be so damn loud, and at the same time so impulsive and crass; but then Dražen, letting go of the railing, aimed his initial volleys of laughter into his hand, but after the fourth volley, set the laughter free. She, however, crouched down since for some reason she couldn't remain upright when laughing – either her knees were too weak, or her bladder was, or she was afraid of people scowling at her – and, amid the waves of laughter, the two of them tried to encapsulate the situation: *Pol-len . . . term-in-al-ly ill . . . wee-ing*, Dražen syllabised; *Only you could say something like that*, she managed to get out; *Real-ly . . . on-ly you*, Dražen sang and extolled their mother as the *Queen of Comparisons*.

She could often be crass – that was undeniable – but she was even more often witty. Yes, a complicated woman was their mother, who stood laughing in front of the entrance to their building as the wind played with her curly brown hair, cropped at her ears. Without real conviction, like a choir conductor unsure of the work in front of her, she waved her arm to get her children to (what irony!) cease this bizarre behaviour before somebody saw them, and kept repeating to no avail, *Dražen, please, stop; you know how loud that bass of yours is, and you, my little—*

✳

'Dunja?'

The voice could not be her mother's. It was too gentle, and yet not unfamiliar – no, anything but unfamiliar.

'Dunja, is that you?'

And Dunja instantly opened her eyes, blinking nervously, with big blinks, until the colours and shapes and smells and sounds in her consciousness gradually and reluctantly, but in the end successfully, organised themselves. Opened her eyes to the harsh August light, which absorbs in itself every shade of blue, especially the blue of the sky. To the revoltingly green apartment building with the revoltingly yellow window shutters and the equally revolting concrete balcony walls. To the long row of cactuses big and small, chubby and lanky, with and without flowers, arranged along the wall of the smallest balcony on the first floor. Dražen's balcony. To the five dreamcatchers hanging from a slat attached to the ceiling of the balcony above, which dangled in meditation over the plants. To the snow-white cat, whose fur would have caused a reaction in all three of them – her father, her mother and Dražen – and which had inserted itself between two dome-shaped cactuses so it could stare at the self-absorbed visitor. To the scent of pines and cypresses, deceitfully encumbered with smoke from incense sticks, oh dear, of eucalyptus/sandalwood/Orientalism/cancer. To the drone of cicadas, which, scattered along the trunks of the conifers, drowned out the noise of the traffic, of the unusually heavy traffic – really, it didn't use to be like this – which was channelled into three new roundabouts graced with islands of agaves and palms. To a boy's furious *fuck you, fuck you, go to hell* (this will never change) and the clap of a football against elbows and knees and trees and *fucking hell, mate, nice boots*. And, finally, to the waving of a firm hand and a face with too much make-up, the black eyeliner and mascara visibly melting in the heat, the purplish lipstick lumpy and, no less so, the layers of the too-dark foundation, particularly on the nose; the hair, bleached to near-white, was tied in a high ponytail, but the smile – just look at it! – made a striking contrast: undisguised and healthy, with shiny white teeth – a smile she had wanted as a girl to pluck out and keep for herself. Oh my God, that smile!

'Oh my God, Katarina!'

She wanted to hug her – of course she did; the chance meeting had in a second thoroughly warmed her, but it could not get past her sense of propriety, which shoved her arms behind her back, as if she were suffering from motor control issues. Her long, billowy white dress, after all, had no pockets.

But *she* – Katarina – hugged *her*. It was a joyful, strong hug, the kind children give dogs: nose buried directly into her neck so she felt its warm, sticky tip; hands on her back, directly above her kidneys; and bosom directly below her own, which took her breath away and made her arms, there, behind her back, even tenser. Looking over Katarina's shoulder, she saw for a moment the other woman's backside, covered in denim shorts with tiny pink and silver crystals sewn around the pockets, and, hmm, Katarina was still much smaller and narrower than herself but she was also fuller, more flexible and softer: this bum and these boobs, she thought, which in the hug had spread to both sides of Dunja's body, must certainly be dominating Instagram. *Sunshine80* or *SunnyKaty80* or *KatyInTheSky* – yes, this could easily be a variation on the Katarina she had once known.

'Yes, it's me,' she murmured into Dunja's collarbone. 'Oh my God, I can't believe it: you're here, right in front of our building! I was sure you'd never come back to the coast.' She placed her hands on Dunja's upper arms and winced – wow, how sinewy, sinewy and thin, like a girl's – but then, considerately, she pushed her away, now not like a child with a dog, but as one might a dance partner at the end of a Viennese waltz. 'I'm incredibly happy to see you, incredibly, *incredibly* happy!'

Dunja – truly, just as one does at the end of a friendly waltz – shifted her weight and smiled. A big, wide smile? No, not that, not entirely. She was, to be sure, finally dangling her arms in front of her body, and even scratching a little where it still smarted from Katarina's exotically lacquered and pornographically manicured nails, but her fright was just now flaring up. A logical delay, she realised, absolutely logical.

And justified. Katarina's hands slid from Dunja's biceps down the length of her arms and interlocked themselves with her friend's hands. Warmly, encouragingly. Katarina-ly. But even so, there was a question. A question the provinces ask the centre, the past asks the present: 'So what in the world are you doing here?'

She stared at the ground, which was scattered with dead rhododendron blossoms. Which every summer, even those she had missed and refused, looked the same, equally scattered. She could answer that she had come back because she too was still the same. Equally scattered, in all directions. She could reply that she had decided to be done with second thoughts and doubts. That she demanded explanations, clarifications and reasons, just as anybody would for their life. That she needed, therefore, a narrative, one that was complete and clear and convincing. That after twenty years she had decided once and for all to find peace. At least the promise of it. She could also tell her about the woman with dementia, the incredibly shy and unpredictable, incredibly different, almost unrecognisable woman, who her mother had become in merely a year, and how unbearable it was to be suddenly bearing this hole entirely alone.

But *could* was only a word. A rhetorical ornament. She lifted her chin and glanced at the chestnut brown that was gazing at her. 'I am writing a book,' she whispered. 'Well, I would *like* to write a book.'

'A book?' Katarina let go of her hands. 'You're going to write a book? About everything? I mean, about that?' She made a circle in the air with her index finger, capturing in the gesture the yard, the car park and the patch of lawn, the tree-lined paths and walkways, the first-floor balcony but also the balconies on the second and fourth floors, the fish market, open only in the morning, and the delicatessen, which in the years of Dunja's absence, had been demoted to a bar, the pavement along the road to the primary school, the secondary school a few miles up the hill, the discount store, which, ironically, was tucked among the fashionable apartment buildings on the opposite hill, the newsstand next to the odorous canal next to the main road, the boat moorings down in the marina, the marina's ice cream parlour and seafood restaurant and the vandalised bus station on the edge of the community, but more than anything else, her gesture captured Piran, *damn* Piran, *fucking* Piran, *revolting* and *evil* and *horrible* Piran, *unjust* and *cruel, so fucking cruel* Piran – the wall of Piran, which had taken, had taken so much from Dunja, the beach of Piran, which had robbed her, had robbed her of so much, and Piran itself, which should have burnt to the ground long ago. Burnt to charcoal. Evaporated. Disappeared.

'Yes.' She collected herself. 'I'm trying to write about *that.*' And again longed for pockets. 'There are lots of things I don't remember all that well, but I'll be here a few weeks, so maybe I'll cobble something together.'

'You're brave,' Katarina said with a barely noticeable, melancholy shake of her head. 'But then you always were.'

She looked down for a moment, as if wanting to verify and evaluate the quality of Dunja's shoes, as if that strange habit still possessed her, a baseless but none the less self-important snobbery, and continued in a half-whisper, 'You've done so much and come so far, Dunja, really far. I follow everything you do, constantly, everywhere – all your books, your articles, and two years ago – or whenever it was – when you got that award, I was so happy for you, Dunja. You know, I cried when I saw you on television, after the award presentation, when you were lighting the bonfire and the wind was blowing and you couldn't get it started and you were smiling and laughing. That novel, you know, I really liked it. It was good, you know, it was very good. You deserved that award, you deserved it all.'

The cleavage between her polyester shoulder straps expanded as she inhaled and fell as she exhaled – theatrically, calculatedly, with thought for the effect everything nonverbal was making – yes, that is exactly how Dunja would have assessed it all if she did not know Katarina.

Did not know? *Had* not once known? Yes, past perfect would be correct, she decided with a slight frown.

'Thanks, Katarina.' She ran her fingers through her hair and scratched the top of her head, although the only thing itching her was embarrassment. 'So what about—'

'Oh, I know my opinion can't mean much to you.' Katarina's chin sank between her collarbones and for a moment became very small. 'I'm sure you must be used to praise from people who know a lot more about everything, but I suppose what I'm trying to say is that people like me, who don't read a lot, well, *we* read you too.' She caught her ponytail in her hand and started stroking it. 'That's counts for something, you know.'

'It certainly does,' the centre said, doing its best to console the provinces, attentive but patronising, as it could do nothing else. She straightened her back, stiffly and determinedly, thrust out her breasts, which despite her best will remained woefully unperky and flat (spondyloarthritis having done an exemplary job on her), and tried again. 'But what about you, Katarina? How have things been for you here?'

The other woman let out a sigh, again theatrical, reached into her back pocket and, a moment later, was lighting a cigarette. 'Not so bad, believe it or not.' She held out the pack to Dunja, who declined. 'For a long time, though, it was pretty rough, you know? I've had three abortions, Dunja. Three. But the next time I became pregnant, I said no. This time no abortion. I was twenty-four years old and you can probably guess who the father was. So I got pregnant and he left me – big surprise – even before Duška was born.' Katy used to hate the smell of tobacco and the smoke had always bothered her, but now the cigarette was glowing like kindling in a fireplace and she was clearly going to light a second immediately after the first. 'But at least I finished school, although it took a while.' She tossed the butt into the drain. 'After he dumped me, Mami helped a lot with Duška, so I found a job pretty fast, but I lost it fast too, then I got a new job, which I also lost, and, well, I guess I went through six or seven, all really badly paid, but Duška was growing and I took what I could get. I would even have worked in a salami factory, you know, if I lived in Italy.' She puffed through the first half of the second cigarette and now rested her weight on her right hip, as rebellious little girls do, those little wanderers who never let their free leg relax but keep it flexed at the heel, so it's always ready to push off, to run, almost to flee. 'It was just Mami and me for quite a while, thirteen years, you know.' She let her left shoe, a slip-on, slip to the ground, and Dunja glanced at Katarina's pedicured but terribly swollen foot and her wide, hard ankles, the feet and ankles of a woman of fifty or sixty, certainly not those of a forty-year-old. It wasn't fair, she thought, that the laws of experience should be so much stronger than the laws of biology.

'You must remember my mother, right?' Katy asked and Dunja nodded at once, even before she had summoned to mind the image of that kind-hearted, shy woman, whose hearing had started declining early and who tried, whenever possible, to conceal the fact by turning up the volume on the radio – *I can't hear you, Katarina! I can't hear you, Dunja! The music, you know* – which she would then turn down when the other person decided to shout. The image of that single mother who, after settling in at a local hair salon, which had a huge clientele and growing revenues, found that her hips, too, had started giving her problems and so (at least this is what Katy had told Dunja) would ease the pain with analgesics in disgusting shades of blue and pink and yellow, which were always making her queasy, so eventually she stopped eating actual meals and instead fuelled herself on snack food, breadsticks, bananas, rusks and, in the summer, apricots and peaches and unbelievable quantities of probiotic yogurt, which had recently and with great pomp erupted in the shops, and within a year or two became as thin and pale as sheet of paper; the image of a curly-headed, fair-haired – and eventually, Dunja supposed, grey-haired – woman with a refined taste in jewellery, in *pearls*, as she called her trinkets, which were anything but pearls – necklaces, bracelets, earrings and rings made of plastic and fishing line and wire, tastefully chosen to be sure, but none the less plastic and fishing line and wire; the image of a woman who would wave enthusiastically at her from their narrow second-floor balcony whenever she spotted her in the yard, often calling out to say how happy she was to see her, how happy she was that her Katarina had her as a friend.

Yes, I remember Cvetka, she should say and ask how she was doing – she could be polite – but the cloud in Katy's look gave everything away: her mother had died, probably not long ago, probably completely deaf, probably from a fall. She would learn everything eventually, but not right then, she decided, when workers had started swarming the building, having completed their morning shifts in the coastal factories, and not right there, in the last of the blazing hot yards on School Street. So she merely squeezed Katarina's hand, sympathetically and firmly, and waited for the veiled eyes to clear.

'Well, we can't just stand here and fry!' Katarina said suddenly. 'Wouldn't you rather come round to mine? How about tomorrow, early evening? It'll be Saturday, and everything is possible on Saturday, right? And if it's not so damn hot I expect we'll have a lot more to say to each other.' She smiled – a big, wide smile, in total contrast to the absent eyes a moment before.

'I'm still on the second floor. Even the name on the buzzer's the same.'

'You know, Kate?' Dunja swallowed the *y*, along with some saliva, then exhaled with a whistle and finally relaxed. 'I would like that very much. I'll be there at seven.'

'Oh, wonderful! That's wonderful!' Katarina exclaimed and hugged her, her magnificent bosom again below hers, and this time Dunja returned the affection. She held her old friend close and took a whiff – Chanel? Dior? Givenchy? Something expensive, something nice, nothing acidic or boozy.

'You know,' Katarina said, loosening the embrace, 'my name is not the only one on the buzzer.' She gave her a wink and blew her a kiss, a kiss Dunja might have believed if the voice accompanying it was not perceptibly lower. 'You'll see tomorrow, you know? You'll see everything.'

She turned nimbly on her heel and marched off to the building, hips swaying. It was clear she had, fortunately, so far escaped her mother's afflictions.

Except men, Dunja thought. Except, maybe, men.

2

He dropped two scoops into the cup, chocolate and hazelnut, and planted a little umbrella in the ice cream. *And* a wafer. She was amazed. There weren't many places left that still decorated their ice cream with umbrellas and wafers. At a certain point, probably when the Slovenian marketplace was penetrated by homemade ice cream, all-natural ice cream, vegan ice cream, low-cal ice cream, non-aromatised ice cream, grandma's ice cream, start-up ice cream and Italian gelato – in other words, ice creams based on the idea of minimal harm or the least possible evil – sinful garnishes lost their right of residence in most ice cream establishments. Before long, the market was banning even whipped cream, that deceitfully fattening substance, so her first thought was that this was a charming gesture – the indestructible aesthetic of Albanians. But when, just before handing her the cup, he added a second wafer to the scoops and then drenched everything in chocolate sauce, which immediately hardened, it hit her: he must have recognised her. He must have remembered her. Remembered her obsessive sweet tooth, her vociferous complaints as a child that the wafers were too small, that they always vanished before the ice cream did, remembered her regular, mostly solitary visits as a teenager, when she would try to leave the wafer to the very end, or at least when she told him and all his brothers (there were seven

in all) that she'd try to do this. Although she never did. On
the contrary, once puberty overtook her, her appetite became
insatiable.

The fact that he recognised her, she thought, was maybe
not so strange. After all, she had a memorable face, with features
that the chisel of age had only deepened, only sharpened: three
little birthmarks, beneath her right eye and on her right cheek,
distributed in the shape of a crescent, eyebrows that almost
joined together, a bloated upper lip on an otherwise narrow
mouth, and the pink eyelids of those who are eternally tired and
underslept. *Sturm und Drang* eyelids, as a classmate at university
used to tease her – a boy who had been in love with her, or so
she suspected.

While all this was true, it was certainly not the whole truth,
she had to admit as she rummaged in her purse for coins. He
had recognised her because for a few months, some twenty-plus
years ago, her family had been in the papers, both regional
and national. In news reports on television and radio stations
of every kind. In local conversations both spiteful and sympa-
thetic. In the houses and flats atop the coastal hills and in the
flats beneath them; in cafés and bars, restaurants, fish markets
and shops. On posters that at first appealed to people's conscience – *Did anyone see anything? Does anyone know anything?*
All information is welcome! – and in announcements that in the
end relied on people's avarice – *All information will be rewarded!*
In the homily at Sunday mass and in the prayers, but also on
the internet, such as it was in those days, in chat groups and
forums; they had even been talked about in schools and kin-
dergartens. They had been everywhere, fucking everywhere,
and everyone on this damn coast would remember that bygone
flood, would remember her, who had once flooded over. Bučko
might certainly be receptive to female beauty, she decided as
she took the cup in her sweaty, shaking hand, but he was even
more receptive, as anyone would be (and *receptive* is hardly the
same as *sensitive*), to tragedy.

She dug two little spoons out of a dish on the translucent counter above the ice cream tubs, forced out a smile and

a thank-you and made a quick exit. Him remembering her was (sure, of course) *almost* natural, but him possibly saying something to her would be cruel. Shameless.

One spoon she dipped into the two scoops and licked; the other she stuck in her pocket. Without looking left or right, she crossed the road at the zebra crossing, crossed it very slowly, and a car immediately blasted its horn – a low-slung BMW, of course, an older model with, if she could trust her eyes in the bright daylight, an illuminated undercarriage. These were two standard components of the coastal folklore: pensive, lazy walking and furious honking; the third was swearing, a mode she quickly, although most unwillingly, switched to. Folklore – she went through various definitions in her mind, turning them over until at last she picked one – folklore, or, *what hides in plain sight.*

She stopped beside the canal of murky seawater, which provided moorings for boats, whether submerged, in disrepair or merely worn out or unseaworthy, and the wooden walkway above it. Behind her were the go-kart track and a place serving fast food – kebabs, hot dogs, bureks etc. – but it was closed (it still kept divided operating hours), and the small pharmacy and one-storey general surgery, round as a cake and colourful as, well, ice cream. In front of their entrances, a narrow car park, a wildly overgrown thorny hedge, and pebbles scattered across lanes and footpaths winding back and forth and around. Beneath the arcade next door were clumsily positioned neon signs of what had once been shops offering nautical equipment, now impossible to lease or sell because of their excessive floor space. Visible in the distance – but, again, not so far away, since in Lucija all distances were actually short ones – were the crystalline masts and blurry contours of sailboats undergoing maintenance and repair. Opposite the marina was the tennis court – intended for managing directors, public officials and Russians, of whom there were none, nor would there be any – and its sinking iron fence, and, immediately beside it, Beach Pizzeria, a playground for drunks and holidaymakers from Štajerska, in the eastern part of the country, as well as, here and there, little hills of gravel and gigantic rubbish bins.

And, most notably, very few people, at least not with their feet on the ground, or to be precise, on the concrete: everyone, old or young, foreign or local, was in their cars, keeping cool as carpaccio – their pets, too. There were not even motor scooters buzzing around, although in the past they would have been buzzing all over the place all of the time, those lords of the littoral, those rulers of the world.

But what *were* on the ground, wherever there were no cars but sufficient litter, were crowds of well-fed seagulls, who never gave up, in neither tempest nor heat – horrible seagulls jostling for crumbs and pecking at each other's eyes. Two particularly fat ones came hopping over and were instantly at the level of her chin, their beaks almost in reach of their creamy prize. She bolted away, into the sparse shade of some larch trees, and the birds, fortunately sated, did not follow her.

She sat on a bench, straddled it, her back turned to the nonplace Lucija in order to study the beginning of the nonplace Portorož. The minigolf, where she and her family, when they were a family, had celebrated all their birthdays, was still the same; she expected that one of the holes, the one hardest to get the ball into, must still have that same defect: a surface that was bumpy where it should have been smooth. The complex of shops next to the minigolf also looked the same: square and grey and overgrown with rosebushes; here holidaymakers, but rarely locals, were always sure to find something they wanted: flippers, water wings, crisps, condoms. She did not recognise the trio of restaurants on the corner, but she did recognise the type: the sort that garishly proclaimed their identity – Mexican, Italian, seafood – but were in fact utterly without identity. Across the road a plantation of pastel hotels rose up, their parking garages bored into the hills, and, just beyond them, the luxurious Grand Casino. Two of the hotels were certainly new, she determined, and two had new names, since a name, after all, is a brand, and the Slovenian coast is a brand, and *Rose* and *Pinetree* give you less branding, while *Prestige* and *Villa* definitely give you more. As for the swimming pool, oh, the swimming pool, raised above the crowded concrete beach and itself also crowded, with stocky

Czechs and Hungarians and overcooked British couples, with cracked tiles and *pommes frites* and milky drinks with fruit and salmonella, with overchlorinated pool water to keep fungi and urine from becoming an obvious problem, with rusty showers and withered palm trees – well, *this swimming pool*, she concluded, only a madman would have branded, never a local. So it remained unnamed, even though *this very swimming pool* represented the key theme in the story of this nonplace of a thousand roses, namely, its slow and noisy and cheerfully hopeless decline.

The ice cream did not disappoint. It was exactly as she remembered it, precisely the best, exactly as sweet and light and fresh as ever, but even so, nearly all of it had melted. She tossed the soggy cup in an arc at the litter bin in front of her and scored. Then watched through the bin's green mesh as the creamy gloop ran down over a mushy banana peel and a plastic carton, over a second plastic carton, over a paper carton, over a chunk of meat.

She had grown up, had truly grown up, she found herself thinking as the liquid dribbled through the little gaps onto the ground. Had grown up in that *morbid* way, if indeed there was any other, she theorised (and finally put on her sunglasses, which at once slipped down the bridge of her nose) when reality constantly curtails pleasure (heat, dust, the melting of ice cream) and when play (dipping the little spoon gently into the creamy substance, smacking your lips and giggling) must often go into exile. Automatically she pushed the sunglasses back up to her forehead, straightened her back and nodded at her insights.

They did not surprise her; of course not. *Morbid* comes from the Latin *morbus*, and *morbus* suggests disease and disease tends to suggest (bring, deliver) death. The trick had all this time been in the language: she had grown up on death and had also been shaped by it, she determined, and shut her eyes. She moved her face away from the sunbeams that were trying to find her through the needled branches, and many had found her. She didn't take well to sunshine, which must be why she could not be sunny. Since, in the end, isn't a person always whatever they most easily bear? The thing they find easiest to love?

As a child, however, she had loved the sun, had longed for it, looked forward to it. She liked the feel of it on her skin, and under her skin, too, in her ears, in her nose, in her mouth, and on her eyelids. In her belly, in her head, between her ribs and deep in her pelvis. She had drawn it and painted it, had sung it and written it: she had inserted it in every picture and tried to domesticate it in each of her poems. She loved it, yes, she truly loved it, until suddenly, like a brick through the window, a tree crashing through the roof, it revealed itself to her completely. Until it showed her that it had never meant anything.

✳

Though still only morning, the sun was shining immense and strong. She rolled up the blind, not without difficulty, and, kneeling on her bed, watched as other children her age kicked a ball around, played badminton or, the more co-ordinated and agile among them, tossed frisbees back and forth on the grass outside. They were also shouting at each other, excitedly, not yet with threats – the game was still young. Every so often their parents would wave at them from the edge of the playground, all showing signs of having spent the past few nights celebrating the country's new independence (a celebration that would later be called – grandly, falsely! – Statehood Day): black circles of satiation around their eyes, the skin on their cheeks red and taut from lack of sleep, Wednesday or Thursday's hair, their movements sluggish but not at all weary, even less bored, their smiles nice and toasty. *I'm coming, just as soon as I eat breakfast, just as soon as I get dressed*, she sang into the warm windowpane and slipped out of bed. From her section of the wardrobe, she chose her favourite outfit – a loose pair of shorts and an even looser T-shirt with a logo on it of some (imaginary or real?) basketball team. She threw off her pyjamas, delighted because at last she had had the room to herself the whole night (Dražen had not yet returned), and in only her underwear, her body still stiff with sleep, performed a clumsy twirl. She bumped into the wardrobe door (*ow*), struck her fingers against the knob (*ow*), and banged into the little shelf (*yeeow, hahaha*).

I hear you moving around, darling, she heard her mother say from the other side of the door, when, freshly bruised, she finished dressing. *It's good you're up. We'll be eating soon – well, when Dražen gets home. Until then, why don't you play by yourself a little?* her mother warbled. *But pull the blind down halfway*, she added, *so you don't get overheated, my little Dunja, so the room doesn't get too hot. So you don't get hot!*

Yes, Mama, she replied grumpily and lowered the blind, again not without difficulty (*Why does it have to be so heavy and awkward?*), lowered it just a little.

She spread her drawings out on the rug, which divided the room into two. Drawings of horses, wonderfully slender, gentle animals trotting across a bright-green, boundlessly open, invitingly sunny plateau, and drawings of wolves, foxes and lynxes, lurking in bushes, watching for prey, openly frowning but not wicked animals, with ribbons of heat pouring down on them from above. She took her coloured pencils and markers out of the drawer – *countless* pencils and markers (*countless* was her new favourite word) – and sprinkled them over the textile and paper surfaces, as the sunlight turned the pink ones to red and the blue ones to deep green. She selected an orange marker – to put right the faded fur on her cunning beasts – but then a new idea came to her: what if she ate the marker? Or washed herself with it? Or, better yet, coloured herself? And so she stretched her leg out across the drawings, making them all a little crumpled, and pressed the marker into her sharp, scrawny knee, a little spud of a knee, and imprinted a dot. Then another. And again, another.

When she had done this for the hundredth, hundred and first, hundred and second time – she was counting each one – there came, as if resonating with the dot marks, a clanging noise. No. It was the buzzer.

Why in the world is he buzzing? Did he forget his keys? She heard the voice of her mother, who had excitedly dashed into the corridor. She saw her (even though she couldn't have) stopping in front of the intercom, that grey, squarish invention, and pressing a button, this time the right one. *Yes, Draži, finally, we've been waiting for you, we're just about to eat so come on up.* She did not wait for her son to say hello, which would have been preceded by annoying crackling. She put all her weight on the second button and held it a long time, a very long time, to a count of ten and then some. So the door would *definitely* unlock. Would unlock for her *son.*

She saw her (even though she couldn't have) frowning a minute later as she approached the door on which a pair of hands were insistently knocking. *Oh, I hope I haven't let in any Jehovah's Witnesses! Dear me! Ljubo! I forgot it was the season for them* — she seized the door handle — *maybe you could get rid of them,* she murmured and unlatched the door, that damn door with no peephole.

Good morning! three times, then *Yes?* only once, in only her mother's voice. Even then she saw her (even though she couldn't have) standing with legs astride, her face flushed for a moment.

Have we got the right flat? Are you Mrs Anko? The man's voice was low, almost a whisper. Her mother (so the daughter in her bedroom imagined her) nodded and, gulping back the worms burrowing into her windpipe, offered a kindly smile.

We apologise for not introducing ourselves below. Again the voice of a man, but a different man; she saw him shifting his weight and rubbing his hands together, as she herself sometimes did, behind his back, out of view. *My name is Peter Birsa, detective chief inspector with the Koper Police Administration* — now he was rubbing his fingers, too — *and this is my colleague . . .* He stopped when her mother — whom the daughter saw, whom the daughter never lost sight of, just as a bird in flight must never lose sight of its fields, for the sake of its food, for its safety, for its protection — went limp. Went pale.

Police detectives? she asked. *Ljubo,* she called. *Ljubo!* she cried.

She heard her father (only heard, never saw) slowly shifting in his chair at the dining table – *My God, what drama* – putting down his newspaper, which was filled with the new country's joyful news, and in his shabby slippers shuffling over to the trio at the door. *Good morning*, he said sleepily, *would you like—*

They're detectives, her mother interrupted – by now the worms were gnawing at her mother's soft palate and trying to reach her tongue – and her father stepped closer, right up next to her, and held her by the forearm. *What sort of detectives? What's going on? This is a mistake*, he might have said, might have raised his voice – *A mistake! What foolishness!* – he might have pushed them away and slammed the door – *Just some crazy, degenerate prank!*

But he didn't. He was grasping her mother's frail arm the way one should only grasp the sturdiest of things.

My name is Simon, Simon Milek. The detective took a step forwards, with the taller man directly behind him like a dog. *Could we perhaps sit down? It would be easier that way for everyone*, he said, modulating his bass, and leaned against the door until it was creaking.

Her mother, whose mouth was burning by now, whom the worms were hollowing out, with her father heavy on her arm, ignored the request and (Dunja saw) shut her eyes tight. Her eyelids were now merely two horizontal lines, signs of stoppage, the stopping of the heart. *You can tell us right here* (at this door, at this damn door with no peephole), she insisted. *It's about Dražen, right? I know it is. I'm not stupid. He didn't come home. He should be home by now* – the worms came dying from her mouth and were ceaselessly multiplying in it. *So what did he do? Just tell us what happened.*

Peter cleared his throat loudly, but Simon said, 'Yes, madam, it is about your son. We found him on the beach in Piran, beneath the church. Unfortunately, he was dead. We are very sorry for your loss.'

When Dunja flung open her bedroom door, the door to the corridor, the drawings flew into the air – the horses broke their necks, the fearsome beasts cracked their skulls and (as in a dream? an earthquake? a war?) the entire landscape went wild. Her mother, who could easily have screamed and stamped her feet, scratched and pleaded – her mother, who always showed her feelings – was now motionless, frowning, but saying more, while her father, who never said a thing, crumpled to the floor, and then (as in a dream? an earthquake? a war?) everything caught fire. (And this was not a crackling fire; this was a fire that destroyed and devoured.)

She, *little Dunja*, crept between her mother, buried, and her father, a kneeling shape in front of the door, and started crying – *Mami? Daddy?* – hunching over – *It's not true! It's not true!* – pounding at the men – *You're lying!* – pinching them – *You're lying! You're lying to me!* – but still she let herself be taken by the flames, by her mother's and father's arms, which wrapped themselves tightly around her. (Yes, she burned to her foundations.) If only she had resisted the flames – this the child pondered a long time afterwards – Dražen would have lived and she wouldn't have lost him.

*

She opened her eyes in panic, like a cat disturbed in her nap by a noise. Her head must have dropped to her chest – it was this damn heat, her fucking rheumatism, she thought. A thousand worms were rushing to her neck – no, what was this? Electric jolts? Electric tingles? How do you say *hot flushes* in Slovenian? Whatever they were, they certainly did not have any poetic name, she decided as she deftly squeezed the nape of her neck with her hand. She also rotated her shoulders a few times (forwards, back, back, forwards), arched her breastbone upwards, sucked it back in (in, out, in, out), and then, five more times, deeply inhaled and exhaled. After such preparations, a person (any other person) might go swimming or running, might go into battle or, as she once saw on YouTube, lift a 250-kilo Olympic weight. She, however, just wanted to stand up, to stand up in a way that would completely conceal her illness, as if, ironically, her preparation routine was not itself a dead giveaway.

She slid her feet to the side of the bench facing the road, glanced down at her attractive, beige, sheep-leather sandals (which had not been cheap!), pushed herself up (onto a horse, off a ski jump, over a vaulting box), and straightened her legs, at which, from the pain of the electric jolts, tingles, unpoetic hot flushes, yes, that *shit*, coursing down to the bend of her knee and up into her backside (hah!) and even higher, to her pelvic joints, she let out a shriek. At that moment, two girls approaching on rollerblades jumped a little and raced past her, while two girls coming up behind her looked at each other and started laughing. The only sympathy she might get would have to come from some old lady, some old lady with a walker, some old lady with artificial hips, some old lady with puffy joints, with joints like jam doughnuts, she thought as she clenched her lips and sat down again. So what now? Should she march on, in her halting march of humiliation and defeat? Ugh, you know, she'd rather not.

She raised her skirt a little and fluttered it, and as she fluttered it she exposed her knees, which, like frightened little girls, fell inward, into an X. She stroked them with her hands: they really were still smooth — freshly shaven and amply lotioned and, especially (so she told herself), not yet arthritic. It felt good to circle them with her fingers, to touch the kneecaps with gentle zeal, and she would have gone on doing this had not something troubled her. She did not even have to squint to see it, sharply and clearly, on her left knee: a phantom figure, a smeary orange letter, composed of many, many dots. A letter that one sunny morning had been intended to announce, spotlight, elucidate *D-unja*, but that in the end had clouded and darkened into *D-ražen*. A letter through which (her hands dropped beside her thighs) a little girl had been trying to show off. She had not meant to damage anything, to spoil anything. She had not meant to destroy anything, *Mami*. Really she hadn't, really. Please believe me, *Daddy*.

3

The flat was *completely* different. The orange-yellow-and-black wallpaper in the little front hall, with the thready details that had made its pattern seem embroidered, as if from a different age (a proto-consumerist age, she would say today), had been replaced by a Catholic white. On the walls of the living room, which was also the dining room, with a kitchen area in the corner – walls that had once been a warm yellow – the white was, ironically, creeping like a fungus. Like a foreign entity. Even the bathroom, to which she had retreated out of nervousness just after entering the flat, was now a snowy, perfectly sterile palace, which left the impression that only already clean people were permitted to shower here, while peeing would be nothing less than sinful. But it was in this very bathroom that she and Katarina had, as little girls, experimentally shaved their hairless legs, arms and bellies and, with some henna they found in the cabinet, a dye they had no idea how to use, darkened a few locks of Dunja's already dark hair, not to mention the tiles and curtain above the bathtub and the ribbed rubber bath mat, as well as, in the process, Dunja's face, cheeks and brow. Katarina's mother, obviously, was not the least bit pleased about this, but she did not have the heart to scream at them. Or to punish them.

Punishment, or rather, minimalism (sorry, I don't always find the right word) was, however, screaming from the new furniture: the obligatory Ikea, but not the cheap-looking kind. Primarily white, with cautious notes of woody brown and anaemic beige. The three-seater sofa – in what, white pleather? maybe actual leather? – had in the past been two shoddy armchairs, an ottoman and a rocking chair inherited from some grandfather, while the white cube table with a wide slot for newspapers and magazines had once been a little table on squeaky wheels, which, whenever they were watching their soap – *Spring* or *Springtime* or *April . . . Blossoms*, was it? Or maybe *Flowers*? – Katarina and Dunja and Cvetka would roll back and forth, from one to the other, like a rattling peace pipe; it would be laden with biscuits and fruit and tea with lots and lots of honey. She also missed the chandelier, which is what Cvetka called the lamp – orange, of course, and shaped like a spaceship – that used to hang low above every breakfast, lunch and dinner. In place of what in the eighties and nineties was allowed to dangle in all its splendour, even if everyone was always bumping into it, now the only thing affixed to the ceiling were discreet *lighting elements*. Indeed, the very idea that something might stick out, might protrude into the space, oh the horror, oh the vulgarity, that would never do. The end table next to the sofa boasted neither figurines nor flowers; on the kitchen counter one found only a knife, or rather five, stuck into a block, and a fruit bowl with an even number of bananas, a pair of peaches and, surely a mistake, *three* nectarines. The windowsill held nothing but two spray cleaners, one for the window, the other for the outside ledge, and, beneath the television (necessarily attached to the wall and displayed like a smug modernist painting, a black rectangle of consumption and plague) stood a white triple credenza, all three sections as empty as the Pannonian Plain.

But. Next to the balcony door, despite everything, stood a big, bushy potted plant. This, she suspected, *must* be Katarina's choice, her first true choice, Katy's personal green lagoon on this island ruled by – for he *must* rule here, Katy was anything but white walls, anything but order, method and otherworldly severity (God, it was a shock, just as she had been shocked below, at the door to the building) – by none other than Kristijan. Kristijan Battelli.

'I see you're a bit flustered,' Katarina said as she noisily placed two white saucers on the coffee table, saucers from an Italian coffee set, before she returned, no less noisily (bumping into the dining table) to the Turkish coffee pot, in which the water was just starting to boil. (Now, *who* was a bit flustered here? Dunja had to wonder.) 'I know you must have a thousand questions, Dunja, or at least one. But I know you and you know me.' She giggled and splashed coffee into the stylish cups, which in her hands became (my God! forgive me, Katy) somewhat bargain-basement – never before had Dunja seen anyone so patently mismatched with the place where they lived and the objects they used; it was as if the grammars of two unrelated languages were being revealed simultaneously, one Indo-European, the other Finno-Ugric.

'Um . . .' Dunja accepted the cup in a clumsy transfer that left drops of coffee spattered on the table and some on the floor, too. She uncrossed her legs and shifted her position in an attempt (a futile project) to ease the pains in her pelvis but also (less futile) to buy herself time: how the hell, she was thinking, do you ask an impossible question, a question that was sure to be humiliating, sure to be depressing, and would, in the process, put a damper on something. A reviving intimacy, for instance. For it's clear, after all, that intimacy can only be revived through mimicry.

'Don't torment yourself,' Katy said, smiling, and sighed. 'I know that Kristijan' (so it really was Kristijan) 'is the last person you'd expect to see here. To see here with *me*.' She took a sip and smacked her lips. 'And I completely understand that it might be a little uncomfortable for you to meet him. But when you told me why you came back, I thought you might be OK with it, that it could be useful to you to see him and maybe talk, and, I confess, this made me a little happy.'

My God – for the third time that day Dunja felt something Christian-like – Katarina's form of empathy, this transparent lack of grievance, was hardly bargain-basement; it deserved to be the fundamental horizon, the fucking aspiration, of all humanity, she concluded, not very Christian-like, and at last settled herself. Looking intently at Katarina, she confessed that, well, yes, she had hit the mark 'as near as could be'.

'As near as could be!' Katy repeated in a carefree tone (at such a revelation, Dunja thought, it would be impossible for her to start yelling at her friend, or at anyone in fact). 'You still have such a way with words.' She sat down next to Dunja and shoved her feet into the slot with the newspapers and magazines, audibly crinkling their pages. She took another sip of coffee, holding the cup just a bit too long in front of her lips, like characters in a French New Wave film who, just when they ought to be putting some object down on the table, are struck by a vague idea, desire or vision – or simply a typically novelistic melancholy – and their arm, bizarrely, but especially *symbolically*, freezes in mid-motion, as if to say, see how the mind zips ahead of the material world, how a thought so wildly surpasses the organic presence of our French hero!

'So the two of you . . .' Dunja began, staring at Katy's extravagantly, minutely filigreed gold ring, a ring she had obviously been too agitated to notice the day before, 'are what? Married?'

'Engaged.' Katarina at last set the cup down. She then removed the ring, but not without difficulty, and with even greater difficulty put it back on. 'But it doesn't really fit. I can only wear it in the evening, when I'm, you know, not so swollen. I somehow never find the time to have it fixed, and I don't even know if they can make it bigger or if they'll have to make a new one.'

'I see. I don't have a clue about jewellers,' Dunja said, and at once concealed her face behind a sip of coffee. What else, she wondered, might not fit this woman? Had she perhaps judged her too hastily? Could it be that Katarina, unlike what Dunja had been sensing, was in fact right for this role? If not in form, then maybe in content? She took another sip and told herself she needed to be kinder in her thoughts.

'So come on, Katy, tell me all about it. How'd it happen?' she asked, with a decidedly amiable laugh.

'Sure, OK, before Kristijan and Duška get back from the beach. They've been there all afternoon. He told me not to make a fuss, since she knows to use sun cream and find shade. OK, so before they get back, I really should tell you the whole thing.' Two beads of sweat glistened beneath her nose, and another on her temple; in the arctic-white room it was easy to forget the tropical heat, which even now, as evening approached, had been penetrating the flat through the cracked windows and balcony door. An air conditioner, she supposed, did not belong here. It would have stuck out.

'I used to wait on him. At the bar where I worked, in Koper. I was there a fairly long time.' She wiped her nose with her fingers. 'He'd come there for coffee in the mornings, quite early, half past six or so. And always ordered cappuccino. And you know, I didn't recognise him – well, obviously.' She reached for her coffee and, without any novelistic hesitation but more from novelistic nerves, with her pinkie firmly extended and her head thrust back, drank the entire cup. 'But he recognised *me* right away – he told me that later – he was just waiting for me to remember. And I did, barely, but only when he invited me on a date and we were sitting in a cake shop on the Koper promenade. Anyway, Dunja, I really liked being with him. He made me feel respected – and he never put any pressure on me, Dunja; he was the first guy who didn't immediately try to sleep with me, and the first one who took me out to dinner, which, I admit, was strange and awkward for me, but it was important to him that I felt comfortable in the restaurant.' She drew up her feet and sat cross-legged on the sofa, with her hands on her ankles, as if she were ten or eleven and telling Dunja about a new love she was feeling, about its new and never before experienced greatness, its transformative power: *I can feel it changing me, Dunja*, or, *With this love, I will never be the same again, Dunja*. Well, that's *almost* how it was, Dunja thought to herself, quickly correcting the comparison. Katarina really was sitting exactly as she used to, only now her eyes were not shining with anticipation and belief (*naivety* and *confusion*, Dunja had thought as a girl) but instead reflected something factual, with a certain resignation and weariness – which may well be the same thing. 'He and I get along *dorro*, really well, and so do he and Duška – great, in fact,' she continued. 'And he was renting a flat in Koper, but after a year or so I invited him to move in with us, and he's really done a lot with the place, which of course you noticed. He works at the port, in logistics. He makes a good salary and doesn't mind that I'm temporarily out of work and have to look for a job again.' She tensed her back, just by a degree, and her position cast a greyish glow on both her forehead and cheeks. 'He's a good man, you know.'

'That's great, Katy,' Dunja said, still smiling; she was trying hard not only to sound serious but to think seriously too. It was splendid to hear that a man finally respected Katarina – and that she had learned to recognise and choose men who respected her – but even so (for the hundredth time, forgive me, Katarina), Dunja had the dark feeling that she was *hearing* one thing but *discovering* another. Respecting men who respected her had hardly come naturally to Katy. She was, indeed, unable to truly accept what she needed most, although she did have sufficient resources to perform acceptance, to put on a show for the public. Only this time, Dunja speculated further, desire was pushing her in a different direction, into some prototypical scene of domestic cruelty and violence, in which Kristijan clearly had nothing to gain, while Katy, well, what could she feel towards him except a strong and pitying revulsion?

'That's really great, Katy!' she exclaimed, to drown out these thoughts, and at once turned red: be kind, yes, be fucking kind, no rash analysis, no matter how accurate it might be. 'You know how much my family liked Kristijan.'

'Your *family?*' Katarina burst into laughter. 'What I remember, Dunja, is how much *you* liked him. And not just liked – you were in love with him!'

Well, OK, there was no need to play dumb. She had been in love with him. *Full-throttle, a hundred km/h.* Whenever Dražen told them his friend would be coming over – his *best friend*, is how their mother put it, although in Dunja's experience he was Dražen's *only true-blue friend* – Dunjica would often put off her

homework until – *Oh, sorry, Draži!* – the boys were already in
the bedroom, with Dražen sprawled across his bed like a cat
and Kristijan leaning against it like (heh-heh) a loyal vassal,
and so absorbed in their discussion it was clear they wouldn't
be going anywhere else. *Nowhere at all.* She wanted to be close
to Kristijan, even if, chained to her desk for an hour – *But Draži,
I still don't get it* – or an hour and a half – *Maths is really hard
for me* – she had her back to him. She was sly enough to keep
quiet most of the time, not to intrude too much. Even so, on a
few occasions her calculating girlish mind gave way to blazing
emotion and, through shameless pleading, she successfully: a)
got them to take her with them to the film *Summer in a Sea Shell,
Part 2*, which to her, because she was sitting next to the love of
her life, became a genuine masterpiece; b) got them to take her
to Bučko's for ice cream when their parents weren't at home, a
treat that Kristijan, who came from a well-to-do family, paid for
with his pocket money; c) got Kristijan, who had not yet won
but was still striving for the title of national youth champion, to
teach her chess: *the Italian defence, the Slavic defence, the Scottish
defence, the Scotch* (what was it now?) – *Come on, try harder; it's
good to have them all memorised*; d) got them to take her with them
on a walk to Piran, where they stayed until dark and the two
rebels – *Now don't you go blabbing about this, Dunči* – could smoke;
and finally, unbelievably, e) total victory: she got them to cram
her like an overstuffed suitcase onto a bus to Koper, where they
all went to sunbathe on the hot concrete and swim in the oily
sea. It was there, as she later reported excitedly to Katarina,
that her love for Kristijan grew even stronger. While he and
her brother were making fun of people they assumed (*Them?
Not a chance, no way*) did not understand Slovenian – *She could
break into a vault with that arse . . . If he was any more bow-legged,
you could enter Narnia through those things . . . Oohoho, Macho Man
has taken his fucking roids, and a little silicon too, just look at those
balloons, up he goes into the air* – she was trying to work out how
she could make Kristijan suddenly redirect all the attention he
was giving her brother to her, after which . . . well, her imagination could not quite make it to the next scene. It was enough for

her to imagine the details of the Big Event: the tilt of his head,
a ray of sun caressing her just as he looked at her, a sea breeze
dancing on his lips, his throaty voice, hers a mere whisper, his
first words, variations on her name, a poem, songs, harmonies.
Whereas Katarina was already anticipating the Big Change,
which was something erotic, the most Dunja could hope for
was the Moment of Being Seen. Still a child, still with a mythic
consciousness, she saw in Kristijan a fairy-tale creature: with
long, blond, sun-bleached hair, soft as down (as the down that
was about to sprout on her legs), smooth skin, eyes the colour
of walnut shells, with shoulders and elbows, wrists, ankles and
knees thinner than paper, more fragile than glass, with a con-
cave belly (even though in fairy tales there is constant eating)
and true fairy-like attributes, pointy ears and a pointy nose, and
movements such as always flying up and hovering in the air. And
not just Kristijan's body, airy as it was, but his character, too,
radiated stories, heroes, saviours and endless goodness, justice
and purity, beauty and reason.

    Hmm, she thought as she brought her memories to a close,
she must have been wrong about his character. What hero or
saviour would *want* to insult ugly people, even if they couldn't
understand the insults? Hah, she laughed, being in love really is
a kind of trauma, and for the very reason that, as Žižek and that
pervert Bataille had taught her, it alters (did they mean to say
improves?) one's relationship with reality. Experience had taught
her that it spoils it, but what did she know? She'd leave such
pronouncements on important matters to the men – oops! – to
the philosophers.

    'I'm glad you find all this so amusing. Of course, I didn't
expect that after all this time you would still be suffering.' Katy
adjusted a strand of hair that had fallen across her forehead
and, for a moment, her swollen ring finger caught the light – it
did not look healthy. 'But sometimes, well, sometimes anger
just keeps holding on, even if we don't want it to, even if . . .'
She shrugged her shoulders and Dunja did the same. It would
be hard to explain to Katy, or rather, she really did not feel
like explaining, how a death in the family has the side effect

of invalidating all dreams, all enthusiasm and all that fucking anguish, especially the anguish of a nine-year-old child, who has no sense of gravitation, or if she does, it's not earthly gravitation – moonly, maybe.

'But let's leave it for now,' Katy continued, brushing it away with her hand. 'Instead, Duni, tell me if there's anyone special in *your* life.'

'Oh my!' She flinched as if genuinely surprised by the question, as if it hadn't been in full view all the time, like the Alps on a clear Ljubljana day, and, without thinking, shifted her position on the sofa, a movement that produced a painful and semi-audible creak in her hip. 'No, there isn't. I'm single. I've been single for a long time now.'

'Oh, but that doesn't sound good. Why, Duni?'

Because, umm . . . (now her mind was creaking, too, angrily) every time she'd been in a relationship she had felt sick. The problem was evident in the word 'relationship' itself, in that crispy word *razmerje* (God, how she loved the Slovenian language): her *mera* ('measure') and the other's *mera* and the obligatory, foreseen 'separation' or 'distance', expressed by *raz-*, *pre-fixed* into the meaning from the very start. It was this, the necessary space between, which she had never been able or known how to preserve: either she herself would, beyond her measure, overgrow the boundaries, or he, the other, like some pest, like some beetle, would feed on her, and, sorry, but isn't that the very worst thing on offer beneath the umbrella of *love*? It was as if there were a line dividing her body in half: on the left, she was the oppressor; on the right, the oppressed. She had invested an enormous amount of her time, and even more of her money, in repairs – ten years of therapy equals how many pay cheques? – but then suddenly, in maybe the seventh year, her intuition told her that it was much too late to find balance. That she would never achieve any real change, that she was working towards a consciousness that was simply not meant for her, that could never be hers, a fake consciousness, then, yes, precisely that, towards lies and illusions, towards some damn hocus-pocus.

'Because, umm . . .' – she stared at her feet – 'it's been a while since I've met anyone, at least anyone suitable.'

'Oh,' Katarina said, as she pulled herself off the sofa, 'I completely understand. I expect you're more demanding than most.' *More demanding than me* is what she was thinking, of course it was, and she was already rinsing out the pot to make another coffee – another coffee at seven p.m.?

'No more for me, Katy.'

'Sure, all right.' She turned around as if in a pirouette, her head overtaking her body – 'So would you rather have tea?' – and the dirty water from the pot splashed onto the skin below her collarbones, and on her pink top, too, which was pinched at the waist into yellow pleats, and, again (oh my, oh dear Katy!) all over the floor. She ran her hand gingerly over her breasts and, grabbing a dishcloth (the one meant for the counter), slowly bent down.

'Yes, I think I would. Mint if you have it,' Dunja replied, watching her friend's kneeling body as she wiped up the blotches of grainy liquid, lazily at first, like a reptile in the sun, but then, when the door handle clicked – and what a sharp click it was – and murmuring entered the flat, well, *whoooosh*, she became as busy as, well, a bee on a blossom.

Then she hastily stood up and tossed the sodden cloth into the sink, which donged from the impact like an intermission bell in an amateur theatre, and Duška ran into the room. The girl's head reached, more or less, to her mother's collarbones, which is exactly where she buried her nose as she embraced her.

'My Duška!' – 'Mimika!' they cried in turn, and their embrace struck Dunja as so enthusiastic it was as if they had lost each other decades ago and only now, after long searching, had found each other again. It ended with a noisy exchange of kisses on cheeks, foreheads and mouths and a giggly joining of hands. The handholding proved no obstacle for the girl, who simply lifted her mother's arms above her head, crossed them and turned around. The big X of the mother's arms across the daughter's chest was X as prohibition, not as variable – *she is mine and I am hers* – and the wide smile on Duška's face was so wide, so much Katarina's, that, if Dunja had not been Dunja (may God forgive her), the *most* obvious thing about the girl would have simply dissolved in it: namely, little Duška was (of course, everything about children is beautiful, but still) rather plump. Good heavens, let's face it: she was definitely fat. But at the same time, if this makes any sense, *empty*. The skin was hanging from her arms, shoulders and neck as if its contents had somehow been *vacuumed out*, while it gathered above her knees in hundreds of folds, which, had there been no ligaments or muscles or bones underneath, would have detached themselves and slipped down her calves onto her bare feet. She had, for her age (which was what, fourteen? fifteen?), rather large breasts, which rested on her belly as if on a shelf that was about to collapse. Her torso was also all in folds, like an air mattress when the air is being let out, while her belly button drooped over the too-tight waistband of her shorts, drooped deep and flat, and Dunja imagined that that bulk-on-bulk must chafe, must itch her. And she had to wonder, even if the question was absurd: would it not have been a bit easier for Duška if everything on her that was constantly swaying and flapping and fluttering had been full? Had been inflated? She felt as though she was watching a body in the midst of a difficult shedding, that Katarina's daughter was indeed trying to shed weight, but (oh, Dunja's magnificent way with words!) she obviously had a very long wait ahead of her.

Her face, however, was stunning! She looked like the actress Keira Knightley, only she didn't come across as dim. She wore her hair short, which brought out her hazel eyes and cute, twice-pierced ears adorned with small round earrings, as well as her perfect teeth. Although Duška had just returned from the beach, Dunja could have sworn she had mascara on her eyelashes, a trace of lipstick on her lips (or was this the purplish, salty remains of the day?) and yellow eyeshadow on her eyelids. Her head had found its way onto her body from a totally different sort of book.

'So you must be Draga?' Her voice was like honey, which is not unusual with portly people.

'It's *Dunja*, darling. Her name is Dunja,' Katarina corrected her daughter, leaning over her ear, and then awkwardly
repositioned herself behind her back.

'But you look just like a Draga,' Duška said in a calm voice
and, surprisingly, without a hint of insult; the frank expression
on her face was, more than anything, an invitation to discuss the
issue – to discuss the meaning and content of names, the juic-
iness, plumpness and stickiness of quinces and the propriety,
angularity and homeliness of people named Draga. She could
barely stop herself from responding to the girl as she might to
an adult – *how Shakespearean of you to say so!* – but instead, she
loudly cleared her throat (those damn pills, with their eternal
river of phlegm) and, to top it all, burst into a coughing fit. But
what she really, *really*, wanted to do was laugh.

After this bizarre display, the only option was silence. The
guest gazed at the floor, the mother at her daughter's shoulder,
and the daughter at the edge of the table, amused but *understanding* – at least that's how Dunja pictured her, although she
could not have said why. Did Dunja think that fat people were
somehow more saintly, more compassionate than most? That
when people are tested, when they bear myriad stigmas, their
hearts always expand? Oh please.

She heard water running in the bathroom. From the sound
of the stream, this would be the shower, where Kristijan must be
washing off sand and sun oil and microplastics with particular
enthusiasm. She realised, when the atmosphere in the kitchen
relaxed and she again felt Duška's penetrating eyes on her, that
she was not the least bit offended that Kristijan had sought refuge in hygiene from her unforeseen visit. Although she herself
had provoked this cross-pollination of past and present and,
what is more, knew very well that past processes rarely expire,
that the present is nothing but a multitude of becomings born
in various once-upon-a-times, even so, the will to enter her own
(and others') beginnings often got stuck. Like a lump in the
throat, like a breath in the windpipe, like Christmas dinner.
It was – a cheap metaphor came to mind – as though she had
rung up the past, all the while hoping that the lady would be

unavailable and those expensive long-distance minutes would be in vain. The only thing that impelled her to keep calling again and again was a sense of urgency, a suspicion that something important was there.

'OK,' said Duška, with a playful glance at her mother. 'Enjoy yourselves, Mimika and *Dunja*. Now it's my turn to take a shower. My skin is itching all over and even stings a little.' She wriggled out of the maternal pretzel and stood in *relevé*, looking just as she sounded – elegant and confident. What a remarkable child, Dunja thought, and followed her to the door with her eyes. Are all Gen Z kids like this, so at home in themselves, with full rights, or at least with more rights? Or are they merely more adept at constructing the illusion that they don't give a damn about society's demands?

Passing through the door, the girl turned not into the bathroom, where no water could now be heard, although the rituals seemed to still be in progress, but into the bedroom. Wait a second. Could that be *her* bedroom? Duška's room? Surely she did not sleep, as Katarina once did, on a cot next to her mother's bed? Would Katarina and Kristijan soon do what Cvetka had done and move to the sofa, so as not to cause the adolescent girl embarrassment or shame? What if for a change, she thought, impatiently backing into the sofa cushion, she simply asked Katy about it?

'It was a fair bit of trouble, but we split the room in two and now Duška has her very own space – not a large space, but at least it's a room,' Katy explained as she pulled out a chair and sat down at the table. She placed her hand on the table's surface and started tapping her fingers, which, Dunja knew, was to keep the desire to smoke at bay. 'I didn't want . . .' She laid her hand flat and, as if hounded by a ray of light, turned her chin away.

'She didn't want Duši to grow up the way she did, you know,' a bass voice chimed in, so low that Dunja, perhaps from the shock, felt the tissue between her ribs quiver. She automatically grabbed her knees (how incredibly defensive of her) and looked up to say hello (how incredibly polite of her) to Kristijan.

And . . . looked down again without a peep. Her stomach, which so far had borne the evening with relative calm, at once knotted up and did a flip. Not from disgust, as was its habit, but from excitement, the kind better suited to the anticipation of spring. She felt feverish all over: who was it actually standing there, tall and solid above her? She spread her arms a little, to check if her armpits stank, and cursed the polyester when she realised that they did. Of course they did.

'Hello, Dunja.' He held out his hand beneath her nose. 'I won't say I can hardly believe you're here, because I'm sure you're hearing that all the time these days.'

Another quiver, only now it was the tissue in her throat, weakening.

'Still . . .' – a true gentleman, he waited a moment, bending awkwardly – 'I guess you know that's the only thing I can say.'

She extended her arm like a frightened child in the presence of authority, her fingers more or less *swooning* into the offered hand. At the same time, her neck froze up, so with all her strength she strained her eyes, lifting them higher and higher, to show him that she did indeed possess something like a soul, that she was not merely some monstrous wreck. When they finally managed, yes, like in some stupid romcom, yes, to make eye contact, the scene was not banal: the lines of Kristijan's face, around his mouth, across his forehead and cheeks, were sombre, verging on pained (or anxious?); they were in fact (she studied him intently) the same as *hers*. This mirroring moved her. She was not the only one, she thought, whose life was not predominantly about having fun. She could barely compose herself enough to utter a soft, burbling 'Hello, Kristijan.'

'Are you staying for dinner? I'm cooking today,' he said, again standing upright above her, and she could not help thinking he had pronounced *today* as if it meant *always*. Katarina was already settled comfortably in her chair, and there was a certain finality in her comfort – *You see? Things are no longer in my hands.* Yes, that's exactly what it said. Which, strangely enough, Dunja did not find appalling. When she saw Katarina's hands folded in contentment, it was only then, perhaps, that she truly grasped the division of labour her friend had yearned for all these years. Surrender to protection – this might well have been her motto, even if it meant a white-walled flat and, almost always, the relinquishment of certain rights and the relaxation of certain duties.

'Oh, I . . .' Dunja was about to devise an answer, when Kristijan interrupted with a decisive 'Honey, could you hand me the dishcloth?'

'Of course, dear,' Katy replied and leaned over to the counter and then back to her partner.

'Sorry, Dunja,' he said, crouching down with sniper-like concentration and gently nudging her knees, as if to say, *Please lift your (old-person) limbs.* She really did feel as though a nurse from the old people's home were visiting her: *So how are we today, Miss Dunja? You're looking very well, Miss Dunja! Are we feeling peck-ish?* How many times had she seen those people kneeling in front of her mother as they spoke to her *from below*, with bulging eyes and saccharine tongues, as if the old lady could not *feel* the difference between humility and humiliation. She obeyed him and extended her legs across the three-seater sofa, leaving her feet to dangle over its end, as Kristijan crawled like a ferret to the space below it, wiped there with the cloth, went on to the space under the coffee table, wiped again, and also twice repeated the subsequent procedure, of twice folding the rag. She glanced at Katarina, who shrugged and smiled, and then it dawned on her: the coffee. The drops of coffee. *Between* the sofa and the coffee table. *Under* the sofa and coffee table. Small, dangerous droplets. Which would certainly have left a mark.

'All done,' he said as he clambered into the open, his still-damp hair brushing against her along the way. It was a strange sort of contact, a strange and unexpected intimacy, which, for her, was like two hot points touching.

'So, Dunja, what were you going to say? You'll stay?'

'Oh please do, please stay!' Katarina exclaimed like a child. And, as Kristijan came up to the sink behind her, patted his thigh, a gesture of gratitude that was more feigned than sincere – did he sense this? Wouldn't anyone, at some level, sense it? And wouldn't anyone feel hurt to realise this?

'Maybe another time, if that's all right.' Although she was a solitary person, she always felt tremendous guilt when she refused company (*People like you are why we talk about the atomisation of society*). Fortunately, her host and hostess (the host even seemed a bit relieved) spared her the protocol of entreating her to stay, which serves only to prolong scenes that have run their course.

'So let's make it another time. We're busy the next few evenings, but Wednesday is good. Maybe at six?' said Katy, and expectantly, but also, again, with a pinch of play-acting, looked over her shoulder at Kristijan, who nodded quickly and, unconvinced, let out a laugh.

'Good, it's settled,' Dunja affirmed. She was, in fact, gripping the pleather and calculating which steps and positions might, ironically, help her to walk gracefully, but then Katarina intervened – an intervention for which she was ready to erect a monument to her friend. Clearly, in the lattice of a relationship all that is bad and ugly gets magically evened out: a person is a jerk in the first nexus only to be a hero in the second.

'By the way, Dunja, I told Kristijan why you've come, and he said – didn't you, dear? – that he'd be happy to meet with you to answer any questions you might have for him.' Katy gave her a wink and, a moment later, was smirking. 'Now don't you two worry – I won't be hovering around you, I promise!'

Dunja, her fingernails deep in the artificial leather, at once seized the opportunity. If she had hesitated a second too long, something uniquely hers would have made itself known, some pathetic character trait – shyness, for instance, which was nothing more than unpreparedness for life dressed up as gentleness. But Dražen, when all was said and done, deserved a sister with balls.

'Really?' she exclaimed. 'That would be splendid! I know you said you don't have time for dinner until Wednesday, but Kristijan, would you have time for a morning coffee? Maybe tomorrow?'

The tall man, a least a head taller than Dunja, blushed, and it seem that he too, like her a little earlier, had got something caught in his throat. He ran his hands across the kitchen counter as if checking to see if it was smooth (or clean?) and only replied when Katarina flicked her hand behind her chair and nearly slapped him on the knee.

'Well, suuure.' He smiled apologetically. 'Would ten be all right?'

'Perfect. I suppose it's obvious I'm not on a schedule here,' she said, returning his smile. And this time she wasn't feigning or lying. Her — what was it even? research? *investigation?* amateur whodunnit? police procedural? — had no schedule or method or any real to-do list. Kristijan was her only starting point, and even he had simply *strolled* onto the scene. Of course, she wanted a structure for her narrative about Dražen, but a writer doesn't work her way to the structure until she has first chosen (or in her case, *recognised*) the times, places and characters — certain fundamental situations in her protagonist's development. Anything beyond that is digression, and Dunja *had* been digressing, and felt a great deal of guilt about it. For even if digression is the best way to conceptually capture human lives, she was well aware that it could not have the same validity when it came to human deaths. Death, she knew, demands discipline. Demands organisation. And discipline and organisation are hardly enough to shape a *narration*. This circle was complete in the most fucked-up way possible, but the promise of the Sunday chat over coffee gave her hope that at some point she would finally stop being scared of it. That at some point she would finally begin it.

'So where should we meet?' she asked. 'You know, I don't know what's here any more.'

'Do you remember where the summer farmers' market used to be? Well, just across the street, there's now a small shopping centre; most of the shops are closed, but one of the places still open is my bar, with a small patio that looks across the bay towards Savudrija.' He turned his head left and right as if in pain.

Of course she remembered Miss Lamija and Mr Almin, and the blood oranges in red string bags and the mounds of tomatoes and the little piles of slender peppers and the pyramids of courgettes and the bunches of parsley, but most of all she remembered (hee-hee) Lamija's little moustache and how much Almin loved to talk. But a bar?

'So what's the name of the bar?'

'*My Bar*,' he replied with a scowl, and Dunja could only agree: the hospitality industry too often brings out the worst sense of humour, the worst ideas. But what can you do? They deal with ordinary people.

'Good. See you tomorrow, then.' With a stately gait she proceeded to the door that led into the front hall. Katarina and Kristijan followed politely. She turned to the little cabinet for shoes, intending to put hers back on, as any well-mannered guest would do, but . . . she realised she had nothing to take off: her feet were still sweating in her pricey sandals. A remnant, she thought, of old habits, when a few tiny smudges on the floor would not even have been noticed. At the same time, she caught Katarina's eye, to convey a humble apology: *Sorry, I didn't take off my sandals!*

Katarina raised her eyebrows and pursed her lips, which Dunja knew – knew even after all these years – meant: *Don't be ridiculous, Dunči! It's fine!*

Don't be ridiculous, Dunči, it's fine, she repeated in her mind, and standing in front of the door of the flat that had once been like a second home to her, she almost believed it.

4

At sixty euros a night it was hardly surprising that the air conditioning, which might have helped her fall asleep, was not working. She had to rely on keeping the balcony door wide open and the natural cooling of the night – but nature, clearly, had a different idea. Around three in the morning, after her body had heated every scrap of bed linen, and she had stripped to her skin, and more than once pinned and repinned her hair up so it wouldn't glue itself to the pillow, to her face and to her back (aargh, if it would only disappear!), after she had grabbed her phone, unable to sleep, and stickied and soiled her fingers on the pornographically self-righteous, aggrieved and victimised posts she found there, after the air she had let in filled the room with a vile and sordid odour (yuck!), like a drunken writer at a New Year's Eve party (*Hey, little girl, aren't you a treat!*); so it was that around three o'clock, after she had been in the bathroom, rinsing her neck and cooling her wrists over the sink and admitting to herself that relief (and, the following day, new attacks of arthritis pain) would come only on the floor, although not even there really, since the tiles were absurdly warm; so, in short, around three o'clock, she became so exasperated that she was almost hallucinating. She stamped and she screamed and eventually she threw herself face down amid the tangled sheets and started pounding at them – good grief, what a child.

She railed out a few couplets and surrendered: whenever she could not find peace, what rescued her from her turmoil, even from the arthritis attacks, was, as a rule, weed. She dug it out of her *nécessaire*, in which she kept all her toiletries (if marijuana was not a necessity, it was at least a toiletry: it freshened her up at times, beautified her), arranged on the mattress the stoner's triad – grinder, roach cards, papers – and, ten minutes later, *voilà*, a joint, *finis*! She wrapped herself in the nearest dress, which was draped over a chair, grabbed her lighter and slipped onto the balcony.

Outside it was the complete opposite of the overwrought inside: tranquil, almost kind. The air was vaporising the sea, which stretched out beyond the treetops like an endless dark tarpaulin; it flickered in the moonlight, gently lapping, wavelet after wavelet over wavelet into wavelet, splashing with greater force against its (our?) edges, as if it were trying to push them away, molecule by molecule. What is it about the sea, she wondered as the tip of the joint started crackling yellow before her eyes, which tends to banish all individuality, so that anyone who stares at it long enough suddenly realises they are hollow inside and there is nothing around them? That they are, well, small? Why does it fill with yearning anyone who isn't totally dense (whoa, she was already feeling it – indica really does not take its time), with the yearning to put aside all *feeling* for your present, to reject this ultimate psychosis and experience a kind of apotheosis, even if it is merely an *assumption into the sea*, to attach yourself to the past, to the universal, no, even better, to be more precise, to the primordial, to dissolve into a place before anything ever came to be – especially not her – but had always, from the beginning of time, existed? *Shiiit!* She realised how hard and deep the stuff was hitting her, and yet how shallow her thinking was: she wasn't getting anywhere with these ideas; in fact, all that water was probably having the very opposite effect. The sea stimulates melancholy, and what is melancholy if not the feeling that you're missing out on a life you never lived, but what is that (she drew the Indian smoke inside her and held it in her lungs, the way a spiderweb holds a raindrop) if not a kind of vision? A vision based on all that is unfulfilled, deferred, rejected, on remnants, crumbs and sediment? To gaze at the sea (she exhaled the smoke and sat down on the folding chair in the balcony corner — she felt a little dizzy; this was strong stuff, as strong as could be; next time she would buy something milder; she would definitely ask her dealer for more detailed information about his product and not just grab the first thing he offered, umm, OK, so where was she? Right, *to gaze at the sea*, that's where she had stopped: to gaze at the sea is to see (heh-heh) the fabric of the future in the making, but a future woven out of odds and ends, out of rags, out of knots and snippets and scraps, out of materials the seamstress didn't need but kept anyway. And why did she keep them? Why does *any*body keep *any*thing, if not simply because the very act of keeping is a fundamental warranty for future possibilities; if not because without a box of scraps there can in fact be no future?

Uhhhh, so what if all that is true? She giggled and inhaled and, oof, that drag burned, it really hurt; oof, it hit her right in the centre of her consciousness, right where there is no metaphor, no metonymy, where truth accepts and in the end takes its promissory note: the sea (yes, this has to be true) washes up a huge variety of colourful visions, which arise out of thousands of discarded items, but her discarded item — ouch, how could she call it that? — was always and only one, even if it had two bodies; it was always Dražen's and always her father's, her father's and Dražen's, shared *decomposed* body, while *her* fucking vision (she started to cry and the burnt-down joint fell from her hands) was always their — always and only their — un-lived-out life.

Leaning her elbows on her knees, her wet face cupped in her hands — that fucking sea was now on her cheeks — she felt in her gut, she actually *heard* — what exactly? Was that Peter's voice? Or Simon's?

✳

Simon's. It was always – only – Simon's voice speaking to them, even though it scorched and burned them (don't bombs fall precisely so the fire does *not* stop burning?). He was found on the beach, Mr and Mrs Anko, by an early-morning bather (Simon was rushing, yes, rushing over the words) and he must have fallen from the cliff, from the church wall probably, and had lain there, by our estimation, since three a.m., and, Mr and Mrs Anko, it was only luck (*luck!* he said it right in front of them) that he wasn't carried off by the tide. (But water douses fire, doesn't it? Water soothes!) The boy's actual identity (Soldier Simon kept on lighting the fire, but with a voice smouldering like embers) was deduced from his ID card, which was still in his pocket, inside his wallet (a child's wallet, the old green one, the one with velcro), but, Mr and Mrs Anko, deducing alone is not enough; we must follow procedure. The two detectives then croaked in unison, You know . . ., but again it was only Simon, Tank Driver Simon, who continued: It will be painful, Mr and Mrs Anko, but the boy (he rumbled) must also be identified by you. We understand, the two of them said, leaning towards each other until they touched heads, two sad ostriches in the middle of hell; Mr and Mrs Anko would much prefer not to, but if it was necessary . . . So today or tomorrow, Mr and Mrs Anko. Take your time, the blond man said, there's no hurry. (Fire is fire, after all.)

Her mother, wincing, said, *Tomorrow*, and her father, now only an echo, a bullet shell, repeated after her, *Tomorrow, yes, tomorrow.*

Only she, the charred little girl between her exploded parents, asked him, asked with her eyes, eyes full of soot, being at a loss for grammar: *But what was it? What happened? How could someone fall, fall from so high up? How could* he *have fallen?*
Why
did
Dražen
have
to
fall?
My brother Dražen?

We can't yet say for sure what happened, the fair-haired detective said, absorbing all questions so the dark-haired one could more easily summarise: Behind the wall next to the church we found evidence of drinking, two empty bottles of inexpensive wine, but we still don't know who drank them. Forensics will explain a few things, and the autopsy will clarify others: was Dražen inebriated when he fell? Did he perhaps fall by accident? Could anyone have wanted to harm the boy, who was only a teenager? Did he maybe jump deliberately, because he was unhappy? But we'll be discussing all this later, and with you, since you are the ones (he slowed down amid the ruins) who knew Dražen best. But without a doubt, Mr and Mrs Anko, the detective assured them, there are witnesses out there who don't yet know what they saw, and witnesses who maybe suspect something, and witnesses who know but are still in shock and too afraid to say anything, but they will find the courage, and it won't be long before they do. (*Who know, who will, we know, we will* – what a pathetic rhythm, the rhythm of striking a match, the rhythm of a march not an elegy.)

'We're very sorry for your loss,' the men said when they had run out of things to say. 'Sincerely. There is nothing harder in this world.' Her mother, hollowed out, nodded at *very sorry* and at *witnesses* and at *won't be long*, each time digging her chin into her daughter's hair. With her hands she covered her daughter's eyes, ears and nose, and the two of them became a pile of ash, and her father, also ash, somehow put his arms around them – his embrace had always been a gentle, most delicate smothering. (Remove the oxygen and you put out the fire.)

And, truly, they were not breathing. How could they be when they had lost a—

—heart rising to her throat, trying to push through her ribs, to shred itself on them, front and back, to pierce her lungs and graze the surrounding organs, to flood them with its raging boom-da-boom beat. The nausea was cannabinoid, new, now, but also then, and—

—she felt like she was going to throw up that day – the day after *that one* – when her parents came home (oh, but it wasn't a home any more, it was a haunted house) and their vacant eyes told her to sit down, to sit *between* them, to sit alone in a space meant for a *spectrum*, for a brother and a sister, a son and a daughter, a space that had always been soft but was now only sharp. (It pierced her, not like a flame but like a sword.) They put their arms across her shoulders, but those translucent arms did nothing to soothe: there beneath the cliff, it really had been Dražen; there beneath the sheet, really Dražen; lying on the gurney, really Dražen; there in the morgue, Dražen,
everywhere there,
unmoving,
Dražen,
and what could this soothe? Remove? Console?

The silence was long and became the day, yet another sunny day, as if on purpose, to give them a rehearsal of life in hell, and Dunja, cocooning herself in herself, had almost completely climbed into herself, into her nausea, when her mother *said.* (Slanting the tin between them so that for a moment – since tin melts in heat – it would fill the crater.) That Dražen's *corpse* (yes, she actually said this, but she meant well) looked incredibly peaceful and sweet. That it was even smiling a little, *such a mischievous smile, Duni! You know what I mean, Duni, like when he would lie to me about smoking, or, you remember, when he was telling you about breast-feeding and made it sound so disgusting you started screaming in horror, or, well this you won't remember but your father and I do, when he let that fat blind man into the flat, just into the front hall.* That it didn't (she kept saying) have unruly, shaggy hair (the way Dražen's always was). That the hair had been shaved off, but even like that it looked (*the corpse,* she kept saying, meaning only the best), even like that it looked handsome. That its skin was *silky,* with azure flowing beneath it (*Since I'm different, I'm special, I'm blue-blooded*). That its eyes were closed, but even so it was looking at her, *as if teasing me, you know, but, Duni, always with affection.* Yes, this is what she told her daughter, because what was lying there was not composed of words.

(*His skull was smashed*, she did not say.

Just a hint of eyes, no shape at all, she did not sob out.

His nose wasn't just broken, it was, oh . . . she did not burst into tears.

His lips were all that remained of his face, his lips were how we recognised him, she did not scream.

And they were expressionless, a straight line, soulless and blank, she did not wail.

Nor did her father say that the blue was *stony, not azure or aquamarine, but poisonous.*

Nor did he tell her how *when they pulled the curtain open I collapsed onto the floor and your mother and Simon and Peter helped me up.*

He kept quiet about how *she looked at Dražen through the glass, with glassy eyes, glassy limbs, a glassy throat, a glassy chin, she was all glass.*

He did not say to her, *I looked only at her. In the glass. Made of glass.*

He did not shatter that *I saw him only through her, Dunja, only through her. Because through glass, Dunja, you see enough; you see everything.*

He did not inhale that *she shut her eyes.*

And burst into shards.

He did not exhale, 'And that's how I knew.'

They did not exhale, 'And that's how we both knew.'

Nobody *told* her anything.

Nobody.)

Never, but still—

—there had always been an *image* running beside her – no! running *behind* her – and it was running even now, as Dunja wriggled out of her wrap and, hunching over, pulled apart the curtains to that fucking room and covered her mouth with her hands, which had gone numb, which she wouldn't have felt at all if she hadn't glanced at them a moment before. She could have sworn it was that *image* which caused her to trip and was laughing at her, loudly and snidely and with cruel delight, when

she bumped into the sharp edge of the damn table and yelled −
dammit! − and hit the wood with her fist − *shit!* − slightly graz-
ing her knuckles, breaking the skin a little − *shit!* − as acid and
fatigue were nearly pouring from her gullet and she gurgled
out − *ffffuck you!* − flapping her arms like a bird that can't get
off the ground because in fact she never learned how. She stumbled over to the bathroom door and − what, in such a rush, was
she really going to hunt for the light switch? − and the *image*
pounced at her from a corner, shoved itself against her, invisible
but dangerously blinding, this fucking inheritance, and Dunja,
little sis, had no choice but to give in. She collapsed onto the tiles
and vomited out her overpriced, oversalted seafood dinner, shut
her teary eyes as tightly as she could and hoped against hope
that when she opened them again the *image* would be swimming in the vomit, a digested, metabolised, *decomposed image*, its
soggy fibres, as thin as could be, now just a puddle in a puddle,
which she could wipe up, wring out and throw away. She hoped
against hope, but even so she had her eyelids squeezed shut for
so long that, behind them, leaning against the doorjamb, naked
and sweaty, sticky and dazed, she finally fell asleep.

*

It wasn't just a single headache she had; there must have been
a hundred. They descended into her neck and shoulders and,
combining forces, defeated her morning arthritis pain, that
total stiffness of pelvis and spine, and this was most welcome.
The problem was that Dunja's antirheumatic medications,
which she had to inject often, did not allow her to take other
drugs, not even fucking aspirin, paracetamol, or ibuprofen, let
alone ketoprofen − none of the effective classics on which the
effective world is founded. The classics which the sullen bus
driver who drove her from Bernardin must surely have used to
wake himself up; which undoubtedly were helping the fisher-
man, weighed down with coolers in front of her, to walk; on

which (it could not have been otherwise) the impatient Polish father relied as he herded his four children over the pedestrian crossing as if they were goats; with which, of course, the woman had armed herself who was hurrying along the pavement beside the roundabout and heading up to the campsite, where, Dunja suspected, she had spent the night in a damp tent on even damper soil; and last but not least, the classic drug the waitress had washed down with her first coffee at the bar where Dunja was meeting Kristijan – a girl no older than eighteen, hidden behind a pair of enormous raver sunglasses, which, however, were too small to cover all the pocks and blemishes on her cheeks and chin.

Dunja, therefore, before leaving the hotel, had been obliged to turn to something that was at odds with her pragmatic life-style (but did she really believe that self-stereotype? What sort of thirty-something pragmatist plays detective?) – namely, Tiger Balm. She had rubbed it lightly into her forehead and temples and applied it thickly under her clavicles and across her trapezius muscles, and then run in a frenzy to wash her hands. This, she believed, was why she now exuded an even stronger, even more annoying odour, and as she perused the menu – sundaes, ice cream coffees and ristrettos – she experienced a new bout of humiliation: her choice of Tiger Balm, she decided, enrolled her in the ranks of senior citizens. Young women are *fragrant* with flowers and fruit, with jasmine, bergamot, lilies and the like, while old women *reek* of spices, herbs and wood, of mint and sandalwood and those fucking cloves.

'I'll have a caffè affogato,' she made her choice when a breeze carried the little barmaid bee to her table – *she* (bingo! Dunja's hyperbole had not been amiss) was indeed all roses and ylang ylang and patchouli. (Good taste, absolutely, a tinge of ecstasy and ketamine, undoubtedly, haha.)

Dunja, in her own cloud of menthol and camphor, leaned back and observed the hills over Savudrija. And the hills over Lucija. And the hills over the salt pans. And the hills over Lucija's wild beach, where visitors bathed at their own risk and junkies plunged into their own veins. Hills she had never visited and which she had never observed quite long enough for them to merge into what they were constantly touted as offering. Fucking natural beauty, something fucking unique, some fucking *rare experience*. The essence of the Adriatic hinterland, its green and prickly and thorny heart beating to the rhythm of the insects.

And apropos of a beating heart, a heart gone wild, in fact: at precisely ten o'clock, approaching her between the closely placed tables, Kristijan appeared. She rubbed her palms like a child between her crossed thighs, an action he most likely he did not see, and started grinning idiotically, which only a blind person would not have seen. Although Kristijan was already sitting down in front of her, and looking at her quizzically, she simply could not conceal her feelings; sometimes feelings cannot simply be switched off, the way we switch off our computer, telephone or television; when it comes to feelings – *to feelings, from feelings, about feelings, with feelings* – things sometimes can get very difficult.

Especially feelings not deemed particularly moral. For it must be understood that neither during that first, incidental meeting nor during this second, planned one was Dunja reduced to idiocy by the force of memory (*Oh look, my childhood love is suddenly right here in front of me!*) – no, it wasn't that at all. Dunja was struck, and greatly struck, by Kristijan's new, *incredibly* attractive body. If, as a teenager, he had seemed mysterious and ethereal, now, as a man, he was clear, *chiselled*, and somewhat generic. But generic, when it comes to the forms and textures of (pardon the expression) *meat*, is not necessarily bad; it does its job (and very well, too): it stimulates, and at the same time cures, desire, if only in the imagination – a property, Dunja was thinking, that cannot be ascribed, at least not incontrovertibly, to experimental formats that are *markedly* erotic, that are, therefore, erotic by will, through a germ of reflection, of decision almost, through something distinctly human, and less through something animal. Something un-thinking.

Kristijan, then, had transformed himself into a hunk, but not the bulging-muscles kind, which, again, is completely misguided in that it reduces body culture to the vulgar adventure of appearance, to an appearance that is incapable of enlisting any sort of thought and so does not hide anything, just as it doesn't show anything either. No, Kristijan had refashioned his body, undoubtedly through enormous effort, into the Ancient Greek kind of hunk (the Ancient Greeks, after all, were adept at creating the appearance, haha, that they put big ideas before everything else), which made him look like a man who, *right here and now*, could throw, hurl, move, push and pull, lift and lower, squeeze and (not violently, but because it had to be done!) trample and crush something; like a man who, *right here and now*, could take action, start something and finish it – a revolution, even a war maybe . . . Oh my God – Dunja at last slammed on the brakes – her feelings were certainly making things difficult, not only because they were not entirely respectable, but also because they were turning out to be so reactionary!

'Hi, Dunja. Are you OK?' Kristijan, sitting down, supported himself on the chair's armrests, which made his biceps blossom.

'Uhh . . .' Dunja at last pulled her hands out from between her thighs and placed them in her lap. 'Well, yeah. I just didn't sleep very well, and it's so hot, much too hot for me, and if I don't get coffee soon my head is going to explode.'

Not bad, she thought – a reply that straddled the border between public (the heatwave) and private (the headache), a reply that invited something comparable in return; yes, a suitable response, she decided, but it would have been *excellent* if she had not uttered it so damn flirtatiously, *and* if she had stopped herself from making that motion, which Kristijan might not even have noticed since it had long been a kind of white noise among the women of Lucija: namely, she had run her hand through her hair, first grabbing a thick strand at the forehead, which she then wound into a bun on top of her head and let fall, just as it was, still on top of her head. This *borrowed* action did not merely serve the submissive function of attractiveness or beauty; rather (again, in true Lucija style), it officially opened the battle season that characterised local heterosexual relations.

At the same time, it signalled a lack of weaponry and foretold surrender — but only under conditions that would, over time, be revealed, change and, especially, *collapse*. Dunja should definitely have not let something like that slip out.

'I couldn't sleep either,' Kristijan said, looking (of course) magnificently rested. 'But for now I've resigned myself to the situation — these are our new summers. Because you know — you probably remember — it didn't use to be so fuckingly, brutally, miserably hot here.'

Although no longer as refined as they had once been, Dunja thought, his modifiers still came in threes: charming, wonderful, beautiful! Fantastic, outstanding, striking! *You must play confidently and aggressively, but also carefully, Dunja. There are no second chances in chess*, she suddenly heard him saying, and in response cocked her head to the side and lowered her chin, which made her eyes look bigger. Honestly, they looked enormous.

'It's true, a lot has changed since I was last here,' she said, giving him her you-especially wink, and she was just about to flutter out *but you always were one of the gorgeous ones*, when the waitress, now sans sunglasses, wafted over to their table in the company of a gigantic conical glass festooned like a carnival float and littered with whipped cream and chocolate sprinkles like the road afterwards, a glass so difficult to set down the girl had to crouch a little and, in doing so, revealed to Dunja and Kristijan the fact that her billowy black top was, *literally*, the only thing she had on above the waist.

'And what will you be having?' she asked, standing quite close to the man, who looked straight ahead, at the top of an empty wicker chair, and demanded, coldly (as cold as ice water, you might say), an espresso.

The girl disappointedly (not having been noticed) buzzed back to her sweltering work habitat and Kristijan removed his eyes from the wicker chair and something — Dunja had no idea what — flashed across his face and for a split second lingered on the shiny copper of his brow. It was the difference between the glow of rising and the glow of setting, she might have said if she wanted to be poetic, but that would have skirted the essential thing, which was that Kristijan's rudeness was now, for no apparent reason, seemingly by chance, progressing into, what? Hatred? Disgust? Towards whom? Towards her? Towards them both? Towards the dark-complexioned, hungover waitress?

The first two possibilities simply did not make sense to her, while the third she would *never* accept. Kristijan, *that sort* of person? Kristijan, one of *those* people? Kristijan, a *fasc*—

Instantly, as if she'd been handling a mangy rag, she dropped her coy demeanour and attempted her most consummate harpy (but hardly a convincing, effective, terrifying etc. harpy – her voice was trembling and her hands, oh, they were dancing around like dust in a draughty room).

'I believe Katarina told you why I've come,' she said and repeated what had been explained the day before. And what could Kristijan do but nod vigorously? 'I didn't know exactly where to begin, but as luck would have it, I was, in a way organically, brought to you.'

'I see.' And a nod.

'You probably knew Dražen better than anyone.'

'Perhaps.' And a nod.

'It's important, I think, that I begin with my brother, with the person he was.'

A nod.

'Because, at the time, the two detectives – so my mother told me – did not exhaust every avenue, and I expect that's true because we still don't know what happened.'

Again a nod.

'Not that I think I can do a better job than they did, since, supposedly, they were good at their job.'

And again. Twice even.

'At the time, of course, everything was kept from me.'

Again and again.

'I would interview the detectives, too, you know, but Simon is dead, and Peter, well, he's a drunk – I know this for a fact – and he'd probably refuse to talk to me.'

Yeah.

'There's a lot I could learn from my mother too, only she doesn't remember much any more. Mama has a severe case of dementia, you know.'

'Oh, I'm sorry to hear that,' he said, nod-nod-nodding.

A pause. If only the consummate harpy could get everything off her chest! She nervously slid her chair back towards the wall and weaved her arms high into the air — *orchestra, you may begin* — and the first beat fell with the piercing blast of a trombone.

'Kristijan, what I am really curious about is why you and Dražen stopped being friends back then. What happened?'

Because something *must* have happened. If, for a year or even two years (her memory, after all, did not provide a precise timetable), Kristijan had been part of the furniture, a portable lamp glowing in the corners of their flat every afternoon, almost without fail, then in March, or maybe it was April, in the year of the country's independence, he was tossed out with the rubbish. This might not be the best metaphor, but Dunja needed somehow to evoke the sense that one of them in this story got *dumped* by the other; that, despite all appearances, their friendship was not exactly ironclad. Her brother, during those weeks, would pace irritably from room to room; hardly a day went by without him griping about her or their mother or their father or some neighbour or the world or the universe, making accusations and cursing at them for one thing or another, her to her face, their parents behind their back: because he couldn't study, because they were so poor, because he had to walk around looking foolish, because they ate bad food, because he didn't have a bicycle, because people were crazy, because people were depraved, because you never knew, because even when you did know it was unbelievable, because anyway it's all overrated, because you're little and stupid, Dunja, and annoying as hell. Because! After a while it became clear even to her, little and stupid as she most certainly was, that he was insulting everybody except the person who, most of all, was no longer in his life and would therefore have been the easiest, if not the fairest, target for his insults and accusations. On the contrary, with regard to

Kristijan, whenever their mother asked him about his friend
(which did not happen often, since, ultimately, their mother was
a thoughtful processor of teenage emotion), he would employ
an oppositional language, which connoted the extent of the rup-
ture exclusively through small signs and short words, through
fillers, basically: 'No, Mama, *really*, Kristijan *won't* be coming
here again.' 'You're *wrong*, Mama; I don't have any plans to meet
him.' '*No, please*, there's no need to make an extra plate for him.'
'*Now look*, Mama, I'm *telling* you, I just don't have time for him
any more.' In order to create the impression that the source of
his instability lay elsewhere and not at Kristijan's door, Dražen
had been exercising the classic method of displacement (this
idea came not from the past Dunja, but from the present one),
but these exercises (as all the Dunjas understood) had been
utterly worthless. Something had definitely happened.

'So they really *didn't* tell you anything,' he began, and this
time, thank God, it was Dunja who nodded. Thank God, she
thought, Kristijan, too, was nervous; thank God, he put his
arms behind his head as if wanting to stretch, but then suddenly,
like two restless seagulls, they returned to the arms of the chair.
'We fought over a girl, Dunja.' A certain restlessness remained
in his hands. 'A girl we both liked. Well, were both in love with,
actually.' The twitches in his right hand he brought up to his ear
and, with thumb and forefinger, sharpened his right sideburn
to a point (*yuck*). 'I suppose we fell in love with her around the
same time, but these things tend to come out later, you know,
especially between boys. Still, I expect teenage boys tell each
other more than grown men do – it hits them harder, throws
them off balance, or whatever they call it these days.'

He's digressing, Dunja (now Dunja the detective) realised,
and intervened: 'So who was the girl?'

'Mirela. A classmate, of course.' Now he sharpened the
left sideburn as well and, as in an aftershave commercial, patted his chin with his open palm, and *a little bit* of his neck
too. That wasn't done intentionally, was it? Surely it was an
act of physical necessity and not meant as, maybe, a sign of
social availability, maybe, flirtation? But if it was that, then

the invitation did not come from her, right? So he initiated it
himself? Maybe? Oh dear.

'I don't remember her. Is it possible I never met her?'
Dunja said, detaching her eyes from the pampered skin of
his neck, on which she detected, hmm, either a love bite or
(speaking of aftershave) a shaving cut, which Katarina's face
powder – yes, it was definitely *her* face powder – had rather
poorly concealed.

'I'm not surprised you don't remember her,' he said with
a spiteful laugh (wow, completely new teeth, too). 'I barely
remember her myself. But, hundredpercent, she visited your
home at some point, because that's what Dražen and I fought
about. I don't like to admit it, but that really is what we fought
about. It drove me crazy back then that he was bringing her to
his place. I was jealous, you see. Totally jealous.'

Had some Mirela person been in their home? Dunja
struggled to remember, but it was a fog. If she hadn't been so
obsessed with Kristijan at the time, she would probably have
been more attentive to external details, if it was even proper
to refer to visits by a teenage girl – a girl who, *hundredpercent*,
took up a certain amount of space in the room and also made
noise – as a *detail*.

'At the time Dražen told me it was my own fault for not
asking her out first, but the big thing was that . . .' He had
started talking like a teenager. He leaned forwards, with his
elbows on his knees, and said, 'So where's my espresso? What's
taking so long?'

He looked over his shoulder: the waitress was at the other
end of the patio, giggling and chatting with a customer – he
must have been her friend, since, she assumed, people only
share lit cigarettes with friends, and when they pass them back
and forth, it's not about the tobacco any more, but about the
touches imprinted on and mediated by the cellulose, by the
filter, and a bit by the wind too. It seemed that – no, it was
evident that – the girl had forgotten Kristijan. Dunja took no
offense, because, well, if she herself had been as hungover as
that girl was, she would have taken the day off, with streaming

TV, phone-ordered pizza and a soft blanket. Kristijan, however, was more than just offended by what he saw. If this had been a cartoon, foam would be bubbling at the corners of his mouth, puffs of steam would be shooting from his ears, and his eyes would be spinning in their sockets, but, *of course*, it was not a cartoon, so the foam and the steam now spewed from his tongue: 'Hey! You over there! Are you gonna bring me my coffee or not? Do I need to talk to the manager? We're friends, you know, and I don't think he'll be very happy about this!'

At the word *this*, at that last chunk of spew, he again turned towards Dunja. His facial features had narrowed into slits, flattened into contempt and, and . . . *OH! SHIT!* It was choking her (mentally, of course, only mentally), forcing her to sink her chin into her neck – *KRISTIJAN IS THAT SORT! KRISTIJAN IS ONE OF THOSE!* And it was clear, as clear as in a laboratory, that this same thing, although not in the same benign language (hers must be, fuck, going metastatic) had definitely been seen by the girl, THAT POOR YOUNG WOMAN, whose lower lip now swelled and drooped, whose cheeks were now rippling and twitching in a remix of anger and thickening tears. Dunja felt all the more for the girl (for God's sake, why didn't she know her real name? *Lorela* would have to do for now) as they had both run aground in Kristijan's Aegean waters; they had both, to put it more clearly, been misled by his beauty, and Dunja had no choice but to conclude that this – to mislead and, by misleading, to lead away – is, in fact, the primary and sole intention of beauty. Beauty can be anything but truth; this, you know, it actually cannot be.

Lorela (let's just call her that) disappeared into the building to fetch that *fucking* espresso, and Dunja, oh, Dunja had received from this repugnant incident sufficient ammunition, enough real ammo, not just blank cartridges, to defend herself against Kristijan, against his outward appearance and, even more, his inward reality. She calmly and for a long, long time stirred the ice cream into her coffee with the long spoon, until the white turned entirely brown; then she tapped the spoon loudly against the glass, which rang with a nervous, nerve-wracking sound, and at last slammed it, slammed it *hard*, onto the saucer. It's a good thing, she thought, that the affogato dishes here aren't porcelain.

'Well, your *espresso*' (she pronounced the word with disgust) 'should *hundredpercent* be here soon. Could you perhaps go back to that *important* thing you wanted to tell me about?'

As if a gigantic lead ball had just swung in front of him, he swiftly leaned back. Maybe she was exaggerating (when did she not?), but he seemed surprised by her reaction, as if he had expected her (how should she put it?) to be passionately inflamed by his mean, despicable outburst and even more passionately to take part in it! Fuckingshit! She was shocked to see what her coastland had become: the fact that Kristijan could lay into Lorela so shamelessly, in front of everyone's eyes, could only mean, first of all, that the environment endorsed such behaviour – that it had elevated it to the level of fucking acceptability – from which it then followed that the environment itself must be irrational and rotten.

A torso as taut as Kristijan's would normally produce a sound that thundered; Kristijan's voice, however, now stumbled into thinner tones and sounded, well, like an adolescent's. Its very timbre, she suddenly realised (to the honour of prosody, or was it poetics?), contained meaning.

'Yeah, umm, I was talking about Mirela. So the big thing was, you see, that Dražen and Mirela had this, like, really big common interest, which made it easier for him to invite her home. Because Mirela was also a big – I wouldn't even say big – she was a *huge* Michael Jackson fan. *Huge*, I tell you.' As if offering her treats – *Look what I've got, Dunjica, chocolate truffles and chocolate-covered marshmallows. So which would you like?* – he cocked his head in a grandmotherly fashion and, boy, did he *not* get the response he wanted. Far from it. What, did he think she'd forgive him just like that? Give in to the granny and forget the fucking *fascist*? Pretend that nothing had happened and see him once more as the god of sex appeal? No fucking way. She had no intention now of accepting any of his slimy filth – *Get the hell out of here, Gran-Gran*, she almost muttered; *You can scrape*

those truffles and chocolate-covered marshmallows straight into the bin,
Grandma fucking Kristi!

'Yeah, well . . .' – he was obliged to continue, since Dunja,
clenching her teeth, remained silent – 'it was really Michael
Jackson that brought them together, because compared to that,
she and I didn't have much in common, except maybe that neither of us was very popular – her not with the boys and me not
with the girls.' Then he quickly cocked his head to the other
side – *So how about some cream rolls, Duni, or I could bake you some*
other tasty treat. But from Dunja, practically nothing. She licked
her lips. Angrily, *but what a temptation.*

'Of course it was ridiculous, you know, the two of us fighting. I mean, it's not like I had any deep love for her. If I'm
honest, I fell in love with her because she was the first girl in
our class to get, well, you know, *breasts* and, well, *other curves.*'
How bashfully he said this! Like an adolescent boy – it struck
her that he still had pockmarks from puberty, and she felt a little disgusted. 'Other than that, as far as I can recall, she didn't
have anything else that attracted me. But you know it wasn't
all that different, all that special, for Dražen either; Michael
Jackson was the only thing they shared. But still, we became
rivals, Dunja. It was just a big delusion.'

His gaze left Dunja's face, or that general area – they were
simply not looking each other in the eye any more – and for a
moment went *south-east,* an established metaphor for, umm, not
exactly suffering but maybe endurance? Yearning? Obviously
(how could it have been otherwise?), when she saw him like that,
at that moment, Dunja, but only and exclusively for a moment,
had to soften. Something, after all, joined her to Kristijan; well,
probably not just *something,* but an essential intersection, probably the feeling that they had both (it was, of course, impossible,
but what can you do when guilt and logic are so mutually hostile?), once upon a time, caused all of this, all of *that.*

That's OK, she was about to say, consolingly, but then it hit
her, the great detective (we should capitalise this in the future),
it hit her in a flash: in matters relating to Kristijan at least,
nothing was impossible. Didn't she come to this *fucking coast*

precisely to resolve *all of that*? And how was she supposed to
do this if she hadn't yet armed herself — not with anything? If
she was still so *unsuspecting*! If she was walking around these
nonplaces as if on some memory safari, with potentially dangerous beasts lurking everywhere — underfed lions, leopards
and rhinos — and her *so fucking oblivious*? Next thing you know,
she'd be taking her picture with them, complete with selfie stick,
stupid duck face and peace sign.

So she shook off (*hooray!*) the impulse to console him and
gave her head a quick shake: there would be no selfie or duck
face or peace sign today.

But . . . but what to do *next* (her breakfast did a loop in
her stomach, and in a panic she reached for the water that had
come with the coffee) — but what to do *next* , since there was
no way she could openly *interrogate, pick apart, double-check* and
cross-examine Kristijan. If she did, she would lose the advantage
of naivety and force him to defend himself, whether or not he
had actually done anything. Aaah, she greedily finished off the
water; her unsuspicious pause was running out, but she still
had one more obstruction in front of her! *Shit.* She set down
the water glass and, at last, started on the ice cream coffee. She
plunged the long spoon right to the bottom of the glass and,
dragging it up the side, fished out, hmm, not something particularly nice to look at — a muck of milk and sinfulness — but
certainly tasty. And *voilà*! Diving and fishing and smacking one's
lips might easily serve as an allegory for the investigative process! After all, doesn't it often happen in genre fiction (or could
this be true of all fiction?) that the key element is hidden not in
excessiveness but in some ordinary, everyday, *mind-numbingly
tedious* thing, to which the heroine suddenly becomes hysteri-
cally attentive, in so far as hysteria is always the site of a battle
with truth and, at least in crime fiction, with justice as well?

Yes, something of the sort might well be that golden rule,
but, as Dunja set down the ice cream glass, nothing, *really nothing*, was occurring to her. So she blurted out the first thing that
popped into her mind, since Kristijan was by now eyeing her a
little suspiciously.

'So was Mirela in love with Dražen?'

'Big time! Which is why it all seemed so pathetic to me. You need to know' (Lorela, her face red, appeared behind his back) 'that it meant a whole lot more to her than it did to us. She even persuaded her father – she told me this herself –' (Lorela, now at Kristijan's shoulder) 'to buy her a second copy of Michael's first album. And then she gave that second record to Dražen, as a gift, and at the time' (Lorela gingerly setting the coffee in front of him) 'it was – you should know this too – like a precious treasure. Dražen was over the moon, since the vinyl record wasn't the easiest thing to get; it was constantly sold out, and of course, in Yugoslavia, buying it on order was basically impossible.' He did not even blink at the sight of that damn espresso, while Lorela herself was, as far as he was concerned, something *loathsome*. 'But you know, Dražen also made fun of how devoted Mirela was.' Dunja quickly thanked Lorela and wished only that she could also give her a hug, that she, the white saviour, could assume part of the girl's burden, could comfort her for all she had recently lost. 'He did not truly appreciate her friendly – no, it was more than that – her *loving* gesture. He told me – and this was the day we quarrelled, so you see how bizarre our fight was – that he was going to convince her to get her father to buy him a second record too, I think maybe *Bad*? I'm not sure; it was a long time ago.'

'I don't think I . . .' Dunja began, extracting herself from the imagined hug. 'Well, maybe I just don't remember any records, and I don't remember Dražen bragging about owning any, but I know for a fact that our family did *not* have a record player, so why would Dražen want records?' This felt really good – shoving Kristijan so *casually* and *confidently* between the horns of a dilemma; with any luck, she gloated, he'll get himself a little beat up. GOTCHA, FASCIST!

'Well, you were obviously too young at the time to understand, but vinyl records were a status symbol, Dunja. Even if you couldn't play them, it was still fantastic to own them, to collect them. Believe me, if Dražen was alive today, he probably still wouldn't play them. But he'd be showing them off.'

OK, so he didn't stumble after all, the Great Detective determined, but the skin around his mouth and nose and on his forehead was again furrowed – a new attack of melancholy, that fearful symmetry between them. All the same, Dunja had learned something these past twenty minutes, and now, suddenly truly worthy of her moniker, she became sharp and bold, which is to say: *creative*. The time had arrived for her to play the one trump card she actually held (and she had to admit that she would have *let him be* – as people say on the coast, as she herself used to say – if Lorela hadn't drifted into the story).

'Fine, I get it.' She feigned a smile and held it a bit too long – on purpose, of course: she wanted to see how durable, how solid, Kristijan's poker face was.

Not very. Dunja's little smile was stirring awful doubts in him, and clusters of new furrows had percolated to his forehead, which he clumsily tried to conceal in a gesture meant to signal *My head is hurting*: hand to brow, fingers boring into the skull, leaving marks of pink behind them.

'So what about you and Dražen the evening before his death?' (Had she really used that phrase? It sounded so sad and cold.) 'You didn't see each other at all? The two of you didn't go anywhere together? Dražen told our parents he was going to spend the night at your place. But you know that, right?'

My head is hurting was turning into *My head is splitting*: the fingers had relaxed across the surface of the forehead, and the hand – an incredibly shapely hand, a fine, long-fingered hand, damaged only slightly at the side and knuckles – was now covering the eyebrows too; but it lingered there just a moment, after which it glided down, over the eyes, the nose and the mouth, past the neck and the sternum, until finally, rigid, like a cheap extra phallus, a phallus of plastic, it rested on his broad thigh.

'But Dunja,' he said, agitated, '*you* know, don't you, that Dražen's lie was dealt with at the time. Not only did he not sleep over at our place that night, we weren't together at all. But you probably know that. And I'm sure,' – his voice became a shade more caustic – 'I'm sure you remember, too, don't you, that it wasn't just anyone who looked into this – it was the police.'

Oh puh-lease! Of course, she knew that Kristijan's parents had stated that they *saw* Kristijan lying in his bed that Friday night, and that they saw *him* lying there – saw his blond head on the pillow and his body softly rising and falling under the blanket, and *not* some arrangement of pillows, clothes and a wig, a trick he could have easily picked up from films like *Home Alone*, *E.T.* or *Gremlins*. Central to Kristijan's alibi (if we can ascribe such a thing to children) was his younger brother (what was his name? K-something. K-lemen? K-lavdijo? Or maybe K-alibi!), who told the detectives that he, too, had been into Kristijan's room that night, since he couldn't sleep, and his older brother, that Eternal Role Model, never once, not even *that* night, left him waiting at the door, that no matter how comfy and cosy in the covers Kristijan was, he always heard him knocking and pleading, always heard his little brother saying something had scared him. The only thing that supposedly remained of Dražen's *deception* – little Dunja, huddled behind the kitchen door and straining her ears, had repeated the word to herself, a word that smelled of mildew, rot and decay – all that was left, then, was a tiny note, a note on the margin of the report, written in a clumsy hand, neither underlined nor circled: her brother, *your son*, had been seen on the path that went to Kristijan's house, which stood on the slope opposite the blocks of flats on School Street; he had been seen by two women (of course, she knew exactly who they were: two sisters on the third floor, a pair of gossipy, grouchy, grey-headed mice) – *How horrible, how shocking that the poor boy died! We haven't slept a wink for days and have no appetite for food*, they must have said. *But you know*, they certainly added, *on that Friday the boy must have sensed that his end was near; why, he just hurried right past us, you know; he didn't even say hello, and he was walking like a madman, looking down at the ground with his hands in his pockets, and he was making a strange sort of jingly noise!* Nobody else, *supposedly*, actually *saw* Dražen – *which is unusual, Mrs Anko*, the two detectives agreed; *it was light out that evening, at least until nine, and this wasn't the kind of circus that vanishes into thin air*; and then hours later he appeared in Piran wearing different clothes – instead of his baggy tracksuit (little Dunja, tearful and in pieces, had decided) he was in his favourite black trousers and best white T-shirt – new-ish, worn only twice – the one with nothing printed on it. On Tartini Square, now no longer in a hurry but just walking around, he supposedly greeted (and with what a greeting!) a girl from school (what was her name? K-something. K-lara? K-lavdija?); she and some other girls were just leaving a pub where underage boys were allowed to act up, drink a lot and smoke even more, so they could more easily hit on underage girls – *The things you see with that sort of people*, Simon let slip, *but forgive me, Mr and Mrs Anko, that's a different story altogether*. Basically, K-lavdija said she thought Dražen seemed a little, *but really just a little*, drunk; *I mean, the guy was hugging me, he'd never done that before, and then he kissed me on the cheeks and his face was a little red.* But in the same breath – *She was a bit panicky, Mr and Mrs Anko* – she added that maybe it wasn't quite fair for her to say that, since in fact she'd been pretty drunk herself at the time and couldn't really distinguish colours or gestures very well, and if she had had *even just a bit more* to drink she would have passed out. K-lavdija's friends, however, were less equivocating: *Dražen was definitely drunk at the time, he was definitely high, definitely not him-self; the guy was wild, the guy was all wound up*, the oldest girl had said – but not because they had all been sober that night, but rather because they had made their statements in front of their conservative parents, who would not have tolerated the idea that their little girls – who always obeyed the curfew! – were in fact not as well behaved as they thought. *Something was definitely going on with him, Mr and Mrs Anko,* Policeman Peter summed up the situation, *but what's more important is that your son was in the square, alone by the monument, after which, it must have been around midnight, a witness said they saw him going up one of the streets that lead to the church, one of those steep, zigzagging streets, and the witness saw his face, and not from a balcony either; the witness was walking towards him and they passed each other under a street light; so it was definitely him – they described him. But the witness also described, and this is what I wanted to get to, a second figure, who was waiting where the street turned, and this figure waved to Dražen, a short, frightened wave, but unfortunately the witness didn't get a good look at this individual, that is, they didn't see their face.* But later, in the course of the investigation (Dunja's parents wondered why it wasn't that same day, *porco puttana*, in that same damn deluge), they learned that the *figure* was slender and *fairly tall*, taller than the witness, about Dražen's size if not taller (short people have trouble telling height differences between tall people; at a certain height they reach their event horizon, beyond which they see only a blur, darkness, the cosmic mystery) and was *maybe* wearing a dark-coloured tracksuit with a hood, which of course they had up, and was holding a plastic bag, *maybe heavy; the witness said it seemed full*; Peter and Simon made a point of this and announced that, *for now* (which then became the unbearable *for ever*), that was the extent of the eyewitness testimony.

OK, fine, *dorro*, I remember the whole thing, *dorro*, so what? (Dunja suddenly squirmed in her chair at the forgotten coastal way of speaking.) Since, *vaffanculo*, none of it meant a thing, *testa di merda*. Because why wouldn't Kristijan's parents lie for him, *cazzo di merda*, why wouldn't his little brother lie? Why wouldn't they try to shield and protect him – *How* disgraziato! *Of course he was sleeping! They should be bothering somebody else, not our sweet, innocent boy!* The sex of the individual waiting for Dražen had never been clarified, oh, but the height, *the height* would fit, *vaffanculo!* Definitely! And the tracksuit, yes, that would fit too! Since Kristijan's tracksuits had all been black! And that fucking bag, *testa di merda*, that would also fit! He and Dražen were always bringing bags to the beach – *Backpacks? No way! What are we, packhorses? This is more than enough for just a towel* – but what fits most is that guarded, what, aura? of yours, or should I say *vibe?* – the aura of someone who's hiding something, the aura of someone who's frustrated by something, the aura of someone who, like me, is permanently divided, picked clean, used up and, from overuse, unimaginably tired.

Uhhh! Dunja fell back in her chair. So what exactly was Kristijan's *aura* supposed to fit? Had she possibly gone mad? Right at the start of her, umm, *investigation*, her, umm, *amateur crime novel*, had she let herself be beaten down, be befuddled by despair? Was she really ready to hang a *murder/homicide* (did you hear that? *a murder/homicide!*) on the conscience of the first person who displayed a few (to put it diplomatically) unpleasant character traits and, well, questionable personal convictions?

Aaah, she took a deep breath and exhaled. OK, then, the denouement was still uncharted, and she had only now – aaaaaaaaaaargh! – got started.

'*Dorro, dorro,*' she said at last, 'so who else could Dražen have been meeting with? As far as I recall, the police never found any serious replacement for you.'

She needed to land a knee in his chest, or even better, his balls. He grimaced, shifted back in his chair and stared at her. Was it safe for him to answer? More importantly, was it wise? Would this woman (the thought flashed across his cheeks) make a shambles of things? Would it help her if he were candid? Would it help her if he lied? Would it help her . . . ? Ehh, ahh, umm, they were obviously both thinking.

'Now, back when those two policemen were asking me about this, well, back then, I didn't say anything, as if I was drawing a blank, as if I had no idea, but to tell you the truth' – the truth was not exactly *falling* from his lips – 'I felt like I knew, although it was also sort of impossible, if you get my drift.'

No, Dunja didn't get his drift.

'Look, it seemed to *me*' – he too was only now getting started, was only now pushing off from the top of the ski jump, and his words were rattling like skis on a bumpy ramp – 'it was that girl, Mirela, because I don't know who else it could have been. Dražen was not exactly – how should I put this – swimming in acquaintances, let alone friends, and she would basically be the logical choice, except that, apparently, this was extremely unlikely, she was apparently at home, because her father, you know, she had this really tyrannical father, oh my God, and he would never have allowed her to go out like that on a Friday night, and certainly not so late, and we all knew what a prick her old man was, what a *stronzo* he was, and of course she was afraid of him, so she would never have disobeyed him by climbing out of the window, if you get my drift.'

Yes, this drift she *did* get. Not because she herself had ever truly lived the teenage life, but because she had watched other people living it. How they tried to make the world they knew, the world in which they were born, bend to their will like (pardon the simile) branches in a storm, and how the world they conceived in their mind was constantly escaping them, slipping out of their hands like a fish, how their imagined world was simply *incapable* of birth or existence, since this – to be born and to exist – would require something of the world they were doing their utmost to leave. She watched them, oh yes, she observed them intently, and only wished that she too might know such wilfulness, but her wish was not realisable: to be self-centred, you first needed a self that was *apart from* the world; loss, however – ha! LOSS – cocoons you in the world, every ounce of you, for a long time, and keeps any drop of fantasy from ever reaching you.

'OK,' – Dunja winced – 'so do you have any idea where this Mirela is now? I could speak with her, and maybe she could shed some light on things.'

At this, Kristijan's face undoubtedly lightened, undoubtedly for the first time, and this was, without a doubt, relief. And what relief – unabashed and clear, without a speck of dust.

'Mirela's a social worker now. Katarina knows her. Once when she was out of work – this was before I moved in – Mirela helped her with arranging social assistance. She works in Piran, at the Centre for Social Work, of course. I expect you can find her number and email address on the internet. She'll be happy to see you, I think. She remembered Katarina, you know, and I believe she knew she was somehow connected to you and your family.'

'Good,' she said, but the thought of another *interrogation*, yet another (and another and another) vacillating, disingenuous, grubby meeting, drained her of all energy. 'Good. That's good.'

Kristijan seized on the refrain – no, not the *refrain*, the part that comes at the end of the song, the echoing of the key words: *you, you, love, love, right now, now, now*, that idiotic recap – seized on it with eagle speed: without turning around, he lifted his hand, extended two fingers, with which he signalled to Dunja's Lorela, who was sitting on the patio, signalled for the bill, signalled the way you might signal to a dog – no, not even that, since you would say something, shout something, to a dog; dear God, you would have a conversation with a dog! He signalled to her the way you would – well, there's nothing to compare it with! – and Lorela (this comparison is obvious) slinked over to the table *like a wounded animal* and, from the device hooked to her belt, tore off the little slip of paper that demanded its euro. This she then placed on the table . . . And Dunja wanted to give Kristijan a wallop, she really did, she wanted to give him a fucking christening (ha!), but she restrained herself and, instead, effectively, *to good effect* you might say, sublimated at least a fraction of her aggression. The coins which un-Christian Kristijan clinked onto the table she shoved back to him – *Away with this filth!* – and quickly, with a warm smile, rummaged her own coins from her purse – *Let this be a civics lesson for you, stronzo!* Then, through the air, like a stork with a baby, she delivered them into Lorela's hand, which gratefully opened to receive them.

'Thank you,' said the girl, but at the same time she said, *You are not a racist; you look at me the way no racist ever would.* Meanwhile, at this brief exchange, Kristijan finally got the message that *he* was now the one being excluded, overlooked, rejected and, fuck him, *despised* – all these things – if only for a fraction of a moment. That morning a crumb was enough for Lorela and Dunja; the important thing was that the prick had been caught off guard.

'You're very welcome, and I'll be back.' Dunja looked over at Kristijan and, when Lorela left, gave him a wink. 'What an incredibly nice girl!'

In response, he stood up first, and Dunja, her gaze planted in him like an axe, slowly followed, after which he said, 'OK, so I guess that'll be it for today, right? I need to start cooking soon.'

'Yeah, that's it for today.' They were now staring into each other's eyes, like in *The Good, the Bad and the Ugly*, and Dunja, without knowing why and not really wanting to, held out her hand to him. 'Well, have fun cooking,' she said as Kristijan's hand slipped into hers like (really, even if it is a cliché) *a fish*, a soft, pliant, but also hesitant and limp *fish* – but at least it was warm. The contact was unpleasant, extremely unpleasant, and not just because of the fish – she was used to those – but because of the contrast between it, the wriggling vertebrate, and the sturdy, rigid, *toxic* whole. The Mannerism in Kristijan's fingers did not come from that body: although annoying, it was expressive and gentle – and seemed to surprise and upset him as well, for he immediately folded his arms across his chest (once more the *sicario* Francisco Ortega), stepped back and stood with legs astride.

'I'll manage. Thanks,' he said in the deepest possible voice, and Dunja, well, Dunja just cleared her throat, because otherwise she could only have laughed out loud at the muscleman, racist and fish.

5

Digging up a telephone number – what could be easier in the Age of the Internet? Reaching a person *by way of* a telephone number – well, that takes effort. On Monday (our Detective mustered her courage) she called the Centre for Social Work in Piran at least fifteen times, morning, afternoon, even midday, when according to the listed office hours the centre was closed and so, in her estimate, the chance of catching Mirela by the hair of a guilty conscience would be at its greatest (since no matter how hungry or thirsty a social worker might be, she must never, but never, leave the phone to ring, since a phone is much more than a device, it's a victim of violence, a hungry child, a toothless old lady, the jobless masses). But Dunja was mistaken, of course: the peak of one's own hunger and thirst trumps the troubles and sufferings of others. Mirela answered just minutes before the end of her workday, which at the Piran CSW must have been honest-to-God awful and chilling and tense and taxing, worthy of a miniseries on Netflix or HBO (but most feasibly on TV Slovenia), given that the branch's primary issues were amphetamines and heroin dependency (and people say there's nothing special about living near a port!) along with their shy pal schizophrenia.

'Long nails,' Dunja thought when Mirela finally picked up. Pointed too, she amended when she twice heard (ooh, shivers!)

scratching on plastic (which went on and on throughout the conversation).

'Mirela Čirić speaking. How may I help you?' Even her voice sounded scratchy, but not from boredom or dissatisfaction, not exactly, and not from an excess of cigarettes or coffee, not from high cholesterol or a passion for alcohol, nor from any of the other likely afflictions of the female civil servant – really, none of that. No, her voice was scratchy the way it is with tired people who, nevertheless, maybe automatically, are trying their best to be kind. Helpful. To speak in a damn major key.

This affected Dunja, too, who straight away dropped her minor and introduced herself into the receiver in a pleasant conversational tone, although, well, the pleasantness was not truly *natural* – it trod the line of sycophancy.

'I do apologise for disturbing you in the middle of your workday, but I didn't know how else to reach you. I really do apologise, and I hope you won't be upset.'

'Dunja Anko, did you say? *Dunja Anko?*' The scratching of her claws and voice had accelerated and was now almost a thrashing, like the limbs of a rabbit trapped in a tight snare. Dunja responded at once and Mirela was o v e r j o y e d to hear from her. (Was every joy, Dunja wondered at that first little shriek, so, umm, neurotic? Did joyful people always sound so, hmm, unbalanced? As if they had suddenly lost something and not, in fact, gained something exceptional? As if some essential cog had rolled off somewhere – the very cog that maintained their connection to reality? Was it only this stranger, this Mirela, who was so intense, or was that true of everyone? Was she herself so very different? Yes, when it came to joy, there was a lot she had forgotten.)

'Why, this must be fate!' Mirela decided, singing out the words, and in her song Dunja detected something extraneous, a tone from a different register – maybe every joy, regardless of its content, regardless of its cause, expires like this and ends in a minor key. Its energy always eventually runs out and, in the minor key, the joyful person, perhaps even unwillingly, can rest a little.

'Now, I don't know,' Dunja sycophanted on, 'if I'm interrupting anything at the moment; for all I know, your workday isn't over yet . . .'

'Please, just tell me what you need,' Mirela said politely, and Dunja realised that, being a social worker, she could not be naive.

'I have a few questions regarding my late brother. But don't worry; what I'm curious about is not so much his death, but rather, who he was when he was alive.'

'Yes, yes.' (That *other* tone, though barely perceptible, was spreading, and Dunja, morbid as she was, could not help but hear it.) 'I understand. Well, there'll be a lot to say, you know; he and I spent a lot of time together, so there will really be a lot to say.' She breathed in and out as *slooowly* as possible, as if she weren't in her office but on a yoga retreat at some ecovillage. 'There's a lot to say, there really is a lot.' Apparently, this was now a mantra for Mirela, and, as people say (indiscriminately, but accurately), it was getting on Dunja's nerves.

'I'm sure that's true. Well, as I said,' – she had, after all, put her stock in good manners – 'I certainly do not want to interrupt your day. But if you could find some time for us to talk, this week, or even next week – that would also work; I'll still be here – I'd be very grateful.'

Another *looong* intake of breath followed by, hmm, not an outtake but – could she really be *holding* her breath? *People! Oh my God!* Dunja grumbled to herself and felt an attack of misanthropy coming on (but it hadn't got hold of her yet, hope still burned). Who made us such pathetic creatures? Us – the crown of creation? Yeah, right. More like the tight arsehole of the universe. To encourage Mirela's response, she released a (harsh and disgusting) cough straight into the phone.

'Of course we can, of course we can talk,' the other woman said, finally exhaling the carbon dioxide, which (through her teeth, was there a gap in her teeth?) produced an esoteric whistle.

'So when would be good for you?' Dunja asked. She was starting to feel annoyed.

'I'm sure we can arrange something; of course we can.' (For fuck's sake. Dunja almost coughed a second time.) 'We can even meet today, this evening, sure, today, this evening, we can do that.'

'That would be great, thanks. I *can*' (that word, again!) 'come to Piran. There seem to be quite a few buses running, and I gather they even have air conditioning – if they want to carry live passengers.' All right, that might do, Dunja chuckled, offering up some dark humour, a bit of her true self, to loosen Mirela up a little, but, um . . .

'Yes, by all means, take an air-conditioned bus.'

Fuck! She was really getting annoyed. This social worker. Sure, she's nice enough, but horribly stiff. In any case, Dunja did not understand where people got the idea that social workers in particular overflowed with sarcasm. Wisecracking was maybe just the first sign – a loud sign, to be sure, but easily overlooked – of burnout. Mirela may have once been witty, even very witty, but now at age, what?, forty-five, jokes had most likely lost their impact for her – which did not bode well for long life and happiness.

'OK.' She went back to mere politeness. 'So when and where could we meet?'

'Oh, that won't be a problem, no problem at all,' Mirela replied, to a question Dunja had obviously *not* asked. But *salvation in patience lies* (as the saying goes), for what came next was: 'I live just above Piran. I need to go home after work, and I'd prefer to stay there. I have cats, you see, and I can't be gone the entire day; they're alone a lot, too much. So why don't you just come to my place? Come at six.' Then the obligatory breeeathiii-ing and the required variation: 'So come to my place. That'll be good. At six o'clock.'

Fuck, fuck, fuck, Mirela. 'Now, where is that? Where do you live exactly?'

'Oh right, yes. Above Piran, near the cemetery. Across from the cemetery, actually, where Olive Tree Way splits into the Fiesa and Arze roads. Do you know where that is? Do you know where . . .'

'Yes.', Dunja's stomach was instantly in shreds. Nausea
seeping into her nerve plexuses, through them and across
them. Then spilling into her knees, where it yanked apart, blew
apart, the ligaments, and she was lucky – what fucking luck! –
to already be sitting down. Next, fever crept into her elbows,
wrists, fingers, so that for a moment, a frightening, pinching,
all-pervasive moment, she felt nothing whatsoever. Instinct had
to rest her elbow on the table; instinct had to place her forehead
in her left hand; instinct had to keep her mobile phone in her
right hand; instinct was raising and lowering her sternum, lifting it and dropping it; instinct was lacing up her backbone. To
keep her from falling apart, so she could keep being a sort of
person – instinct, sheer instinct, the body's connective tissue,
yes, even if this same body, her body, was seizing up beneath
the icy eaves and *plink plonk plink plonk plonk* and
in a droplet, in a boxlet, him
tiny, so tiny
so small, it's too small, Mama!
in a droplet, in a boxlet, in a coffin of poplar
in a droplet, in a boxlet, odours, but no, not the odour of wood,
not the odour of time
but
Mama, but
the odour of disinfectant, of fresh linen
our smells, *the smells of home!* and
in a droplet, in a boxlet, earth, so much earth
dug up earth, dented earth, and
chrysanthemums, *so many flowers!*
and the people carrying them,
swarms of these people and
Mama,
why are they all murmuring and
who are they talking to,
not me, Mama, they're not talking to me and
Mama, we knew that there was nothing, *nothing* to be said,
to tell him, to name the thing and
Mama, why are they bringing him anything at all and

Mama, how will he accept anything at all and
Mama, why are they making fun of us and
Mama, why don't you tell them to stop and
Mama, talk to them, tell them, please! and
plink plonk plink plonk plonk and
plink plonk
plink plink plonk
plink plonk
plink and . . .

*

The sky turned dark not long after her call with Mirela streamed
to its close – streamed the way water splashing off the roof
of a canvas tent streams into a canal, first burbling and swift,
then leisurely and quiet – but Dunja, well, she didn't have her
umbrella with her and, initially, she didn't really understand why
she decided not to take it. This wouldn't have been the first time
that walking around holding an umbrella when it wasn't even
raining seemed like a stupid idea to her, a sign not of caution
but paranoia. This wouldn't, ergo, have been the first time she
was lazy, and certainly not the first time laziness had led her to
look with disdain at people who were in fact well prepared and,
therefore, prudent.

But as she was walking uphill from central Piran – on the
street, a windy corridor, that curved out of town – and inter-
cepting with her body the fat and aggressive but still only sparse
raindrops, she had no choice but to open her eyes. It was simple,
so very simple: she *wanted* the drops suddenly and dramatically
to thicken into rain and soak her, truly soak her, to the very
skin. To skin that would burn slightly under her heavy, dou-
ble-layered, polyester dress. To skin that would redden all over
and break out in horrible gooseflesh. That would bristle, yes,
bristle into little needles. And to skin that would sting. To skin
that would chill, badly chill her, so Dunja would be shivering

from head to toe. To skin that would get colder and colder until, with any luck, it reached hypothermia. And eventually to skin that would need to be dried, warmed and reclothed – and where best for it to be dried, warmed and reclothed if not at home, even if this was just a temporary home, a room on the second floor of a hotel. Dunja wanted to go back; she needed a reason that would make her turn around and either cancel the appointment or rudely ignore it. No, Dunja did not want, not yesterday, not today and not tomorrow, to be in Piran, and when she saw the inscription above the entrance to Dražen's and her father's – what was it? She couldn't bring herself to think *burial ground*, *happy hunting ground* or that stupid phrase *eternal resting place*; she couldn't bring herself to think *grave* or *tomb*; she couldn't bring herself to think, to think up, anything, full stop – so when she saw *that* entranceway *there*, she simply stopped, in the absurd hope that it would finally start pouring, that the roof of the canvas tent over the little town would finally give way (collapse, split apart), that piercing thunder and lightning would strike full force, strike *her*, that chaos would finally again show its strength, would, fuuuuck, suddenly save her—

—but no, of course it didn't; walking towards her (no, not walking, *marching*) up the Arze road, she saw Mirela, who was nervously, with her arm high in the air, waving at her. Perhaps, Dunja thought, they both wanted the same thing; perhaps this was not a greeting, but rather a desperate skyward plea for the heavens to open right now and get the damn mayhem started!

And indeed, a moment later Dunja saw with relief that she wasn't mistaken: Mirela, too, was averse to this meeting. She had stopped at the crossing, next to the empty road, and was looking directly at her visitor and, as if unable to move either forwards or backwards, as if trapped under a glass, hmm, maybe even a *bell jar*, just stood there stepping from foot to foot. She was a little too far away for Dunja to say if her eyes were actually fixed on her, but when Mirela did eventually cross the road, she conveyed only nonchalance towards Dunja.

Her attire, however, conveyed anything but nonchalance, if that can be a synonym for *calm*. Dunja had never seen anyone

more decked out, more garish, more (she was searching for
words) stylistically tricked up — if Mirela was a sound, she'd
be the noise of road traffic, a night club, a factory, an airport,
all combined: her nails were outrageously long and pointed and
pale purple; her wrists were laden with hoops of metal, silver
and plastic; her skin was wrinkly and tanning-cream orange;
her lips were glossy and pink, glaringly pink (the cosmetics
industry has made enormous strides with its pigments) and her
cheeks were no less intense, while her eyelids, *oh, her eyelids*,
were the colour of the Queen of the Night, dark blue and turquoise and, oh her God, did she really detect green, too? Nor
did Mirela's dress offer respite: pulled in at her childishly narrow waist, across her breasts (heralded by Kristijan and indeed
bountiful) it became something truly wondrous, as ruffled as
a permanent wave. Peeking out of this garment were two little
arms, thin as paper, and two little legs, long and as narrow as,
well, carrots, with feet shod in a pair of white Adidas trainers.
The only thing on her tall body that struck a different chord
was the enormous handbag hanging from her shoulder; it was
clearly almost empty, jingling only with keys, but its green, lilac
and turquoise stains made it eerily expressive.

For a moment it occurred to Dunja that, maybe, when
she observed a woman she didn't know, she wasn't looking at
cacophony but rather at an unfurled recording of free jazz,
which always seems totally random but which also reveals again
and again that there is no randomness without a theme, without, one might say, a *question* that propels it. Dunja, therefore,
suspected that Mirela's style was *deliberate*, that behind it stood
a mind that was, what? Expansive? Yes, certainly, but also at the
same time (watch out: a most unpleasant word) *idiosyncratic*:
complicated and cosmic, cunning and brittle as a pretzel, neurotic and possibly, just possibly, as pensive and poetic as (here
you go, a teensy cliché) a road swathed in mist.

'Hello.' Mirela did not offer her hand but instead hooked
it onto the strap of her bag. The raindrops were becoming
more frequent, and two or three or four had already marred
Mirela's face, but she didn't seem particularly worried by

that. Her little mouth, slightly warped at the edges, remained straight as a ruler.

'Hi there, hi! Thanks for coming out to find me. Shall we get moving? Otherwise we'll be drenched.'

'Yes, of cooourse. Let's gooo,' Mirela breathed out, ohhh myyy, ohhh deeear meee! But in this regard, luck was kind: apart from 'this way', 'here' and 'this is it', Mirela said nothing all the way to the fence of her home. Her silence had another advantage, too, Dunja realised as they turned onto a little path behind a garage/carwash/mechanic's: it gave her a chance to consider her strategy, since every *interrogatee* (hoho, Dunja's new idiom had become rather bold) is, of course, different, specific.

So she *did* consider it. And the Great Detective was just about to initiate her procedures when Mirela unlocked the gate to the garden of a two-storey house – the lock creaked à la Mary Shelley and for a moment seemed stuck – and it struck the G.D. that maybe she would have to proceed more slowly. Some people are rowing boats; others are galleys.

Because, OK, *to a certain point*, it all seemed thrown together, not particularly well cared for and typical of the Slovenian coast. An apricot building with an orange-tiled roof and windows bordered in white and a central semicircular balcony thrown in. Around the house, agaves, palm trees, two blossoming oleanders, a gardenia no longer in bloom, a patch of withered lavender and a patch of trampled grass. Along the garden's edges, cypresses and cedars, for shade and charm, and in front of the house, an attempt at a grapevine, furrowed and sparse, dolefully brown, and only barely still climbing some wooden structure, from which it cast, hmm, well, certainly not shade. Beneath it, three loungers, a table and, of course, an ashtray. The dot on, well, not necessarily any *i*.

But beyond that point, oh, beyond that *fucking point*: HA!

First, a wantonly luxuriant bougainvillea, which, unlike the other vegetation, somebody must have been caring for devotedly, and which had scattered the area around it with so much purple, tons and tons of it, that Dunja was a little carried away. What, just a little? *Completely*. To the degree that her heart

shoved into her windpipe. Which made her windpipe scurry up
through the Eustachian tubes into her ears. Which made her
ears immediately start ringing. At first in a good way: an aesthetic experience. But then in a bad way, the worst way: jogging
her memory. This – this deep, penetrating, intense *purple* – had
been Dražen's favourite colour, although he never wore it –
Because I'm not, honestly, I'm not; this colour doesn't mean anything,
I just think it's pretty; other people think so too, even guys; c'mon,
Dunči, you're so annoying; don't look at me that w—

—but Dunja could not stop looking! Mirela led her down
the walkway to the front door and there, in a semicircle above
the door, on the *outside* of the house, on the *outside* wall, and not
in small letters either, but very visible, not just painted with a
brush, but chiselled *and* coloured (if black counts as a colour),
were the words: *If you wanna make the world a better place/ Take a*
look at yourself and then make a change. Behind the door, Mirela
had obviously installed her own variation on Neverland, and
what a variation it was. Even the front hall was occupied territory: on top of the shoe cabinet, *waiting for mother* (haha),
were no less than twenty plush toys – kittens, puppies, rab-
bits, seals, teddy bears, fish, snakes – crammed together like
sardines. Dunja wondered if the little animals had maybe been
glued together, if they were a single plush organism. Again, she
had the feeling that with a little effort she might discover some
grand *system* in their arrangement.

As she might, too, in the next room, a hybrid dining/living
room in the middle of which stood a long oak table, undoubtedly an heirloom, undoubtedly from the Gorenjska region –
there was something patrician about the whimsical curlicues of
its ornament, while the carnation blossoms at the end of those
curlicues felt plebeian. This was surrounded by seven chairs of,
hmm, industrial origin. On top of this giant object were two
candlesticks with a red runner beneath them, as well as (the
first cliché) four cats, orange and grey and white and black, who
greeted their mistress with raised tails and hops to the floor in
the direction of a leather four-seater sofa (definitely leather:
there were scratch marks on the sides, the kind that bloom only

on skin), where stood an array of bowls containing water, kibble, and some, well, rather disgustingly ravaged chunks of meat.

OK, fine, the kitties and their paraphernalia did imply filth and, especially, parasites (shiver), but such implications quickly gave way (perhaps, too, because there was no notable odour in the room) beneath the weight of something *far more obvious*: the walls were covered in no less than a hundred posters and flags and drawings and trading cards – whose subject, of course, was predictable – while the shelving displayed yet more cubic metres of plushness, a stampede of various monkeys, elephants and unclothed dolls. Other shelves held the precious and prestigious temple flowers: Preamp, Amplifier, Player, Speakers and Turntable – and in the corners, in *every* corner, were stands filled with CDs and vinyl records, as well as, naturally, a section for DVDs.

The records and DVDs were all from the King of Pop himself and each of them, the G.D. noticed as she scanned their thin spines, had its own – what? remastered? autographed? in some way evil? – twin. The compact discs, which were more numerous, had recieved a more casual treatment: arranged neither alphabetically nor chronologically, they encompassed a variety of genres, if not, one might say, musical *ideologies*: present among them was pop – 'N Sync, Usher and Whitney – but also Kanye and Kendrick.

Dunja had the opportunity to take such a precise swab of Mirela's dwelling place thanks to the owner herself, who had disappeared into the kitchen to get, as she softly said, *a refreshing beverage*, and who now returned with (yet another excursion into the distant past) two cans of Pepsi. She offered the drink to Dunja the way a *connoisseuse* at an art opening might force on her interlocutor a glass of wine snatched from a waiter's tray: confidently but distractedly, with eyes focused on the main exhibit.

'That one I got from the Colosseum Cineplex in Ljubljana, and it wasn't cheap.'

Aha! the Great Detective noticed, standing closer than ever to her hostess: Mirela's wheeze was actually a duet. A duet of mouth and nose, which, oh dear, was aggravated by a kind of old person's shortness of breath.

'They had it hanging up as an advert,' she pressed on, 'over the main entrance, and when they stopped showing the documentary, or no, even before, I called their Ljubljana office and convinced them to sell it to me. Then, as you probably noticed, Dunja, I trimmed it to fit. It was too long for this room, too long, Dunja, simply too long.' She was still in the gallery, still enamoured of the piece on the wall, which was probably why she had not invited her guest to sit down. And the guest desperately wanted to sit down; the wind and the raindrops and one small shock after another had tired her, and her face, she thought, must be noticeably flushed; so, like a scheming woman in a Jacques Tati comedy, she shuffled backwards to the sofa, stopping just before she hit it.

But from Mirela: nothing. Or rather, *everything else*. She took a sip of her refreshing beverage (where could she even buy Pepsi?) and started wheezing out a monologue, which (it was an alarming thought) Dunja herself must have somehow elicited, if only by her presence, by something about her that might be hostile to Michael or, more precisely, to Mirela's love for Michael, and that might even cause harm.

OH YES! OF COURSE! She was talking about the notorious documentary *Leaving Neverland*

• which 'they made solely for profit, Dunja';

• which 'of course will completely, yes, completely, mislead all the uninformed; only true fans can understand what's really going on here, and it's horrible, oh it's horrible';

• which 'ignores the entire context, and the context, Dunja, is what's important; all those mothers and fathers – I don't blame the children, I really don't – but the parents are nothing but money-grubbers, just your basic white trash; believe me, Dunja, believe me';

• which was 'full of inaccuracies' – yes, she said *inaccuracies*, and also *disinformation* – 'and outright lies, too' – after which she cited some facts that Dunja quickly lost track of – 'and the director couldn't be bothered so much as to verify their statements or even – that *stronzo*! – at least compare them';

• which was 'a complete disappointment; I had hoped that ten years after his death they would at least let him rest in peace, but no, of course not; his money is still alive, and his money will outlive every moral principle!'

Her indignation, of course, was not confined to just a few bullet points; it was so circular that eventually Dunja was spinning too. Not only had she suppressed how menacing Dražen's own obsession had been in this regard, what a thick and long and sinewy tail it had had, and how, with this tail, it had been able to sweep away any realities that did not belong under the rubric of Michael's, hmm, affluence? his *Gesamtkunstwerk?* – realities that reeked of mass (the mass of bodies, the mass of consciousness), since at the time he still believed in something like mass, in something like being unmarked by detail. Not only, ergo, had she overlooked that fact that Dražen must have been a terrible misanthrope, cognitively receptive only to that which was far above human nature, but she had also always suspected that Dražen's, and therefore, of course, also Mirela's, and therefore, of course, ANYBODY'S obsession was the product of a false consciousness, a consciousness that had sustained an injury, that was on the verge of fracturing into an approximation of truth, but this same consciousness had quickly, too quickly, and vehemently, sealed the epistemological fracture – since, on the one hand, it's not easy to lose the object of one's desire, which is to say, to see it for what it is, while, on the other hand, the false consciousness must never allow things to get to the point of true loss, to more than *the wobbling of the counterfeit object.*

'I expect Dražen would have been as outraged as you are, if not more so. I remember how painful it was for him when people didn't understand Michael's eccentricities and started calling him Wacko Jacko.'

'I remember that too, Dunja,' said her hostess and, with her by now probably empty can of Pepsi, finally gestured to the sofa, against which Dunja's calves were now well and truly perspiring. During her rant, Mirela's eyes had been flashing fire, and now, even as they cooled, they preserved an intensity that was not so much *psychiatric* (as more cynical readers

might predict) as, well, thoroughly *normative* – a sadness, or
rather, a *regret*, mixed with an anger mixed with involuntary
memories mixed with embarrassment mixed with guilt mixed
with shame – since guilt and shame always act in tandem, don't
they? And this redemptive tandem was, in the end, mixed into
the expectation – *of what* exactly Dunja was not sure; after all,
she could not divine everything from the story of an eye . . . But
when, however, she at last was *pleased to sit down*, the dominant
hue in the palette of Mirela's emotions – influenced, surely, by
the cataclysmic darkness that then penetrated the room (how
the rain came down!) and cast a shadow across her face – was a
promise, nuanced partly as triumph, partly as doom.

'But you know . . .' – Mirela turned away from Dunja and,
curiously, sought a chair at the huge table, where two cats were
again presiding – 'in a way it's good he didn't live to see everything that happened to Michael. Really, so much happened to
him and Dražen would certainly, yes, he would certainly have
suffered from it; it would have worried him so much. So that's
something; in a way it's good.'

WHAT THE FUCK! Dunja, dumbfounded, leaned back
on the sofa and unclasped her hands, which until now, as The
Guest, she had, of course, been holding serenely in her lap (for
a guest is good only if she does not occupy too much space
or touch too many surfaces, only if she acts as though her
body, which cannot help but leave traces, is somehow something superfluous). So she unclasped her hands, and her arms
dropped down to her thighs like the limbs of a corpse. So WHAT
THE FUCK, then, WAS MIRELA GOING ON ABOUT! Were
those cynical readers right to suspect something psychiatric?
Was Mirela's personality, as one might further say, a borderline
phenomenon? Was the *social* worker *socially maladjusted* (which,
while perhaps not delightful and certainly a problem, was also
not seriously destructive or harmful)? Did she realise that she
had abandoned something that a rather large portion of the
population (thank God) still adhere to, namely, the ritualistic,
cohesive minimum of shame? Did she realise this but not give
a fuck? Did she realise this too late? Did she realise this but,

what? Good grief, Mirela, however it happened, what you said was ghastly!

'Dražen alone, I expect, would have understood every-thing, anything, connected to Michael – and understood it the way it should be understood. Really, he was the only one.' Mirela's tone had suddenly softened, had become, damn, even reverent. Her behaviour, on the other hand, was the complete – really, *the complete* – opposite: she reached for the fatter of the two cats, pulled it off the table, like a card from the top of the deck, and draped it over her shoulder, rather abruptly, which made the poor thing meow in distress, and then slapped it on the back as if it were made of Teflon. But that was not the end, oh no. She then thrust poor puss into the air, so that its little paws were sticking out in astonishment and its meow became a siren; then she started rocked it, *yee-hee*, to the left and, *yee-hee*, to the right, and wheezed ethereally, 'Yes, yeees, hiiim and me, weee were the oooonly ones.' Or did she say, *weee were the oooonly ONE? SINGULAR?*

'Mirela, I'm sorry' – no, after *that* episode, she wasn't, not even a little; the phrase had just slipped out, as phrases do – 'but I have to ask you this, I guess I should know, but even though he was my brother, well, I don't. Basically, what I'm curious about is this: were you and Dražen ever more than just friends? Were you, in fact, a couple?'

The kitty, which was actually a tomcat, wriggled out of Mirela's hold, but strangely, as if accustomed to misery, did not hide from her. He only crouched on the edge of the table, at arm's length from his custodian, and stared – predatorily? accusingly? disdainfully? – at Dunja. For her part, Dunja had (at last!) managed to arrange herself the way a person normally sits during a visit: one leg over the other, forearm over forearm, spine like a broomstick (ha! as if it wasn't already).

'A couple . . .' Mirela again looked at the cat. 'A couple?'

And she too became a broomstick. A *tableau vivant*: hand on feline's head, arm extended, already vibrating, the illusion of an Adam's apple (from the tightness of the neck, of course) and, again, that weird look in her eyes, a mix of triumph and relief, of defeat and tension, but at the same time, all of this, hmm, in retreat? In remission?

So even before Mirela explained anything, the hurt Dunja had felt just moments earlier completely passed: Mirela, she thought, and felt sorry for her, had not just had some fleeting teenage crush on her brother; Mirela had most likely, probably, possibly (but those eyes, those eyes! – they supported her suspicions) *loved* her brother with a mature and adult love.

'No, we weren't a couple.' The confusion in Mirela's eyes again recombined. 'But we would have been soon. It was just a matter of time; it was almost inevitable. We were in love, and everybody knew it, everybody saw it.'

Everybody *except* the sister; it had never entered the sister's mind. No matter how she racked her brain, Dunja had no memory of teenage Mirela. The most she could come up with (or, in all probability, *produce revisionistically*) was, first, an *atmosphere* of Dražen and Mirela sniggering behind the closed door of her and her brother's room – but since Dražen was not allowed to lock the door, Dunja, when she entered the room, must have *seen* Mirela, must have *known* her, have *met* her – and, second, a short but kaleidoscopic scene involving a phone call: Dražen, facing the corner, holding his arm across his mouth, his voice as sugary and gooey as a papaya, a Mating Voice, and a little gurgly too. She had spent the remainder of her Sunday trying to piece together these things from whatever fragments presented themselves, but, ironically, nothing presented itself except *memories of a certain awareness* (oh dear, this was getting complicated), an awareness of *a certain presence*, but certainly no three-dimensional presence, certainly no body that, say, was moving about behind the aforementioned closed door – rather, more likely than not, a presence *in Dražen's life*, a certain content that for a fair amount of time had inhabited his consciousness, taking up copious room in it, radiating it with something foreign, as if, well, *from other people*, maybe from an even then somewhat peculiar, exhausting Mirela – so think! The fact she was unable to recall *such a person* might easily mean the marijuana had made mush of her brain – but, ahem, well, the notion that her brother, under the pressure of testosterone or, in more refined language, *his age*, had simply been changing – well, what sort of information was that? Could she have come up anything more universal, anything less meaningful? Fuckingshit! How she had wandered off!

Mirela – she had to accept this – was an empty shelf to her. A shelf she had only now stocked with the appropriate psychedelic souvenirs.

'So had you and Dražen been friends a long time?' A polite approximation of: *Why did I not know about you? Why did I never meet you?*

'Well, our class was pretty big, thirty students or so, and you had to dig your way through a lot of manure to find the gold, the real gold.' Mirela drew back her arm from the fat cat and looped it professionally into her other arm. 'For a long time we were just looking at each other. Our first conversation, I think, happened early in second year, and by winter we were . . .' – a little bubble popped in her nose, and she plopped her hand on the tom, who, poor thing, had just started to purr – 'yes, inseparable, Dunja.' The poor puss again stole into her lap and, although he gave her a look of horror, Mirela did not let that bother her. She was pressing him like an olive, and maybe, it occurred for the first time to the Great Detective, Mirela actually believed that her treatment of the animal was nothing less than tenderness. That she was showing him care. Showing him *love*. Maybe, the G.D. thought, it was possible, on the basis of these gestures of Mirela's, to explain other actions of hers as well. There was a splendid clinical term for such phenomena, but Dunja could not remember it; that's how much the Scylla and Charybdis of her indispensable marijuana had thrown her off course.

'But Dražen – this I do I remember – used to spend a lot of time with Kristijan; they hung out a lot at our place. So I guess the two of you hung out somewhere else? Maybe at your place?'

'Kristijan! Oh, God! Kristijan! Ugh!'

That unfortunate cat. He was staring at Dunja, a little cross-eyed, and swallowing his meows, and ONLY NOW did she notice the beautiful colour of the poor thing's eyes, a colour

many people portray cats as having but which is actually quite
rare among them: emerald green. It's not especially common
among people either, but it was the colour of Dražen's eyes,
and it frightened her, so much so that for a moment it took her
breath away and, in the vacuum, she missed the intro to Mirela's
wheezy tirade—

'. . . was so annoying! I swear, he clung to Dražen like a
barnacle, and I don't think Dražen was happy about it either;
I mean he told me he wasn't, he said it got on his nerves. But
Kristijan didn't understand that, or maybe he didn't want to
understand – he wasn't particularly bright, you know, so probably he just couldn't understand. I mean, OK, he was bright
intellectually. I mean he played chess and all that, but he wasn't
bright emotionally!'

Dunja's breath had still not returned; it was as if someone had bricked up her lungs. (All this from a colour? C'mon,
Dunja!) But by some miracle – really, it was a miracle –
she managed to squeak out her detectively response: 'So did
they fight?'

'Absolutely!' Mirela said, releasing the poor cat, who, mas-
ochist that he was, did not jump to the ground and hide from
her but instead climbed back onto the table – only now, at least,
he went to the opposite end, safe from Mirela's grabby hand,
and Dunja was safe from his emerald gaze.

'And what did they fight ab—'

'About *me*, Dunja!' Mirela said triumphantly. She smacked
her lips, barely audibly, spread her arms and, so there'd be no
mistake, added combatively, 'Nothing else, Dunja! He was hanging around Dražen because of me – Dražen told me all about
it – *that's* why Kristijan got on his nerves, you see. And I know –
because Dražen told me all about it – that the only way Dražen
could get rid of him was for them to fight. He had to put him
in his place, he had to show him that I belonged to *him*, that I
was *Dražen's*, because Kristijan would never have understood
that on his own. He was bright, sure, but only intellectually, not
emotionally.' (Circling and turning, turning and circling – pfft,
Mirela's own unique discursive style.)

So nothing new then. Mirela's and Kristijan's narratives went together like sausage and sauerkraut, Dunja thought as she greedily inhaled. But (as she even more greedily exhaled) seriously? Was she really supposed to believe the main message here? Kristijan in love with Mirela? Judicious, jocular, judgemental Kristijan in love with eccentric Mirela? Judicious, jocular, judgemental Dražen in love with . . . ? So, OK, was Mirela even eccentric back then? Or did she acquire this trait later? But isn't being a teenager all about the eruption of every possible and impossible trait and tendency and passion, while adulthood, speaking hypothetically, is about the pragmatism that keeps a tight lid on the impossible traits? Which is to say, did Mirela have to be worse back then than she was now? And anyway, whether Mirela had been worse or lovelier, what gave Dunja the right to even make such judgements? What gave her the right to (there's no nicer way to put it) such *classism* in matters of love? Was she being cruel or merely practical when she viewed falling in love, and hence love itself, from a *realpolitik* perspective? When she ignored its possible ethical dimension, which prepares a person, first, to step into the experience of the other and, then, even to become as the other? When she was interested in the practical aspects of character and lifestyle and not in (caution: poetic moment) the content of the individuals' souls? When, for her, falling in love was not entirely irrational but, rather, essentially and always, well, a little calculated, ergo, a *narrative* in keeping with what can be socially affirmed, with what suits the social logic, multilayered and complex, to be sure, but always existing in the tension between the good and shining forces of cohesion and the dark and evil forces of segregation. No, I'm sorry – she was about to shake her head but caught herself in time – I'm sorry, but a person cannot fall in love with just anyone. Kristijan and Mirela – correction – Kristijan's alleged feelings for Mirela – were simply not logical. And if such feelings really did blossom, well, then Dunja must be . . . she must be . . . – c'mon now, what rhymes? aha! – an opossum!

To cool her thoughts, she reached for the Pepsi, which she had placed not long before on the coffee table in front of her.

She tipped some into her mouth, and into her nose and onto her chin — she was one of those people who had never been able to drink from cans, who drink from them as if they are swarming with germs — and . . . the beverage was flat. It had an earthy taste and, hmm, an earthy smell too. She swallowed quickly so as not to spit it out, and glanced discreetly at the container: the sell-by date was some two years earlier. My God, Mirela, Dunja wondered as she stared at the poison, what else could you be hiding in your cellar? She grimaced and, even thirstier than before, nudged the Pepsi away.

'So . . .' — now her mouth was sticky and, ewww, foam was gathering at its corners — 'Kristijan never actually confessed his love to you himself? You heard about it all from Dražen?'

'Yes,' Mirela replied as she stood up and pushed away the chair, at which the black cat looked around warily and the other three, as if on cue, rearranged themselves about the room: one jumped from the windowsill behind the sofa *onto* the sofa, but, thank God, not next to Dunja; the second emerged from beneath the table and trotted over to the food bowls, while the third occupied the chair that Mirela had nicely warmed. 'But that was quite enough, because Dražen would not have lied to me.' She turned away from Dunja and, hello, another wheeze. 'Why would he have lied to me? Really, he would never have lied to me, not Dražen; he wasn't the sort to lie. He was very . . .' — she turned her head and shot an accusing look at Dunja.

'Yes, you're right. I completely understand.' Dryly licking her lips, Dunja retreated from this blasphemous territory, *although* . . .

'Would you like another Pepsi?' Mirela asked, turning towards the kitchen.

'Thanks, but I'd prefer water. Pepsi is maybe, well, a little too sweet for me.'

. . . *although* she had in no way insulted her beloved brother's memory by implying what she had. For Dunja knew something that Mirela very likely did not, namely, that Dražen — hmm, how might she put it now, as an adult? As a little girl, she had howled, *Mami, he doesn't care about anything, about anything at all!* — by which she meant that Dražen wasn't considerate or moral, and that whenever he managed to outfox someone or, as he put it, *pull a fast one*, he would boast of it as if he were a genius. The world and the people in it all constantly owed him something, and his entitlement to status and things and money was, it seemed, comparable to the entitlement kings were said to have. Unattractive qualities, to be sure, even in a youth, qualities that could easily have developed into nasty and, yes, quite dangerous character flaws. More than once she had wondered how hostile, how antagonistic, she and her brother would have become to each other as adults. Well, think about it: the mature Dunja, a writer, an ambivalent soul, unsparing in her thoughts yet also unsparingly sensitive, detached from the start yet also immersed from the start, entirely calm yet constantly stimulated, highly rational yet absorbed in vast and deep and always dismal fantasies, analytical and cautious yet also spontaneous, solitary yet at times even very outgoing and sociable, ethical and empathetic yet in equal measure idle and selfish. And next to her, the mature Dražen (she was maybe exaggerating, but all the same), calculating and self-important, socially adept and, therefore, were he so led, politically flexible, a vampire, perhaps, of the neoliberal type, a man whose convictions would certainly not be among the most robust, since in fact he wouldn't have any convictions, or if he did, they would be adjustable, the way the temperature in a car can be adjusted to suit the passengers and the weather; a Dražen, then, who (maybe, just maybe, she was exaggerating) would exploit people, since *people are animals, Dunči, they're animals to be used*; her darling brother, then, who (surely she was exaggerating!) would make puerile fun of weakness and deprivation and deficiency, since *everyone is responsible for their own material position, or any other position they're in, and it's up to them to save themselves*; her darling brother, then, who (but she must be exaggerating!) would privately sneer at the struggle for social justice, equality and human rights while publicly extolling it; her perfidious, darling brother, her brother the meritocrat, her brother the opportunist, her brother, who (damn, this hurts!) without a second thought would do anything for the sake of his precious lifestyle, or more precisely, his precious prestige.

If, indeed, Dunja were not exaggerating, then she would have to infer from this ideological antagonism all the classic dilemmas about the relationship between nurture and nature – only she had a minor problem with the notion. If her analysis was in error (and she doubted she was erudite or, well, clever enough for a proper analysis), nature would at some point collapse into nativism (just as nurture would be reduced to determinism). Still, putting all fears aside, how was it possible for two such different birds to come from the same nest? One, a bird of paradise, a bird of the jungle; the other, a bird of the woods and fields? Was it, in fact, naive to even speak about the same nest – the same parents, the same social class, the same educational possibilities, fuck, even the same room *the whole damn time* – if, within this nest, she and her brother occupied different positions: Dražen, the first-born *boy*, Dunja, the second-born *girl*; Dražen, for seven years an only child, *alone* and *at the centre*, Dunja, always *the other* and *in between*, sometimes as mediator, sometimes as apologist, but also as (Dražen's) advocate. In short, Dražen's position was, in a way, *fixed* and therefore (heh-heh) profitable, while Dunja's was changeable, vague – might we say, *precarious*? So wouldn't it be more accurate to talk about being from the same *bush*, but different nests? And wouldn't it be better – it occurred to her when Mirela still had not returned and the scarecrow cats had also disappeared – to leave such thoughts about nests for a little later? But wouldn't it be most appropriate, *right here and now*, she thought, surveying the room like a falcon, to keep to the rules of detective/crime fiction and use her hostess's incidental absence to uncover something that might expose her duplicity?

Certainly. Exactly. But, hmm, in a novel Dunja's attempt would inevitably end with her being so nervous, *right then and there*, that she would knock something over, or, even before the scene could develop, say, just as she was digging into the first shelf, with a furious Mirela catching her in the act.

But, hmm, the G.D. thought as she moved to the edge of the sofa, not even this second possibility seemed any less fictional. What a conundrum! She got to her feet, gritting her teeth as the arthritis bit into her pelvis, and intentionally ignored the kitchen door, through which her hostess might – hah! – *right then and there* swoop in on her. What a *fucking* conundrum! Life and art (conceding that genre fiction, too, can be art) push towards an interdependence and, therefore, can easily, as easily as rain slipping into a river, adopt a very persuasive guise in which neither appears to have any demonstrative primacy in the relationship.

What, then? Were they both happening to her at once? Quite possibly, but when she started poking around (and, yes, she still knew how to poke around – it was a skill she had mastered in the bedroom drawers of both Dražen and Katy), the question lost all importance. The mystery of the difference between the twinned albums was suddenly made *clear*: there was no difference between them, if we discount the different degrees of wear and tear on the covers and the extraordinary vinyl records inside them. What, therefore, consequently, ergo, was *clarified*, was precisely *niente, nada, ничто, rien*. Dunja would have normally been discouraged by such an impasse, and would have quickly sat down again, but the G.D., oh, the G.D. – *she* had to show what she was made of. She skipped the first four releases (since, *Dunč, this wasn't the real Mike – not yet!*) and pulled out *Off the Wall* and opened it, hoping to find a dedication, a note, a mark, a slip of paper, a letter, a message, anything! She then pulled out the second *Off the Wall* and opened it. She did the same with the first and second *Thriller* albums and, disappointed, pushed them back into the row. She went on to the first *Bad* and, oh dear, oh no, what a treacherous little madel—

—hey, Draži, that song 'Smoof Kreemeenal' was on the radio, and Mami started dancing to it and Daddy almost died he was laughing so hard – if only I had a video camera – do you think they're very expensive? – we could film her dancing and make our own music video. Do you think that—

— Dunč, c'mon! Learn some English, why don't you? It's pro-
nounced 'Smoothh Crĭmənəl'. English! Really . . .
    — OK, Draži, I will, I promise. But what do you think? Could we
save enough for a video camera? Everyone would—
    — Don't be crazy, Dunč. We don't have enough money for that,
and anyway, we don't know how to make a video, and I don't want to
embarrass myself. C'mon, Dunč, really, you can—
    — 'be so childish, Dunč'! But why do you have to always say that
to me? I'm not trying to hurt you, Draži, but—
    — You gotta behave more like a grown-up, Dunči. Why do you think
Katarina's the only one who puts up with you? She's just dumb enough
to hang out with kids younger than her, she's just dumb enough to—
    — Dražen, please, why do you have to be so horrible to me? You're
really a creep sometimes – creep creep creep – and only to me, Draž—

—eine, what a cruel madeleine! And was that the day before
it happened? Two days, maybe? Was it the same week? Were
Dunja's memories still so in thrall to her guilt? Was guilt dic-
tating her memories' space and content, their ground and sky?
Guilt, because . . . ? Guilt for . . . ? Guilt . . . shit! Why, but
fucking why?

And her eyes were burning, as if sooty and dry. But then
were suddenly washed in tears, which ran down her face like
water down a steep slope, and she could no longer see anything
clearly, not the list of songs, not even the cover, which had once
been a poster on Dražen's wall, which showed *Mike at his most*
beautiful! Look at that jacket, Dunč, just look at those trousers! And
that hair! She was crying, *our Dunja* was crying, so hard her hands
shook and the record nearly slipped out onto the floor, and, well,
wasn't it that same guilt (just think what Dražen would have said,
how he would have raged at her!) which now caught the record?
Guilt, or maybe fear? Pick one. Both get the job done.

She almost certainly got the cover a little wet, but it would
dry; the important thing was that she removed herself in time
from that fucking collection of *tea biscuits*, which crumble and
stick in your throat and prick your stomach like thorns. She took
a step back and, standing exhausted in the middle of the room,

started drying her eyes on her long (of course it was long, it was always long) skirt.

Not that such a thing is deafening, not that silk is particularly loud (still, did she not realise that all *pain* is exceptionally loud?), but she utterly failed to hear Mirela enter the room.

'. . . are you doing?'

Her voice was strict, maternal (ha!), and Dunja – with her wondrous instinct – at once retreated into a *little girl*. She let go of her little skirt and lowered her little head almost devoutly, crossing her hands in front of her pubic area so Mother would see how very, very innocent her young lady was. Even so, she had no explanation at hand (really, G.D., what a stupid, amateurish mistake!), only: 'Oh, well, I just needed to stand a bit, you know.'

Mirela's 'I see' carried an echo of 'I'm *sure* you did' – not chastising, the way our mothers liked to sprinkle it around, but dejected, for which she could find no true reference in the register of motherhood, not a single reliable cliché . . .

Not just Mirela's tone was, again, misplaced, but so was her whole presentation. She had brought from the kitchen two wine glasses, each containing a yellow liquid and quite professionally accoutred – a trace of sugar along the rim, interrupted first by a slice of peach, then by a slice of lemon – as well as a transparent stick the length of a straw (which it probably was). She swept past Dunja submissively, with bent neck and lowered eyes, as if she were the maidservant.

'You know,' Dunja began, hurrying to the coffee table, where her hostess had deposited the *lemonade*, 'I've been thinking . . . I recently met with Kristijan' (oh fuck, she was shocked by the way Mirela simply collapsed into the armchair – the name struck a nerve) 'and he told me that *you* must have been the last person to see Dražen alive and that you must have spoken to him, too.'

'Darling, darling, darling!' Mirela shouted and (a dramaturgical twist? This book is like that? An ad-lib whodunnit? Hold on to your hat!) hid her face in her hands. From somewhere, the green-eyed cat darted onto her thighs and Mirela, in a nasal voice, showered him with praise and muddled gratitude. How doubly touching, Dunja noted and felt a little nauseous – not because Mirela was being consoled by a *cat* but because this could not have been the premiere performance. It was apparently a much-staged ritual in the Mirelian culture.

'I'm used to all kinds of malice,' she moaned and, with even greater emotion, took the cat in her arms. 'But this is the worst, Dunja, the worst.'

Burying her right eye and ear in the cat's fur, she gently closed her eyes and even more gently pressed the top of her hand to her nose, drew in air and mucus, pressed it a second time and then, with her fingers, seemed to be checking if the nose's tip and root were still in place. Then she was sobbing, at times like an adult (you know: when tears stream down a barely altered expression) and at times like a child (when someone is more *grimacing*, with teeth showing and the face in furrows, than actually *weeping*), as, with her free eye fixed on the floor, she provided the details in a cracked voice. 'Oh, Dunja! People say all kinds of things about me, they'll say anything about me, just because I'm different, because I've always stuck out, ever since childhood, because it's hard to categorise me, because I don't seem to fit anywhere. Do you know how they all teased me at school, and at university too, or they would have if that had been normal? Really, like I said, I'm used to all kinds of malice; even clients whisper behind my back, and I do everything for them, all that I can. I try to be good to people, even if they're not good to me. I'm always giving something back, I'm always giving, even though people want to take everything from me. But fine, I'm used to it. What I'm not used to is – oh dear God, Dunja, this is the worst, the worst . . .'

The worst, yes. Dunja tried to quieten Mirela. Her lament was long and repetitive, as such things usually are when grown people keep returning to the events that reduced them to victims, to the moments when the world, or its privileged children, decided to exclude them, to make them subservient, to the periods of vulgar social conflicts, which must not be underestimated since they easily do damage. But, shit! – Dunja could not stop herself – the *way*, that awful, annoying way these things keep coming back. The way of self-pity! A self-pity that tended to block or impede the very compassion it was asking for, was begging for. A self-pity that wanted what compassion did not want to give: validation, not of the content of the suffering or of the suffering per se, but rather validation of – hah! – passiveness, of *sufferingness*, validation of the possibility that neither the content of the suffering nor the suffering per se would ever change.

It's OK, it's OK, Dunja tried to calm her, but maybe poor Mirela should not be faulted for her wearying reaction; after all, Dunja was suggesting that Mirela, at the very least, was concealing something and, at the very most, was responsible for a person's death. In fact, Dunja reflected as she crept contritely back to the sofa, to the end nearer the armchair, Mirela's response was *benign* – unpleasant and irritating, sure, but hardly menacing. Mirela, she thought, and moved to within touching range of her, was not some *sinister* presence, but probably just odd, which is rarely inscribed as a lovable or winsome essence.

'Mirela, forgive me for even mentioning it.' She leaned across the armrest. 'Forgive me for putting the question the way I did.'

'You know what really hurts?' She removed her face from the cat's fur. 'It's that you even wanted to ask it, that something like that could even cross your mind. But at the same time I understand you. How could I not?' In her nose, from the weight of the crying fit, a barrage of new bubbles seemed to be bursting, which was again followed by breathing in, breathing out and gentle pressure on the root and tip of the nose. The cat, meanwhile, having apparently completed his work in Mirela's lap, now stretched himself gladly across it.

'Oh, Dunja, I know you're trying to figure out what happened to Dražen; I completely understand that: you want to know. And I want to help you.' She was petting her Darling and gazing past her now rather pale guest. 'But no more for today. We need to rest.'

'Of course.' Dunja nodded to her hostess and was about to stand up when, out of curiosity – and also Dunjaesque politeness, since it was hardly proper to upset Mirela and dash off — she was tempted to try the fancy drink on the coffee table. Carefully, she removed the fruit slices and, in expectation of some sweet-and-sour refreshment, tilted it to her lips, tasted the white crystals (it was indeed sugar) and . . .

'Wow! Oh wow! It's really strong — and delicious! What is it?'

'A cocktail.' Her hostess looked at her blankly. '*Maiden's Prayer* — an English name. It means—'

'Yes, I know what it means.' Dunja, whose medications did, in fact, allow this, took another sip and, with a smile on her face (and what a smile), thought that while there was certainly an awful lot that separated her and Mirela, prayer, and *maidenly* prayer in particular, was something that awfully, and fundamentally, connected them.

6

As far as Dunja was concerned, Bernardin could easily have been a Potemkin village. Those few houses on the hill – scenery; the villas tucked behind the tall, dense shrubbery and trees along the road to the complex of hotels – scenery; the cars with the foreign number plates parked along that same road – scenery; the grass-covered beach on the other side of the railing – scenery; the hotel complex on the (haha!) *riviera* – scenery; the motorboats and hydrofoils and the lone sailboat moored in the miniature marina – scenery; the travel agency in the hotel complex – scenery; the ice cream and cake shop – scenery; the newsstand – scenery; the people ('Germans', 'Dutch', 'Austrians') – all scenery, or rather, she quickly corrected herself, all *actors*. Of course she was being unfair. To the *villagers* of Bernardin their dwellings must have seemed solid, but to her, if she put aside the smell (or rather, 'smell') – the stench of sewage, the stench of dead fish, of shellfish, maybe even coral – this *village* had never, from the time she was little, from the time she could barely say her own name, seemed real. It had never seemed to truly exist in time. Fuck, or even in space. Because scenery doesn't take up much space. Indeed, even now, as she walked onto the promenade next to the first in the line of Bernardin hotels, the one meant for Slovakian (or was it, haha, Slovenian?) tourists, who never rented a beach *lounger* because, given all the

other expenses, they couldn't afford it — it was more important to eat (*Smoki puffs*, *Bobi pretzel sticks*) and drink (*pivo*, *birra*,
beer) — but preferred to spend their holidays lounging on their
own beach *mats* (It's a good thing the beach is grassy! It's a
good thing the pebbles are clean!) — so that even now, after
more than a fifth of the damn century, she had no choice but
to say that Bernardin still failed to meet the one measly, pitiful
criterion of existence: hardly anything had changed. Here on
this, what, two square kilometres?, despite the original Yugoslav
construction, it was still trapped in the transitional nineties, still
trapped in the period when most of this Potemkin village grew
up and, for the length of a held breath, even thrived. Indeed,
Dunja counted only three globalist interpolations — er, sorry
for the jargon — three interpolations from the current (no less
monocultural) period. The first, a pub with dark-brown wooden
furnishings and just as cheerlessly dark walls, decorated with
ironic, quasi-political pictures and signs — *Your* [sic!] *in America*,
speak English! — where one was served the obligatory burgers
and their even more obligatory vegan variants (this was also the
only place where, in the end, Dunja found refuge); the second, a
small shop offering eco/bio snacks (she suspected it had appro-
priated its space from the equally small pharmacy); and last but
not least — oh, yes, least, truly, culturally the very least — a place
for renting SUPs, those sad simulacra (not that simulacra are
ever jolly or hopeful) of *physical activity* (blech), the apex but
also nadir of holiday *#funjoyment*. Fuck, it struck her as she
picked up the pub menu (that is, of course, as she picked up a
little piece of paper tied to a little board with a cute little bow) —
fuck, it was here, in the middle of this illusion, that she had to
lose her soul. Fuuuck — she decided on just a wine and (*Are you
sure you wouldn't like a beer instead, madam? We have microbrews*)
shyly ordered it — fuuuck, this illusion was really not for people
who were both critical AND sensitive, and, fuuuck, well, maybe
that was why Dražen liked Bernardin so much. Liked it best.
Our own special empty treasure chest.

   'Uhh, thanks.' The wine had arrived at the table. 'And,
uh, could you maybe bring me a burger too?' It was, after all,

dinnertime. 'I saw you had a bacon burger. Well, I'll take that.'
The waiter, a pierced, tattooed, tousle-headed boy, all, of course,
super-contemporary, nodded and sped off to the kitchen.

She was sitting inside – for the air-con, naturally, the air-
con *and* the peace – next to an enormous window with a view of
the concrete beach, where there were still lots of beach towels
and beach-towel owners, of the boulders, maybe naturally but
probably artificially arranged in a line, which children (because
who else?) must have covered with clumps of seaweed, and,
finally, of the bay.

She had never forgotten that feeling: closing her eyes,
taking a deep breath, holding her nose (at age six, but not at
age nine), and with a hop (at age six, but at age nine, like a
dolphin) submersing her head of long, always long, hair, which
underwater (at six, in the tepid shallows, but at nine, in the
colder deep water) blossomed into star points. The six-year-old
would rise quickly to the surface, a little panicky but mostly
proud of herself, while the nine-year-old was already compet-
ing, against herself and others, and especially against *Draži*.
*See that pole on the shore over there? I bet I can swim that far under-
water.* And off she went, a little sea serpent – two, three, four,
five, six, seven, aaah, eight, ooooh, nine, ohhhh, ten underwater
strokes – *maybe I'm already there* – coming up for air and, *ohhh,
yeeesss!*, the pole is far, far behind her. *Did you see that, Draži?*
she had shouted – on this very beach, Dražen's *favourite* beach.
She still remembered exactly where she was standing and where
her brother was, who, *because Mama told me to, Dunja,* had taken
her with him; she remembered exactly how her brother then
yelled at her, how horribly, how wildly he roared, *What a stupid
little girl you are! Stop calling me that in front of other people. My
name's not Draži, you cow! I'm just Dražen, get it? What about that
can't you understand? Now everyone will think I'm a . . .* shouting
so horribly that he attracted far more attention to them than
that lousy *Draži* ever could, and so wildly that the little old lady
who had settled nearby – she saw the shocked, bewildered look
in the woman's eyes – was thinking about her own safety and
protection. She remembered very well how the pride she had

felt at finally making progress in something, at actually beating
Dražen at something, was washed away by stupefying shame
and burning, white-hot anger, and how, when she grabbed her
backpack, tossed her towel around her neck and raced off, she
left a trail of little footprints behind her, all the way to the Droga
warehouse, because she had left her stupid tennis shoes back
there with Dražen, and how she had run all the way to Portorož,
to that *port of fucking roses*, until finally, out of breath, such as she
had never been beneath the water, she had put on her dress, the
one *you shouldn't wear to school, Dunja*, and in tears, completely
in tears, and shattered, completely shattered, walked the rest
of the way home.

'Oh, thanks, thanks,' she said, now for the burger, smiling
into the boy's rather thin back, and sliced into the *artisanal* sand-
wich (one doesn't consume anything *artisanal* by hand) as she
tried to reorient her memory, so it wouldn't be always so sad or
traumatic, so much *on the verge*, so it wouldn't feel so ceaselessly
tremory. After all, she thought as she brought the medium-rare
beef up into her mouth (why is one's conscience not piqued by
the sight of bloody meat, but quite the opposite: all that saliva,
craving, delight at the bloody treat?), after all, she thought as
she chewed (oh yum, bacon adds an entirely new dimension),
after all, she thought as she sliced off a second piece and dipped
it in the barbeque sauce, after all (oh look, five *pommes frites*
too), after all (oh God, now what had she been thinking about?
The marijuana's lingering after-effects she recognised most
often in the presence of food, glorious food), after all, she and
her brother had enjoyed plenty of warm moments together! For
example, that time when (wow! the rocket and cheddar simply
danced on her tongue, gently pleasuring her taste buds), for
example, that time when on this very same beach – she was
still calling him *Draži*, only in a softer voice of course – he'd
been so impressed by her swimming, by her crawl and butterfly stroke – *Look at me now, Dražen*, she had shouted from the
water – he was unable to hide his enthusiasm. Or, around the
same time, maybe that same day – hmm, not that they often
spent days together on this beach, they had done that only two,

or maybe three, times — it was when the ice cream stand on the promenade ran out of Capri bars and she was so insistent about having one — *But Draži, a Tom bar is not the same thing, we both know that!* — that her brother, quite brazenly, as if he were asking for the time or directions, suggested to the girl in front of them, who already had a Capri bar, that she *do a good deed* and give it — *no, sorry, sell it* — to his *little sister; her name's Dunja by the way.* (Hee-hee, the burger, glorious burger, was only half gone.) But the story would have been unremarkable if Dražen, manipulative Dražen — *C'mon, when you were her age it would have meant the world to you* — charismatic Dražen — *You gotta make a little kid happy once in a while; peace has a price, you know* — but also Dražen with his Yugo suntan and, especially, his Yugo good looks, had been unsuccessful. The girl pressed the still-intact Capri bar into Dunja's little hand and, oh boy, did she bite into it (and now grown-up Dunja bit in too); meanwhile, the girl was completely unaware that in broad daylight, in a crowd of people numb with merriment, she had possibly for the first time in her life been played. And then there was the time, oh, that time when (the slicer was again slicing) — but *when* when? *what* when? Oof, the image suddenly left her, the way radon leaves a surface, and she stabbed nervously into the burger, bit into it hard and chewed it ruthlessly — yes, that time that time that time, come on now, when exactly? When she and Dražen went, well, when they went — her ears were buzzing with anger — it was, well, when he was already dressing like Michael Jackson, sure, OK, but where were they going? (she swallowed the mush in her mouth, which went down like a concrete brick) hmm, probably just to Piran? Maybe (she tipped the wine to her lips) their mother had merely sent them to the fish market, or to the greengrocers? Something secular? Banal? Sacred maybe? Did they go to a concert — not a good one, but still, she was with her brother — maybe on Tartini Square? Was he taking her to school? Were they coming back from a family visit, where they had played with the pets, him with the dog, her with the cat? And the dog — or was it the cat? — was called Ron? Or was it Roni? Did any of this even happen?

Another tip of the liquid – *in vino veritas, in vino* all sen-
timent, all tender memories – but no, not Dunja; for her (she
sliced and sliced) the *violence* was so much closer. Its causes, its
translations and transactions, its layers of outlets and actions.
She pushed away the plate – there was still a little meat, a
little sin, left on it – and (yes, a fucking symbolic gesture, but
Dunja had always been good at symbolising pain) finally gave
up. Gave in. In place of Dražen the mimic, whose shaggy curls
so annoyingly proclaimed Yugo right on his forehead; in place
of Dražen the provocateur, who played 'Dirty Diana' *to wake
up those two witches above us, Dunja, because they really deserve it
now, hah!*; in place of Dražen the schemer, Dražen the joker,
Dražen the dancer, Dražen the mischief-maker, Dražen the liar,
Dražen the *Dražen*, there was always and mostly, more than
anything else, Dražen the *vanished*. Dražen who (she signalled
anaemically to the boy for the bill), Dražen who was no more.
Dražen who was as if he had never been. Dražen who would
never be again.

She *did* pay, *did* thank and *did* say goodbye to the waiter,
but she could not be sure she had not done it all irritably, even
rudely. As she was leaving, the tattooed boy watched her with
accusing/pitying eyes, which suggested a still-adolescent capac-
ity for real compassion. But to Dunja, who at that moment felt
completely cold, even adolescent compassion was enough. So
before she swung open the saloon doors, she assembled a – yes,
truly genuine, yes, truly human – smile for him.

When she went outside through the next and last door,
there it was: a magnificent, a m a g n i f i c e n t, sunset, burnt
red and orange, powder pink, rosy pink, purple, the child of
many, too many storms, of yesterday's storm in particular,
that Mirelian storm which had given so much of itself. Much
too much.

She had read somewhere that sunsets aroused primarily feelings of depression in people. Not simply melancholy
or romantic feelings. Nor even a gentle sort of dreaminess.
But depression, full-on depression, a reduction of, or no, the
self-lamenting decline of meaning – this is what the splendour

of the sky was said to arouse. But if that's true, then why does everyone flock to see it? Even though it always repeats itself, is endlessly returning, renewing itself – why does nobody want to miss it? That evening too, there were scores of couples, friends and families – large families with teenage children, small families with little ones – taking their seats on the boulders, benches and grass, turning their chairs in the bars to face the horizon, which they were photographing, which they were Instagramming themselves in front of, and which was indifferent to anything they might write, or, well, tag, in their future post; the scores who had put on inventive make-up and dressed specifically for the occasion (why? so the sunset would fucking like them?); the scores sitting in front of it even if its glory was already spent, already empty, who were hugging and kissing and telling each other *sincerely true* things; the scores who acted as if they were not really affected by this narrowing of the essence, and the scores who, on the contrary, acted as if, in the presence of the parting sun, their own essence and purpose were expanding. *As if* – perhaps really, merely *as if*. Perhaps the only reason those scores of people were there was to drown out en masse whatever they were truly feeling, just as applause serves mostly to drown out any emotional reaction, any pensive reflection, disappointment or catharsis. Perhaps the only reason those scores of people were there was to (united and in solidarity!) obtain, from something that was dying, their opiate, the kick they needed for romance. For dreams. For melancholy.

Now don't misunderstand her – she was no better than the others. She too was among those scores of people, and she too found her own sunset view from an abandoned – or, well, stray – sunbed belonging to the Kempinski Hotel (somebody had transported it across the low wall that separated luxury from lucklessness), a sunbed equipped with a thick and silky-soft mattress. Making herself comfortable on it, in a way she never could on a mid-range hotel bed ridden and dismounted by innumerable heads, pelvises and bellies, she relaxed her lower back and hips and neck and thought, fuck, so this is how queens

and kings unwind. So this is how their faces and chins untense.
How their eyelids shut automatically. So this is how even in the
worst heat they are caressed in crispy comfort. So this, this, is
how the music plays – *pianissimo.*

✳

The last time she had sat here the name of this palatial building had been the Grand Hotel Palace. Had it closed by then?
Was it already deteriorating? It might still have been accepting guests, guests whom, people said, nobody ever saw, guests
whom Dunja therefore imagined not as guests but as (hee-hee)
rare, even rarefied *entities* (she called them *beings*), rare and rarefied from money and fame, because a person who is wealthy
no longer needs a body (so it had seemed to Dunja at the time),
since a body is for work, a body is a cross, and so could move,
almost invisibly, from room to room, from place to place and,
as she once explained to her father, maybe even from century to
century – *We can't know for sure because we can't really see them, but
maybe all the guests are in fact the original settlers! Or maybe they're
from the future! From 2020, maybe, or from 1105. You never know,
Daddy!* Her imagination, Daddy had said, was *second to none, so
incredibly profuse* – yes, it certainly was. But when she had last
sat here, sat here with her parents, not on the summer loungers
but in March, on the cold, concrete half-wall, her imagination
had been so incredibly *obtuse.* As if asleep.

 Why don't we sit down, her mama had suggested. *Why don't
we sit down,* her daddy had suggested. No. *Why don't we sit down,*
they both had suggested, in a single broken voice. The wind was
sharp; it was pounding at the awnings, vibrating in the windows
of the empty pubs, tearing at Mami's kerchief, at Daddy's face.
He didn't dare look at her; no, he was staring at the pier, where
someone was staring at the choppy sea, and the sea was staring
neither at that person nor at Daddy – the sea never stared at
anything. But he was holding her by the hand, holding her tight,

the way you hold an object you mustn't let go of, the way she
had seen him the day before holding money or keys in his fist,
money or keys he did not want to lose.

Mama was holding her too, holding her around the waist,
no less unrelentingly. No less firmly. She was also bending
over her — a weeping willow with its slender, flexible, sturdy
branches — bending over her silently, for a long time, as if, what?
To protect her? To soothe her? To hide her? But from what, if
all the pain was there, between the two of them, beneath the
slender, flexible, sturdy branches, which fell like rain from the
trunk of the tree.

She — the weeping willow — was bending lower and lower,
and when her branches were spread on the ground, she said
voicelessly, *We've been to the police station, Dunja dear.*

And Daddy suddenly squeezed her hand harder, until she
could barely feel her fingers; he squeezed so hard that, no, her
fingers didn't pop or break but only melted into his, into his cal-
loused, rough, enormous fingers, until his own weary, pale-red
blood was flowing into them, bringing her his exhausted, pale
oxygen, and the oxygen was carrying his — oh, the little girl did
not understand exactly what *this* was, but it lingered inside her,
sticking to the walls of her arteries, veins and capillaries, and
as it rose unstoppably, throbbingly, up through her aorta, she
wanted to ask Daddy what he had given her, what—

We had a meeting with Peter and Simon, Dunja, she heard
from beneath the willow, could barely hear, there was such a
roar coming from Daddy. *They asked us to go there, Dunja honey.
Quite a lot of time has gone by, they told us, and after all this time they
still don't have answers, not completely—*

—what Daddy had really passed on to her and what she
was now supposed to do with it. Was she too supposed to look
away? To look at the man who was looking at the sea, which was
not looking anywhere, which did not see anything, nothing at
all, because it never has any need to see anything? She wanted
to ask him, wanted, wanted, tensing her stomach, tensing her
arms, tensing her neck, her vocal cords too, tensing, tensing,
and she managed—

—they managed to interview everyone, in detail, they said,
several times, they said, Dunja honey – there were no fairy tales
for *Dunja honey* beneath the hanging branches, no well-chosen
words or even a melody beneath the hanging branches – *they*
were able to place everyone, but they couldn't reach any conclusion,
Simon and Peter told us. They managed—

—only to cry. But her crying was invisible. Was Daddy's
too? She and Daddy were one, they were—

—to find a few witnesses, but there wasn't a lot of incriminating
evidence, not enough, Simon said, while Peter, you know, my darling
Dunja, he said there wasn't any. The investigation, they said, Dunja
honey, now shhhhh, our darling Dunja, the investigation was—

—were right then, she and Daddy, oh, the little girl again
did not understand, again she wanted to ask just what it was
they were—

—it had been a long investigation, they said, now shhhh, shhhh,
my little Dunja, a thorough investigation, they kept repeating, repeat-
ing in their own defence, Dunja, not to console us, but I wasn't angry,
because it didn't matter, it didn't matter at all, shhhh, shhhh, my little
Dunja, I didn't even press them, my little Dunja, shhhh, shhhh, my
little Dunja, when they told us they were going to suspend the investi-
gation, not close it, you know, Dunja, they didn't say close, they said
suspend, but—

—but with the tears streaming down her cheeks and
through her arteries, veins and capillaries she couldn't ask anything, couldn't say anything. She leaned against Mama, against
her sinewy trunk, and just when she did, Daddy let go of her,
the way a river lets itself go into the ocean and completely dis-
appears, and still gazing at the man who was gazing at the sea,
he sobbed out that *they said they were sorry, Duni, that they were*
terribly sorry but they hadn't been able to solve anything, that they
completely supported us. Time might still reveal something, they said,
Duni, but unfortunately, we don't have time, Mr and Mrs Anko, they
said, we just don't have the time, Mr and Mrs Anko, he shouted *Mr*
and Mrs Anko, he wept *Mr and Mrs Anko,* and the little girl, her
face pulled into a fabric of spiky knots, looked for her daddy's rough palm, for his strong forearm, his pointy elbow, his

shoulders and chest, his anything, just so – *Daddy, please, any-thing* – with her little arm flailing and grabbing at air, flailing and grabbing, grabbing, flailing, just so she didn't have to look at him shouting, still shouting *Mr and Mrs Anko*, just so she didn't have to watch him, watch him running, running towards the pier, stumbling in the middle and nearly falling and finally slipping into the man who was gazing at the choppy sea, who was asking, pleading with the choppy sea, but the sea never tried to answer him and never returned his gaze.

*

'Madam, madam! Oh, madam!' somebody was shouting at her; uhhh, yeah, she opened her eyes – it was a young man from the Kempinski Hotel. 'You can't just sleep on these sunbeds, you know. So would you please get up and let me put this one back?'

'Oh sure, sorry, just give me a moment.' Dunja turned onto her side and groaned. From thighs to neck she was a concrete block, a block made up of extremely painful, extremely inflamed smaller blocks.

'Umm, could you maybe give me a hand here? I seem to have got myself a little bit stuck,' she said with a big (exaggerated) laugh, and the young man, a well-bred pup of the *lumpen-elite*, muttered *yes, of course* and very adeptly – very carefully and patiently, with a choreography that caused her almost no discomfort – helped her to her feet. But before she could begin to thank him, extensively, enchantedly – maybe he wasn't just a pup; maybe he was a fine, true dog – he picked up the sunbed and with a grotesque jerk of his head, more birdlike than doglike, indicated she could go.

But Dunja, ah, Dunja did not budge. What fucking irony, she thought to herself sleepily and again, but no longer from embarrassment, laughed out loud. What fucking irony it was that she should first be awakened and then curtly dismissed by yet another boy with curly black hair.

7

'Kristijan makes such good food, at least that's what I think, but I guess you didn't really like it so much. You hardly touched the fish. But oh! Forgive me! I should have asked you first what you wanted. I know tastes change over the years.' She was whispering, with her chin tucked conspiratorially behind her right shoulder.

Like it? No, it wasn't about what she *liked*. She remembered liking sole, liking its creamy, no, *buttery* texture. Yes, she had liked it; it had been her favourite fish, in fact. She had liked the way it melted in her mouth yet was also filling. She had liked this strange, flat fish, which lived or slept or hid itself at the bottom of the sea, a welcome mat (hah!) she was allowed to eat. She had liked that it didn't smell bad, the way other flatfish often do. She had liked that it meant there was a celebration, and a celebration meant gifts, and gifts meant new things, and new things meant wealth, and wealth meant they weren't poor any more, and because they weren't poor any more, she no longer felt ashamed.

So yes, she *had* liked sole. *Once.* For as long as it meant, at the least, food, and at the most, abundance. Until overnight, over a clear, bright night – full moon and highest tide – it became a symbol of her new destitution. Right until he made his home among its long, thin little bones and became stuck to them. Right until her father jumped into them.

✳

He had got up early, extremely early, one Saturday, for the first time in years – it must have been seven years. She had heard him enter – *enter*, yes, not *crash, curse, stumble into* – the bathroom, heard the water booming in the tub, heard the hairdryer, heard him brushing his teeth, heard even his gargling. Heard him combing his hair, neatening it with lotion. She had seen him, seen him clearly from the dining room! How fresh he was, how very fresh, dressed in jeans and a silk shirt printed with little flowers, his most expensive shirt, a surprise from her mother but Dražen's audacious choice; she had seen him open the shoe cabinet and eventually find his favourite slip-on sandals. And when he left the flat she had seen him (had indisputably seen this!) dragging a little cloud of steam or mist or maybe it was a ghost behind him and (yes, she undoubtedly had seen this!) when he came back, with a bag in each hand, the same *steam-mist-or-ghost* thrust open the door, creating a terrible draught.

    I'm making lunch today, he had told her mother, *I'm making sole and potatoes*, he had told *her*, who suspected – she had cocked her head and peered at him, stepped closer and sniffed at him like a cautious puppy – who had frankly suspected that he was still rather drunk, but actually – her suspicions falling apart like an old jacket – he was sober. Extremely, extremely sober.

    Was he cheerful as well? Was his singing and humming, as he peeled the potatoes, chopped the garlic, cleaned the fish, and prepared the baking dish, a kind of cheerfulness? Was his whistling a kind of fatherly merriment? Is that what his rhymes were too? *Dunja, dear Dunja, a fish a day keeps the doctor away; Dunja, dear Dunja, potatoes we'll add to make the soul* (or sole?) *glad!* Were his *I love you, my Dunja* and *I love you, dear Blaženka* and *I loved you all so very much* a kind of joy? If there had been none of this, neither cheerfulness nor merriment nor joy, then why did it seem there was, as he laid the table? And if, as he served the food and the serving platters were steaming so much that she and her mother had to shut their eyes from the heat, if

I'm sorry I've been a bad father to you, Dunja and *Forgive me, Blaža, for leaving you on your own* — if this was neither regret nor apology, then why did he have to say it to them?

And Daddy, what was the point of *Blaža, come on, put on your red dress for me?* What was the point of *Let's go out for a walk, go out into the sun!* on that extremely extremely hot day in July, when sweat had once been flowing down his forehead, temples and chin, when his drink had been flowing, when his vomit had been flowing — his vomit in the corridor, his vomit in front of the door and on the balcony, his vomit in the bar, his vomit on the bed — when his evenings, afternoons and nights had been flowing, all these seven years, all these 1,858 days, these one thousand, eight hundred, fifty-eight days of guilt sadness guilt bitterness guilt desperation had been flowing and welling up — what, *Daddy, oh my Daddy*, what was the point of such a last day? What, *Daddy, oh my Daddy*, was the point of a last day at all? (Yes, the steam or mist can recede, but the ghost — as Dunja herself would learn much later — the ghost, *Daddy, oh my Daddy*, was stronger than you.)

He's gone out drinking; yet again, he's gone out drinking. *It isn't going to stop; I'll have to do something*, her mother had said in tears, when he again skipped dinner, when, without either of them knowing when or how he left their little flat, dressed in the same clothes, dressed so nicely, he simply disappeared. (Steam or mist or ghosts disappear all the time, they are constantly disappearing, disappearing, -sappearing, -pearing, -earing, -ring, -ing, -ng, gahhh . . .) *I have to do something*, -omething, -thing, -ing . . . *You're so sad too, Dunja, so completely sad* — it was already dark in Lucija, total darkness — *but you and I, we understand your father; you know we do, we always have. You understand, Dunja, you understand — such anguish,*

-guish,

-uish,

-ish

-sh

Shhhhhh

Shhhhhh

Shhhhhh

Shhhhhh, Dunja honey, shhhhhh, Dunja honey, shhhhhh, little one, they rocked each other in the guilt of hopelessness, in the anguish of hopelessness, in *oh Daddy, my Daddy*, in *oh Ljubo, my love,* and the morning allowed them to see EVERYTHING; the light, the harsh, endlessly harsh light, burned away the steam or mist or ghost so they could find him, *below the church, Dunja,*
BELOW
THAT
FUCKING
GODLESS
CHURCH
they found your father. (She did not say: *your father too.*)
Found your fa-
-ther
-er . . .

. . . But a year later her mother *did* say, her mother *did* tell Dunja:

'Daddy left two letters on the wall at the top of the cliff; he weighted them down, with stones, I guess. A letter for you and a letter for me. Here, Dunja honey, here it is. Read it.' (One of the letters written for *us who remained.*)

And as soon as she had unfolded the paper, the *steam-mist-or-ghosts* sat down next to her and smacked their lips, smacked their lips and whispered, 'Now there are more of us, but Dunja, we're still yours, always yours. Whenever you want, whenever you're ready, Dunja darling, just come. Just come, it's no—'

*

'It's no big deal, Katy,' she replied in a low voice. 'It's just that sometimes the medicine I take makes me lose my appetite.' Looking out at the neighbourhood from Katy's balcony, on which she had sat a thousand times, she thought, look at that, spread out before her, and behind her too, was all the material she needed for déjà vu: the racket from the dining room – the rhythm of closing and opening, the rhythm of stacking and putting away, the rhythm of scraping and washing, the rhythm of polishing and, yes, wiping too, since for all the couple's Ikea luxury they still had no dishwasher – and the occasional loud but not actually negative sighs, more like mutters, carried in waves on a draught of air through the balcony door; and Katarina's condescending, self-satisfied smirks, her feline squints and pursed lips, and their footwear too – Katy's pink slip-ons with the silver designs and Dunja's orange ones with the red flowers, borrowed from Katy (they were always borrowed from Katy, since her mother *wouldn't dream of buying those ugly things* for her, although in fact she was just trying to save money) – and that footstool, that self-same footstool, always a little wobbly, which had wanted to be a coffee table and a coffee table it became, although today, instead of the latest issue of *Mickey Mouse Comics*, it bore an ashtray, and finally, the very last thing, although first in magnitude and meaning: the question, solicitous and soft, which made them sit up (back then they were sated and drowsy, today only pensive) – 'Dessert anyone? I've got chocolate and biscuits. You can have both if you like.'

'What do you say, girls?' Katy looked at Dunja and Duši, who was squatting (sorry, Duši, but it's funny) like a mushroom on the ground – well, actually, she was sitting on a Friheten cushion she'd brought defiantly from her room to annoy Kristijan. 'Are you still hungry? Dunja, you always had a sweet tooth.'

'Oh Mami, let's go out for ice cream instead!' Katarina's daughter leapt into position; she was dressed in a lavender top and a black skirt as short as a November day. Her adornments were tasteful but also radical: a multiply braided gold chain necklace and gold earrings of complex shape. Her hair that day was slicked into something mohawkish and dyed the colour of mayonnaise, although without particular success (again, sorry, Duši).

No way, Dunja couldn't help thinking as she discreetly examined Duška, no way was this merely Gen Z expressing itself. Something more was at play: this was already the fucking next generation, with a spirit that not only has settled into itself earlier than most but has done so without any, or with only the slightest, friction from guilt or shame – a generation that truly has had no need to feel ashamed. OK, sure, Dunja tended to go too far when she was analysing young people, but still she was convinced that, historically, it was entirely right that next to Duška she should feel like – look, even her words are old and pallid – a *bonehead*.

'Oh I don't know,' Katy replied, 'to be honest, I don't feel like going anywhere, I really don't.' To ensure that her message could not be misheard or, for good measure, mis-seen, she slid down the lounger, with her tail bone resting by the edge, and there it was: Katy's incorrigible laziness. 'But why don't you two go without me?' And then, for additional measure, that little smile, which could always persuade, which always *had* persuaded, Dunja to do almost anything – steal apricots for her at the market, ring the doorbells in their building (and as she was no good at hiding, people would catch her every single time), write a Love Letter to Katy's Great Love, borrow her mother's lipstick for her and then leave it in the sun, on that very same balcony, lie for her to get her out of trouble, saying *It's true – Katy was never on Jan's motorbike*, and, every time, stupidly conceal how uncomfortable she felt doing all of this. How queasy it made her.

Katarina's request on this occasion was, for a change, not unreasonable, but, even so, Dunja wanted to dictate the, umm, conditions and boundaries (as, what, signs of growth or mere crowing atop a pile of manure?). So, sticking out her chest, she said, 'Sure, if Duši's OK with that, then I have no objection, only not right away. C'mon, Katy, let's have another cigarette.'

'Awesome.' Duši was delighted, although Dunja expected she would have gone out for ice cream in any case, even if by herself. 'Awesome. So Draga, when you're ready, give me a shout. I'll be in my room doing myself up.' And then a wink, a charming, friendly, warm wink, and, yes, Dunja thought, Duši is certainly her mother's daughter. (Also because *doing herself up* clearly meant a lot to her.)

'Dunja and Duši are going out,' Katy passed the news on to Kristijan, without turning around, and her not-yet-husband accepted it with a benign *OK, sure,* followed by *I'll just hop in the shower then.* (Maybe, their guest wondered, Duši had caught some of her fondness for doing-up from Kristijan.)

All right, fine, whatever, but by now Dunja might as well be honest with herself: it wasn't just about setting some stupid boundaries, but rather, and especially, about the fact that behind her eyes, in her mouth, on her tongue, in her stomach, and even (haha) in her heart was Mirela, who had attached herself to her like mistletoe to a healthy tree (and just to be clear, in this analogy Dunja, believe it or not, was the healthy tree). And now she could hardly wait – really, she could *hardly wait*, for the official part of the meal to relax into that other context, namely, sweet gossip.

'You know, Katy, I had an unusual meeting the other day,' she began and then, in a single long breath but still speaking softly, summarised her visit.

'*Porco Dio!* Oof!' Katy did not modulate her volume – *she*, at least, had no reason for confidentiality – and lit her Eve cigarette. 'Oof, that must have been difficult.' At *Why did you even visit her?* Dunja looked away, or rather, looked *out* at the slope rising to the school, and mumbled that she *didn't have much choice.* And gave her friend a look that said, *You understand, you must remember Mirela*, after which a few complicated seconds passed so that Katy could, indeed, remember her, at which she exclaimed, *Ahhh*, and added, *Now I understand.*

'But in fact I didn't know her, not back then, well, not personally. She was in a higher year at my school, third or fourth, something like that, but by the end, oh my God, I think everybody was talking about her. I mean, we were all talking about her but none of us really knew her – even so, God, she was weird, *molto* weird, and, I think, was always by herself.' She exhaled the smoke and looked with sympathy at her friend, who was greedily devouring her words – in anticipation, of course, of the real object of slanderous pleasure, the so-called juicy details, or maybe a synopsis of Mirela's bloody-minded awfulness – and, in a quieter but more anxious tone, continued, 'But I think, although this would have been earlier, that she did hang out with Dražen – at least that's what Kristijan told me; I wouldn't have known that for myself.'

There really was no need, dear Katy, for yet another pause. It wasn't as though Dunja felt a sharp chill every time someone mentioned her brother; it wasn't as though her discomfort was always something explicit – she felt it as one might a days-old wasp sting, as a tingling but not paralysing pulsation, like a swaying, a rocking on the stairs between two decks, which presumably has never yet caused anyone to break their promise and not go to the other end of the ferry to buy sandwiches and soft drinks. Nevertheless, she gave Katarina a grateful smile – better Katy's excessive tact than Mirela's, hmm, well, Mirela's loud, rumbling combine harvester!

'You know what else Kristijan told me?' She had to pause again, just for a moment, although she, too, couldn't wait to say it – she was practically chewing, not smoking, her Eve. 'Apart from everything else, they used to make terrible fun of her because of her nose – Dražen and Kristijan too, only they did it behind her back.'

'Because of what? Her nose? Why? She has a perfectly normal nose. A nice one, in fact.'

Katarina leaned forwards, again conspiratorially, but now energised. 'Dunja! She used to have one of those hooked noses. It was really ugly. Kristijan told me they used to call her – listen to this, will you – *swastika-face*! Awful, no? And in retrospect I do feel sorry for her, but . . .' – she sounded more triumphant than pitying – 'but Dunja, how could you not notice that her nose was fake? Even if you didn't know what it looked like before, it's obvious she's had work done. And you, who notice everything!' She said *everything* as if it meant *I guess you're not exactly perfect*. 'I am really surprised. I noticed it the moment I saw her again, when I went to her office. I had some business where she works, you know, but something seemed off even when we talked on the phone . . .' By then Katarina had got herself so worked up that Dunja had to stop her for a second. She

placed her hand protectively on top of Katarina's, which was
darting around over the pack of slim cigarettes trying to extract
a new one, and pressed it to the coffee table/footstool; then she
gave it a gentle squeeze, as if testing an avocado.

'It was her breathing, right? That annoying way she
breathes.' Dunja looked at their interlocked hands (if domina-
tion is also a kind of interlocking) and, well, stared dramatically into the distance – because what else could she do? It was
a double defeat for her. First, because as a writer she should
have been insanely astute and insanely knowledgeable, and
second, she should have been even more so as a detective. She
had listened to Mirela's nose, she had observed it, and she had
seen – if she might now dare, when it was horribly too late for
triumph (what triumph? no, simple *deduction*), to summarise or
assess anything at all – she had seen a symmetrical shape, the
kind rarely found in nature: a delicate, narrow nasal septum as
regular as rain and as short as (haha) a summer storm, placed
precisely in the middle of the nasal cavity, with volume x on the
right and volume x on the left, actually *melding* into the forehead
and not, as is the case with many proprietary noses, crudely
affixed to it, and a slightly turned-up tip, the very kind that
(aha, now Dunja understood) Michael Jackson should himself
have had if he, or his plastic surgeon, or his worthless friends,
such as they were, had had any taste or, for God's sake, at least
been sober. Mirela's nose (it is hard to believe we have already
devoted half a page to the topic – and in a crime novel, no less!)
had, therefore, looked too good to be true. But it had *sounded*
all too true, and this combination of elegant and repulsive had
led Dunja astray (as she was trying to convince herself when
Katarina extracted her hand, along with the pack of cigarettes),
since the point of cosmetic surgery is to remove the repulsive
entirely, not leave something of it behind as, what? A souvenir,
a joke, a cruel reminder?

'Yeah, that. So I later learned from some friends who also
know her – I mean, they *know* her, but that's just an expression
really since nobody actually hangs out with her, you can't with
that sort, that's just how it is. Anyway, long story short, I learned

that, well, after she got her *new nose*' — she smirked at the words and then, poetically lowering her voice, went on — 'well, at first her breathing wasn't so terrible, but then, they said, it got worse over the years, and there are *theories*' — alarm bell! A lot of people, a whole lot of people, apparently, had it in for Mirela — 'that the real culprit was — listen to this — cocaine.' Solemnly, she wagged her Eve in front of her face — *Now pay attention, the chief is speaking!* — and, with a wink, stuck it between her lips. But Dunja, hmm . . .

Dunja now looked at her, looked at her friend's, well, let's call it *oppressor's zeal*, the same way anyone would look at a newly discovered fungus on their feet — not just with a small fear that it might be symptomatic of something worse, some serious illness, but also with disdain and revulsion. *I'm used to all sorts of malice* or *all sorts of evil* or *all sorts of malicious people* — she remembered those words as she lay there on the lounger and (in defence of *Mirela*! You might even think our protagonist has matured!) instantly straightened her back. Had she been able, she would have sat up and purposefully turned her whole torso towards Katarina, but (the spondylitis, sadly) she could turn only her head, which was no longer nodding and smiling.

'For someone who doesn't really know Mirela, you seem rather well informed, Katy.' She threw the first stone, and the surprised Magdal—, er, *Katarina*, dodged it, wincing a *what the fuck?* with her chin. But she said nothing. It was the same old dynamic, Dunja suddenly realised: she as moral victor (an extorted, undeserved status), her friend pushed into a corner. So she continued in a kinder tone (*Forgive me for doing that, Katy*): 'Well, so maybe you also know when she had the nose job done?'

Katy took a deep breath, exhaled and, with more restraint, replied, 'Oh gosh, she must've been twenty, maybe twenty-one, something like that. She'd finished her first year of university. She was in Ljubljana at the time but would come home on visits, and people would see her.' Here she let out a smile, but it was an innocent, completely innocent smile. 'You know how it is. I learned the whole story right away, from the grapevine, you might say.'

'I believe you' (although she didn't, not for a second). 'But how could she afford it? Rhinoplasty isn't exactly cheap, and back then it must have cost a fortune.'

Katarina again showed a smirk, only now she curbed the malice, which inscribed itself as a smeary scarlet bindi between her perfectly done-up eyebrows, before it could go too far. 'Why, Dunja dear' – she looked at her from the corner of her eye – 'how can you not know? That house you went to? It's Mirela's. She owns it. She basically inherited it. So now you understand what I'm saying.'

Umm, no, such details had escaped the Great Detective, but should she have thought them important? Is everything important in a criminal investigation? Isn't psychology alone sufficient? Or does psychology depend on economics? Or economics on psychology? Are character and money mutually dependent? How had Agatha Christie handled the issue, or more to the point, how had Miss Marple and Hercule Poirot handled it? How does Gillian Flynn handle it? Wouldn't it be better, thought the Great De— (well, right now we'll just call her Dunja), if she researched the standard methods used by actual detectives and not by imaginary heroines, who, well, like her, basically don't know what they're doing, who are permitted to improvise and (because they're fucking fictional!) are also permitted to repackage the raw events into nice little stories? But isn't it a mistake to ascribe the decisive value to method and to reduce the value of improvisation? Isn't that the greatest *fallacy* by far? After all – hah! – is not method in itself fictional, or to put it another way, isn't the need for order and control the very thing that, in every instance, gives fiction its foundation, its fundamentals? But does this mean, then, that Dunja the improviser, in her loyalty to unorganised matter, had been right all along?

Confused, she exhaled and thought that, despite everything, she could certainly pay more attention to the fucking material circumstances, and not just in the future, but, damn it, right now.

'I see. So the family was well off – that's what you're saying. They were well off.'

'Rich, Dunja. They were *R-I-C-H RICH.*' Her friend sucked
in the last vapours of the white smoke and, once more aglow in
the flame of gossip, went on. 'That wasn't their only house, you
know. They have another down by Umag – not a trailer, mind
you, a house! Her *dad'* – she said the word as if – all at once! – it
were a little girl talking, a little girl who had never in her life had
a man she could really call *Dad*, a little girl who deeply wanted
a Father but no Father had ever wanted her or her mother:
from the first, real, one, to the last, they had all walked away,
whether to some sort of freedom or back to their first girlfriend
or, indeed, their first family – 'he worked at Droga; well, he
didn't actually work, you know, I mean he held a position there,
a position where he made lots of money; her mama worked too,
but doing what, I don't know.' She ground the cigarette into the
ashtray until it was rubbish. Dropping her shoulders, she leaned
her head slightly back as if, D. guessed, she wanted her eyes
to absorb the welling tears. My God – the observer felt shattered – everywhere and in everyone, only trauma, or at best, *bad
experiences*, and all these damn eternal children and, ohhh – the
shattered feeling went a little deeper – how should she respond
to what Katy was going through? Change the topic? Pat her on
the back? Wait a little?

'Her *father*' – Katy, *oh may she be fucking exalted*, was again
Katarina – 'adored her, he simply adored her. He'd do anything
for her, which is probably why he bought her the nose. But he
was also very strict with her. I mean, he made sure she wouldn't
get in trouble. He wouldn't let her be friends with just anyone,
she was far too *precious* for that – yes, that's how he talked to
her – and as for hanging out with boys, well, that was completely out of the question, we all knew that, it was basically
Dražen who spread that around, although I don't think she
knew it was him; but come on, really,' (nope, this was not yet
Katarina talking) 'as if any boy would want to hang out with
her!' She whirled her hand in front of her forehead and rolled
her eyes.

'But Dražen used to hang out with her. That's not nothing.
I think she also used to visit him at our place.'

'Really?' She did not back down. 'Why, you never said a word about her to me!' Then her tone became more agitated and, oh, rather sharp. 'So why are you asking me all these questions if you already know her? If you know all there is to know about that freak?'

Because, Katy (and Mirela! and Kristijan!) – she could have snapped back at her – because she had a perfect right, a fucking perfect right, to know what obviously everybody knew about Dražen! *Because*, Katy – she could have bared her teeth at her, which she had actually never done – unlike you, Miss Expert at putting things off, at avoiding things, at being all too fuckingly all too humanly passive about things, *she* at least wanted to understand something. *Because*, Katy – *she* could have been malicious – unlike you, *I* am trying to be rational! *Because*, Katy . . . arrgh, Katy! How angry you used to make me, how quickly you and your envy always got to me, how dangerously your jealousy made my blood boil every time! She *could* have been fucking direct, but . . . But directness, erectness, wreckedness, echtness, blah blah blah, be damned, she did not want to damage, like some dog that out of boredom, anger or revenge ruins a brand-new welcome mat, the only alliance she still had on this stupid coast, or no, the only alliance she had *ever* had on this fucking coast. So inside her head, somewhere deep in the back, a door, a heavy door, slammed shut, and, fuck, she just could not snap back at her, could not tell her anything, if Katy was (and how fucking sad is this!) still her closest friend, even if far away and far apart, since, Katy, yes, Katy, *you* stood by me, you truly stood by me, through everything back then – oh the sentimentality, how she hated it! Hated it all the more because, weak and selfish as she was, and obviously *not* steely-rational, she had always given into it – *you* stood by me, you truly stood by me, through everything back then, and our bond is irreplaceable, since it's unrepeatable, because – sorry, forgive me, but what is the likelihood that things would ever again be equally as fraught and that someone would be there to carry Dunja through them (as if she could actually be carried at all)?

'Sorry.' Dunja shrugged. 'Now please, calm down. I didn't mean it like that.' The words *like that*, here, had a remarkably broad meaning.

But, hallelujah, they were enough. Her friend relaxed her tightly folded arms and chuckled. 'It's no big deal. But what is a big deal is that you take Duši out for ice cream ASAP.' She wriggled out of the lounger, turned around nimbly and stared at the closed shutters on the door to, hmm, was it her room or Duška's room?

'ASAP!' she repeated, grinning. 'Because otherwise Duši will hear everything. She'll be eavesdropping on everything we say. Isn't that right, Duši?'

'Oh, Mimika, please!' came a scratchy little voice, probably from just behind the door. 'You're awful.'

Then Dunja, too, 'turned' around, although it would be more honest to write that she *creaked* around, and through the slats in the shutters caught the sparkle of two dark eyes.

*

'So how long have you been doing this?'

'It will be two years soon,' Duši said when, past the last blocks of flats in the School Street cluster, they turned onto a narrow path across a dried-out patch of grass, where there was still a fig tree growing, growing like a weed and full of sweet fruit that nobody had picked because, although the tree was big, everybody, every *lazy* body, preferred to ignore it since they could buy figs, and in a straw basket too, at the Tuš supermarket. Well, it was then and there that Duši turned professional, not just in her words but, especially, in her royal-blue blazer.

'Eventually, I'd like to start selling it all too.' She was talking about the *hair jewellery* she made: hairbands, tinsel, elastic bands, scrunchies, fancy hair clips and even, yes, ornamental flowers of crêpe fabric. 'Over the internet, of course.' As if on command, she stopped next to Dunja, who – fuck Tuš – had stopped beside the fig tree and was reaching into its biblical leaves. She plucked two fat figs and handed one to the child, becoming for a moment Mother – Mother who feeds, nurtures, protects and defends – but really, just for a moment, since Duši did not actually know what to do with the ripened lump in her hand. Staring at Dunja, who bit into the fig almost tearfully, the girl chuckled and stowed her own plump fruit safely in her handbag. So as not to hurt the old lady's feelings by accidentally dropping it.

'Mami promised to help me with the shipping if I couldn't manage it myself, which of course is tops.' She rested one hand on the strap of her bag while the other hovered above her hair, which was combed back from her forehead à la Sharon Stone in *Basic Instinct*. 'That way, in essence, I'd be able to sell more of everything.' Definitely a *businesschild*, even if by now she was laughing ever more impishly, ergo, ever more *childishly*, at Dunja, who was so indecorously sticky from chin to nose that she had pulled out a handkerchief from her own, incomparably more vulgar shoulder bag – what madness had made her buy that damn Desigual bag in the first place!

'Do you think,' Dunja asked, when she had dabbed up the drying fig juice with the fabric, 'Katarina will really have time for that?' Gesturing with her head, she suggested they go down to the footbridge, which passed over the canal and under the road, where the plant life must already be toxic – there was no sign of either fish or ducks – and where dear Katy, at age eleven or twelve (oh, the intruding picture, the questionable image), pressed against the wall (*but it didn't hurt at all, it really didn't*), had lost her innocence with Željko, a boy five or six years older, Željko, whom she would quickly dump but who later, adult to adult, must have obviously desired her again because Katy had been alluding to him, right? A few days earlier, when they reunited? Or was Davor the one hiding behind the words *you can probably guess who*. Or Igor? Or that little blond guy – what was his name? Jan? Jasmin? But no, no, Katarina's *you can probably guess* must have been sarcasm; it must have been disdain for her former decisions, for her former naivety; it must, indeed, have been her faith in *formerness*, a faith that was a lot of nonsense, but a nonsense necessary for her life, so Katy could rise high above that *former self* who had once been erotically and emotionally attached to a man with an inclination for petty crime, a man who by the law of evolution, Dunja thought, must now be a sadist – Željko, then, had obviously again desired Katy so much, and just enough, that *he got her pregnant*. Pregnant with *Duška*. Dunja studied the girl, who, it was clear from her face, from the way her features oscillated between candour and irony, was still thinking about her answer. So he got her pregnant with a child who, what? Did he even really know her? Duška's brusqueness might in general be just as easily explained by *He absolutely does not* as by *Of course he does*.

'Of course she does. She has time. Mimika doesn't work, you know.' Her answer echoed in the underpass, which soon became a footpath to yet another court/car park for some blocks of flats which, although new, were clearly – a fully legitimate term in this case – half-arsed. Dunja expected that everything in those buildings, from pipes and windows to (haha) the residents themselves, must have been leaking from the very start. 'It'll be *dorro* for her to have something to do, but I'll keep the profits. Anyway, Kristijan takes good care of her – I mean both of us – but I have my ambitions.'

Oh, I'm sure you do, Dunja thought, and merely glanced at a second group of new yellow-and-lilac buildings across the main Lucija road; I'm sure you do. Katy had never had any, not really, while Željko, unfortunately, had only one: an aching hunger for money. As for Kristijan, well: 'So what about Kristijan? He's not just anyone, is he?'

Not just anyone? NOT JUST ANYONE? Oh, Dunja, please! So incredibly inept with people and so easily, if unwittingly, rude – and, she chided herself, you thought Mirela problematic! Hah! Duška too, of course, reproached her with a look – quite rightly – which at the same time told her that the only person allowed to insult, or rather, criticise her mother was her mother's daughter.

'Kristijan's fine.' She stepped onto the pavement next to the main road and immediately stepped aside for a boy who had a sleek wireless speaker strapped to his shoulder – a variation, it occurred to Dunja, on the MTV era and its bulky boomboxes – and, behind him, a flock of young Lucija seagulls. 'He's fine. I mean, we get along *dorro*.' She turned to look at the waddling birds and, clever girl, made a face. 'But he's strange, too. Different. But better him than *Željko*. *Željko* is nothing but a *stronzo*.'

Bingo! How *dorro*! – Dunja was delighted – how *dorro* when some essential thing just drops into your lap, when people chatter on about *the hives they live in* – the refrain from that old Neca Falk song popped into her mind, the refrain of her childhood, although it was older than she was, although as a little girl, she suspected, she did not even know it, although she must, she suspected, have woven it into her memories, added it, the way she might weave in or add a few suggestive details to an already completed detective story, details that actually served no purpose but, in her editor's opinion, enlivened the narrative. So, bingo! whenever the dialogue develops in line with the fucking story plan, even though, when it comes to the story per se (Dunja was being very precise here), we always judge in hindsight. But anyway, BINGO! Željko *was* Duška's father, and Željko was still a scumbag.

Just how he was a scumbag, how often the two of them had met, what they had to say to each other, what they did together, what he did in life, how long their meetings lasted, how, how much, what sort, where, when – she wanted to ask the girl all these things. They were walking under some densely planted pine trees and in this shade – in the shade, actually, of both their actual childhoods, a shade that did not need to be burdened with fictions – it was possible to ask anything. *Anything* could be asked, at least of a *child*.

But every story has its fox. Duši nervously shifted her bag a few times from shoulder to shoulder and in a voice no less nervous raced ahead: 'But your dad wasn't a moron, was he? Mami told me she would have loved having a dad like him;

she said she really got on *dorro* with him, and that she felt just
horrible when . . .' When he *passed away?* When he *died?* When
he *committed suicide?* How was the girl going to say it? How
had Katy said it when she was explaining to her daughter who
Dražen, Dunja, Blaženka and Ljubo were? Had she called them
her *second family?* Her *borrowed* parents, who taught her how to
swim? Her *associate* parents, who later taught her to read (first
water, then the alphabet, that's how it's done on the coast)?
Or were they simply *Aunt Blaženka* and *Uncle Ljubo*, who were
always happy to watch her whenever Cvetka couldn't – *Mami's
friends, Duši, who did a lot for me?*

'My father was . . .' Dunja murmured as she patted the
bark of a pine, which, well, was not as soft as her father's chin.
'My father was all right.' She rolled the sap into a little ball
between her fingers. 'Yeah, he was an all-right type. I can't
exactly complain.'

Oh, but she would have complained, how she would have
complained, if her complaints had not made her feel, in front of
everyone – herself and her mother, her therapist and her friends
Vesna and Ana – so utterly ashamed of herself. She would have
said – no, she would have fucking screamed: My father was a
fucking pathetic weakling! My father couldn't deal with anything but harmony! My father was a father only when the sea
was patient and calm! My father was never a father when rain
was forecast! Never when the bora or sirocco was promised or
when heat was pummelling down on us like a raging Fury! My
father gave himself fucking permission to stop being a father –
he dug a damn hole for himself, a deep and fucking spacious
hole, and crawled into it as if he had a right to be there, like
he was climbing into a damn overcoat, and inside that hole he
first got gooey, and then turned rotten with grief – although
our grief, mine and Mama's, he never listened to, and *his* he
never shared, so that fucking idiot turned rotten, like a bunch of
fucking apricots, peaches, nectarines, all crammed into a crate,
and – What? What are you staring at me for? Yes, I would call
him an *idiot*. A *fucking* idiot. I'd say of my own father that he
got *gooey* and then turned *rotten*, since that's the way it felt at

the time, that is indelibly EXACTLY the way it felt! My father did not abandon me *all at once*, I mean, it wasn't when he did that fuckingly tragic thing; oh no, he abandoned me *gradually*, the way a fruit gradually abandons its shape and texture and juice, or maybe the shape, texture and juice gradually abandon the fruit – since it's not so fucking important that the simile is right, because, you know, when it comes to my fucking feelings there's just no elegant way to word them, no fucking rhetorical trope to coax them into, one after another – thesis, antithesis, synthesis, negation, thesis, antithesis, synthesis, negation, thesis, anti, syn, neg, thes, ant, sy, ne, th, a, s, n – no, the most my fucking feelings ever had as a form of expression was stuttering:
W-w-why did you always l-l-love yours-s-self m-more than m-me?
W-w-why did you always l-l-love yours-s-self m-more than h-her?
W-w-what about y-your f-f-fairy t-t-tales, D-d-daddy?
Those s-s-singing b-b-bunnies in the h-h-hills,
the d-d-donkey, the w-w-wolf and the b-b-b-bear,
all y-your l-l-little n-n-ne'er-do-w-w-wells,
and the b-b-birdy k-k-king up in the air.
W-w-why d-does ev-v-veryone always l-l-love thems-s-selves m-more than others?
Is th-this all I f-f-fucking get in return?
Is th-this all you l-l-left me?
Is th-this your inherit-t-tance?

'An all-right *type*?' Duška gave her a wry smile – she must have noticed the other woman's pain and wanted to lighten it. 'Wow, you totally talk like someone from Ljubljana. Aren't you sorry you lost most of your Primorska accent? Me, I'm never going to lose it, no way, hundredpercent not – not even if I go to Ljubljana for university.'

Dunja returned the smile. 'Of course I'm sorry. You know, I really miss our vowels, the rhythm of our speech, but I can still talk like that if I want, if I try. But it's not the same, you know. So yes, *of course* I'm sorry about it.'

But did a dialect have any choice? Did *she* really have any choice? Was a teenage girl supposed to, what, be a fucking hero and remain a double foreigner? A foreigner in her new life, a foreigner in her new surroundings? No, she had been pushed into redefinition, into a fucking makeover and so, fuckingshit, she *did* redefine herself, she *did* make herself over. She built a wall around those broad *o*'s and *a*'s and *e*'s, around words like *stronzo* and *dorro*, a wall around her beloved dialect – or no, a wall around her *very self*. But as for the core of her being, well, fuckingshit, death had cut *that* out of her. Had fucking erased it.

Her mother, however, had made a different calculation. She had calculated that both their cores, hers and her daughter's, their despair and anger, grief and confusion, would relax a little if they moved somewhere else. *There's not much left for us here; there's basically nothing left for us here.* Before the eighth anniversary of Dražen's death, and less than a year after her father's, they really did do something of the sort – *of the sort* is how Dunja might phrase it because it, or rather, *what they did*, was not truly a move; it was merely the imitation of a move. It was a feverish leaving, abandoning, trimming and cutting. It was frenzy and fluster and fear. It was flight – yes, *flight*. From the time her mother announced: that she had found them a one-bedroom (*I'll sleep in the living room, or, well, the dining room, and you'll have a room to yourself*) in the Bežigrad district (*That's the northern part of Ljubljana, you know, as far away as possible from* this damn *coast*) and sold their home in Lucija; that she was taking Dunja out of the school in Koper (*Of course you'll finish out the year*) and had enrolled her in the Poljane Secondary School in Ljubljana; that she had found work in a hotel (*You know, partly housekeeping, partly reception, but it's all the same to me*); and that her sister (*oh, bene, molto bene*) was going to give them her old car – from her mother's announcements to the time when they were riding in the overpacked rental van (*We need to take everything; I only paid for the one trip*) and carrying things up the dimly lit stairs and down the corridor, which reeked, truly *reeeeeked*, of fucking dumplings, and squeezing everything into the orange-painted flat and cleaning and arranging furniture and putting up curtains and trying to find some peace and quiet from *the bombing, Mami*, that is, from the *booming* which came from the army barracks on Artillery Road, it was less than a whole fucking month! At this, of course, you'd probably like to tell Dunja, *Oh come on, a month is plenty of time to say goodbye!* And Dunja would probably like to snap back at you: *You think so? Well, maybe for someone who wants to say goodbye! But someone who doesn't want to, someone who didn't choose this, someone who is opposed to this, well, she will beg and cry, write letters and entreaties to her mami; she will hurl abuse at her mami, yell at her, shout at her, and at night she'll be grinding her teeth!* It took half a year – hear that? *six whole months!* – for her anger to finally subside, like some stupid lipoma; six whole months until: *Look, on clear days you can see the Alps from the window! Did you see the mountains, Mami? It's not a bad view at all*; six whole months until *Mami, would you make us* cremeschnitte? *Do you even know how?*; seven months until *I'm meeting up with Vesna and Ana later; we'll probably go and see a film*; seven months until Tivoli Park became *a great place to go*; eight months until *Let me make dinner tonight*; eight months until *Vesna and Ana are coming over – I can't wait for you to meet them*; and nine months until a gentle confidence was reborn, the confidence that the daughter was becoming more and more a daughter and no longer a stubborn adversary, until *Sure, Mami, of course I'll buy you a canna lily on my way home from school*, until *Yes, of course I love you, Mami*, until *Yes, of course, well, OK, don't worry, sure, maybe, no problem, well, of course, yes, of course, well, OK*.

'Ow!' Her sandal struck the curb in front of the ice cream and cake shop. 'Gosh, I'm sorry, I guess I'm just not used to this heat any more. I must have blanked out.' Duška gave her another smirk: she didn't believe a word of it. 'So tell me, have you decided what you want to study at university?'

'Of course I have,' Duši said, brightening, and made an arc around a Polish family. 'Comp lit and sociology. But Kristijan and Mami have had more than a few arguments about my decision.'

'Really? Why? I don't under-' Duši suddenly started pulling her by the hand '-stand. Why would *they* be argu—' Clearly, the girl was majorly lacking in . . . (Oh, Dunja, really! What ideas you get! She just wants ice cream!) Still holding on to her guest, Duška hastily claimed a place for herself in the queue in front of the ice cream freezer, not unlike (Dunja, who even gave you that damn literary award? And for *originality of expression* no less!) — well, not unlike a pig in front of a fresh trough of swill. She was standing on tiptoe, looking left and right, up and down too, trying, through the other swaying bodies, to assess the various flavours on offer and make her decision.

'Chocolate and hazelnut, or no, vanilla and hazelnut, in a cone,' Duška mumbled into the back of the man in front of her, and Dunja's heart, one might say, leapt up.

'Hey, I'll have the same! That's basically what I always have.'

'Not me. I like experimenting.' She had released Dunja's hand but was still darting her eyes somewhere ahead of her, through the narrow tunnel of elbows, arms, necks and shoulders. 'But it's a little different now because I'm trying to lose weight — which Kristijan is helping me with — and we agreed that I can only eat sweet stuff on *special occasions* — those are his words — and today is a special occasion. I'm really grateful to him, you know. Mami never supported me in this, because she's such a big overeater herself.'

'He's doing what?'

'I told you,' she whispered. 'He's helping me lose weight.'

'But . . .' She leaned in to Duška's ear, when the queue had dwindled to a single sweaty T-shirt.

'But *what?*' Duška pivoted her head like a vulture and, well, like a vulture, attacked. 'You're gonna say I'm not fat? You're gonna try and persuade me that . . .' — she shifted her weight to one side and, no longer like a bird of prey but gently, with the tips of her fingers, lifted the expanse between her breasts and waist — 'that this isn't just a little bit too much?'

Uhhh.

Ohhh.

Ahhh.

Ooooh, dear Dunja was at a loss.

But.

But, well, it wasn't just about the girl's health, Dunja thought, but also about the fact that the hands wanting to provide

it were those of a fascist – a *fascist*, Duška! and, obviously, a horribly manipulative fascist – which Duška, for all her sensitivity, had
strangely overlooked (that her mother – *forgive me, Katy* – had
overlooked the danger was not particularly shocking), and when
a fascist tries to tell a woman what is and is not healthy for her,
what he actually wants to do is to shape and control her body,
to manage it as he would a machine or his own property – and,
for fuck's sake, Duška, don't you realise how humiliating that is?
And no doubt (Dunja was sure she had grabbed the right branch
to save herself on, although her arms were still shaking a little),
no doubt the fascist had not stopped at beauty; he was no doubt
manipulating and terrorising both Duši and Katy in other areas
too, and by other means – *without a doubt* – even if there were no
external signs of their suffering; even if the two women declared
themselves entirely content. Indeed, their *contentment* – Duška's
Kristijan is fine, he's really fine and Katy's Cheshire Cat smile – this
was the very hallmark of his manipulative expertise, his wily, persistent, stupid fucking dominance! Shit, Dunja thought, and now,
just as they stepped up to the ancient ice cream freezer, her jaw
was vibrating along with her forearms – it's shit when an intel-
ligent girl gets caught in the silky web of the patriarchy, which
grooms her always to be getting stuck, constantly to be stumbling – unless (if only Dunja would calm down for a moment),
having no other choice, a girl or woman entangles herself like a
bee in the spiderweb so that when the vile, eight-legged creature
approaches, she can more easily sting him to death! If, of course
(now Dunja herself had got entangled in the metaphor) she even
wants to and knows how. It was urgent, then, that Duška turn to
Dunja for help, for only *Dunja the Free* could teach her the art of
symbolic (and I stress, *symbolic*) androcide!

Dreadfully anxious to embark on her mission, Dunja paid
for the two cups of ice cream with a ten-euro note, gestured
to Bučko to *keep the change*, and rushed Duška into the nearest
shade, on the other side of the road, and onto a bench in front of
the only boutique still open, which naturally sold the standard
Lucija style, which, as the girl immediately commented, was a
big yawn.

So there they sat: Duši, smacking and licking her lips, dived into her two scoops, while Dunja, with a single click of her tongue, attended more inhibitedly to her one. *More inhibitedly* because the Great Detective had to think hard and fast about how to broach a topic that had already tripped her up three times and which, if this were fiction, would definitely irritate the reader. In life, however, dammit, no: such not infrequent situations must be endured. Women writers, she thought, who *oversee the substance of life* (haha!), oh, they endure them with particular *nervousness*.

'Duška,' she said at last, attacking the hornet's nest, 'what did you mean when you said Kristijan was *strange*?'

The girl giggled and, with the plastic spoon, slowly shaped the ice cream into, hmm, an Alpine peak, after which she slowly brought the spooned ice cream up into her mouth. A second giggle. And then a third. 'Seriously?' She looked at Dunja, oh dear, with pity, the way human beings are accustomed to looking at sheep. 'You really *are* as tense as a *Draga*. What I told you about me trying to lose weight really got to you, didn't it?'

'Duška . . .' (it's a shame you can't hear the dignity in her voice, which the cold ice cream only sharpened) 'I don't know how your mother feels about it, but it seems to me quite problematic that Kristijan has been persuading you to lose weight. You are still very young and very impressionable when it comes to the way other people see you.'

Duška tapped on the Alpine shape with her spoon, turning it into, well, the Pannonian Plain. '*Draga* . . .' (it's an even worse shame you can't see the sarcasm in Duška's furrowed brow!) 'Kristijan has not been persuading me to do anything; he's never said a word to me about my weight, understand? It's *me* who doesn't feel great about it, understand? *Me*. I don't try to hide because that's not who I am, but I would like to feel better. And, sure, it's not just about how I feel, it's also about how I look, of course it is, but also, I don't want to have this emotional relationship to food.'

'Duška, in all probability, there was no need for him to say anything to you because you felt the pressure anyway, because you could feel how he was loo—' Oh shit! This is not how she had meant it to go – a bit of an accident! All the playfulness on Duška's cheeks, between her eyes, and *in* them too, of course, went out like – fuckingshit! – a candle! The girl put the cup of ice cream on the ground (the Pannonian Plain was already turning into a river) and folded her arms defiantly across her chest, her hands clenched.

'You're being really obnoxious about this – totally – when *you're* the one who has a problem with my weight. I remember the way you stared at me the other day.' She imitated a farm animal chewing cud. 'And now you've obviously packaged the whole thing into something else entirely so that, what? You can cleanse your conscience a little? Please. So typical.'

By now the ice cream had turned liquid in both their cups, and the mind of the Great Detective, too, was suddenly nothing but a worthless river. A river of poisoned water. With head-splitting rapids. Was Duška wrong? No, of course not! Was Dunja right? Yes, definitely! So how was Duška right? *In the specifics, in the particulars, in the case at hand,* or however it might best be put, but even so she was only right *in part*, while Dunja (the river took a wild turn) was right *in the globals* – ugh, that sounds horrible – which is to say, right *in principle*! Oh, yes (she was scraping along the pebbles of, haha, an admission), oh yes, she was trying to wash her soul, but that in no way meant that her critique was without truth! Or did it? Was her motivation important? Did everything stand or fall on that? Along with her critical mind, was she also supposed to have a good and brave and fucking pure heart? Was she supposed to aim her critique at herself first? Was she supposed to score a fucking own goal? And if she didn't? What? Would the feminist Interpol come after her?

'OK, OK! I'm sorry!' Fortunately, her mind was exhausted. 'But what did you mean when you said Kristijan is strange and that he and Katarina have been arguing?'

'I meant what I said.' She sounded just like her mother when *she* became angry. 'He's weird. You must have noticed how he's always straightening and cleaning things. He's why we have

such a tidy home. But he doesn't just look after the flat, he looks
after himself, too. He works out like mad – that goes without
saying – but he also takes a lot of showers, sometimes twice
a day. He's hygienic, but he's not pushy about it, if you know
what I mean; he never badgers me or Mami about being slobs,
although we definitely are. He's hygienic. That's the word.'

But he's a racist, Duška! What about that?

'Other than that, he's a pussycat.' She was herself again,
even if she still had her fists lodged in her armpits. 'He's kind
and attentive, and if you really want to know, he's the one who
supports my decision; Mami wants me to study something *real-
istic* – that's what she calls it – something that'll bring in the
cash. Law, or economics, or chemistry. I don't where she got the
idea that that's the way to get rich. Kristijan, on the other hand,
keeps telling her – but they don't talk about it in front of me, I
just hear these things – well, Kristijan keeps telling her I'll only
be successful at something that truly interests me, and that she
can't force me to betray the person I am because in the end I'll
be unhappy. Very unhappy. He said that as my parents – see? he
thinks of himself as my parent – that as my parents they had to
make sure that I lived my own – and here I'm quoting him – *genuine, unique, inner truth*. Isn't that . . .' – she unfurled her arms,
catching a breeze beneath her blazer (it's a miracle it stayed on
her) and, hallelujah, this textbook hothead was finally looking
at Dunja with warmer eyes – 'isn't that beautiful?'

Absolutely, absolutely, this *genuine-unique-inner-truth*
stuff does sound *authentic*, just like fucking Kristijan, but
still, Duška's story did not make a lot of sense. A helpful and
understanding fascist? A racist *softie*? A nice little fascist with
a patient attitude and sweet face? Sure, she thought, leaning
back on the bench as if trying to evade some dilemma, the
way she'd lean back when she was revising a chapter she was
ashamed to read – sure, personality is an expanse, not a single
puny location, but . . . the idea of introducing *both* extremes
in a single spectrum? This would surely invalidate the spectrum and create – Dunja stared at the embellished jeans in
the shop window – terrible confusion. But Kristijan did not

seem confused to her; just the opposite, he seemed solid. Or maybe just hard. Or no – *rigid*? Yes, haha, a crucial difference. But maybe Dunja should consider the context: it was not so strange that the little fascist in him should emerge only when he was *outside*, that at home he was a perfectly ordinary sheep, but whenever he went out for a walk, even if only in his mind, strolling along the margins of certain predictable territories, he'd start roaring like a fucking creep. That was it, she thought: *this* equation at least – *blitz! blitz!* like two bolts of lightning – came out even.

But she was no less confused. If only she still smoked cigarettes! If only she had some place to put these annoying, hovering hands! For the hundredth time, Dunja, you need pockets on this fucking coast! Ugh! But since she didn't have pockets, she just sat on her hands and shut her eyes for a moment: clearly, the conversation was trying to assume a circular structure, which was, well, very *un-novelistic*; it was forcing its way back, back, that is, to Željko, to cover all the things they'd mentioned, but Dunja had lost interest in that tyrannical moron. Her only interest was in Kristijan – she couldn't believe he was so completely different from what he had been a couple of days ago – but now there was probably a kind of embarg—

'Oh, just so you know, *Draga*,' Duška began as she finally removed the blazer, draped it over her bag and calmly stood up. 'I am totally conscious of the fact that Kristijan is a xenophobe, but he is *good* for Mama. You know what they say: a person needs to be content with a little, and he treats her well. He never hits her or yells at her or does any of the things Željko used to do to her.' Then she looked away from Dunja, who was now also struggling to her feet, but even so, she felt as if the girl, whose eyes were fixed on an oleander bush, beneath which a cat was getting ready to ambush geckos, was still thoroughly aware of her. Dunja could have sworn that the girl was *looking* at her, if only with her torso and hips, when with a certain shyness – a part of herself she had not yet shown Dunja – or no, a certain *hesitancy*, she said, 'He would never hit her, because he doesn't ever touch her.'

'Whaa—' Dunja droned out sciatically. WHAT THE FUCK had the girl just told her?

Duška then turned around — turned around with a quiet but relieved 'uh-huh', followed by a 'yeah'. And indicated to Dunja that *they could go now*, that *now* they really could leave this roadside bench. Dunja, however . . . well, Dunja was staring at the cat under the bush, which with a pounce, a pounce that seemed more random than planned, had at last caught a gecko. The victim was wriggling under the cat's paws and emitting lizardly squeaks, while the little cat, as if surprised, went on sniffing and watching it a long, long time.

8

The shop by the canal has a sale on polo shirts. Why don't we go and buy one for you? — Polo shirts? Really, Mami! I'm not queer!

Hey, Draži, can I braid your hair? For practice. — Leave me alone, Dunja! I'm not a queer!

Why don't you take that new shopping bag, the pink one? It's hanging in the front hall. — Aw, Mami, please, you can't send me out with that one. I'm not queer, you know!

Wow, that actor is really handsome. His name is Petrik Shvaizi — I read it on the poster in front of the cinema. Do you guys like him too? — Dunja, it's Patrick Swayze, and no, we don't like him, not like that. We're not queer, are we, Kristijan? — Well, I don't know about you but I'm certainly not!

Kristijaaan, are you ever gonna do your hair up in a bun? Cos I'd love to see you in a bun; you'd look just like an elf! — Oh come on, Dunja! No. I am not. Don't you get it? I'M NOT QUEER!

When they started saying this, when they were repeating this sentence so often it became a fucking mantra, did Kristijan already know? Or only suspect? Who said it first? Kristijan? Or Draži? And how much did Kristijan, if he knew or suspected, flinch at the word? How much did it wound him? Was he disgusted by it? Dunja wondered these things as she leaned back in the thick-cushioned hotel armchair and supported her head on her hands. Was it the *word* that disgusted him — or *himself*?

Or was it (she reached for the purse containing the pot, which she had carelessly tossed on the little table next to the armchair) more complicated than that, as such things usually are? Did he not at first, when it still seemed to him that this was just the way boyish (and manly!) arrogance *talked* but not necessarily the way it *thought* and *acted* – did he not take the word to heart? Did it only later (but even so, soon enough) become a weapon, when he saw it in action, in earnest, maybe in the company of other boys and guys and men, saw it wielded as a cudgel, saw it striking and punishing? He must have most surely, and as quickly and as soon as could be (Dunja spread a leaflet across her knees and on it crushed a tiny ball of resin into sand), he must have seen its hellish children, its effects – or at least its diabolical parents, its *causes*? – those wordlings of the Word. Bullying – *What's wrong, queerboy? Need your mama? Didn't think so. Animals like you need a daddy to teach you a lesson!* Pressure – like when Jan came to school exhausted and unslept because somebody had caught him, *Oh, we caught him all right, the way he kept looking at Željko in the changing room, you know, checking out his arse, that fucking pervert!* Blackmail – *Do my essay for me, cocksucker, or I'll fuck you up, you little prick, hahaha.* And violence (Dunja mixed some tobacco in with the hash, mixed it evenly), how much violence he most surely and as soon as could be, as fast as could be, must have seen – in the school corridors, where a *queer* got himself shoved against a wall; in the schoolyard and on the basketball court, where a *queer* got himself tripped; on the beach, where a *queer* got his glasses stolen; on the bus, where a *queer* got himself pushed so hard into a pole that he bled; at the bus stop, where the glass got itself cracked, cracked from the force of the head of a *queer*; in the checkout queue, where a *queer* was buying a snack, which he, the *pervert*, just happened to drop on the floor and so had to pay for something that got itself crushed by a foot; and in the park, oh in that damn park, where a *queer* got what was coming to him, a kick in his *queer bollocks* and a left and right hook. *I'm not queer*: the cue for humiliation, annihilation, dehumanisation, fucking catastrophe (Dunja licked the rolling paper and sealed it with shaking fingers), a cue that

glimmered *in, on, beside, behind, in front of,* a cue that whispered
from every fucking corner!

And the dark whisper was like a fucking c o n t r a d i c -
t i o n to the softened light of August (she stepped onto the
balcony and rolled out the greying sun awning), a light at its
loveliest, its roundest, at precisely six-thirty in the evening, yes,
at that hour precisely (Dunja sat down), a light that whispered
to her how everything wonderful and splendid and exalted and
sublime and whole and dreamlike was still within reach, was still
entirely possible! Oh, a most enthralling and, because enthralling, a most dishonest light! And a most intoxicating – of larch
and pine and salt and olives and sun cream and white bread and
beef tomatoes and morning coffee served on the pedestal of a
night of passion – and because intoxicating, a most deceitful
August scent! And a most melodious – from the cicadas and
the breeze and the sea and the happy insects and the boisterous
bathers and the murmur of the fishing boats and the murmur
of the caught sea breams and the murmur of the lovers and
the giggling of the shy strangers soon to become lovers – and
because melodious, a most misleading August music! A most –
but why (she inhaled and at once moaned), why was she constantly analysing, metaphorising, symbolising, theorising, terrorising, errorising, -rising, -ising, -sing, -ing, -ng, ngaaaahhh,
when the fucking truth was simply (she breeeeathed in as if
she were all lungs), simply that she was insanely, i n s a n e l y,
afraid. I n s a n e l y lost. She would even say (she blew out the
smoke), would go so far as to say, that she was, indeed, insane.

Did Kristijan being gay – the hash instilled her with courage, or, hold on a sec, the hash was making her *careless,* was
erasing for a moment all the fucking implications of the question – OK, but did Kristijan being gay, when it came to Dražen,
when it came to *Dražen's death,* change anything? Did it change
everything? Was it the crucial *secret* (she squeezed the joint
furiously between her lips), the crucial fact? Was it the great
breakthrough? But what sort of fucking breakthrough could
it be, if him being gay, if Kristijan being gay, barely seemed
real! Kristijan as a character from some cheap *Daddies Gone Wild*

porno (she held the joint between her fingers and flicked off the
ash nervously, oops, missing the ashtray), as that hazy figure
from those nebulous rumours whom nobody ever knows, that
silhouette of a man who hides who he is and marries a woman,
who remakes himself as an alpha male (of course) boasting that
holy trinity of muscles and crudeness and cars, like the hero
of some fan-fiction novel, badly written and based on an even
worse psychology – fuck (the joint was again in her mouth, the
buzz from the hash so much better than that poisonous skunk)
but fuck, OK, Kristijan as all of it, as all those templates and
stereotypes, but Dunja – she had to admit it, since thinking
about *all those templates* didn't put an end to anything but only
juxtaposed Kristijan to the truth that must already exist in the
template for it to be a fucking template in the first place, and
so, patiently caught up in it, she imagined the template as binoculars, or was it the truth she imagined as binoculars? – oh,
forget it, Dunja was simply too stoned for such acrobatics. She
gazed lovingly out at the horizon, but in her skull she was still
creaking with *fuuuck!* and roaring with *shiiit!* and crackling with
daaammiiit! Yes, OK, Duška had implied that Kristijan was gay,
and Kristijan *was* gay, whether or not novelist Dunja – oh, sorry!
Great Detective Dunja – thought this likely, whether or not it
suited *her* narrative (maybe, haha, Dunja was just another of
those writers who try to avoid clichés by resorting to unique-
ness, which is nothing other than a tricked-out naivety, the
refusal to accept the fact that people are tediously repeatable).
In short, and let's make this quick: Kristijan was *a gay man in a
relationship with a woman who had a child*, whether or not he was
trying to bury his head in the sand about it!

And all at once, her heart was in her throat, although it
was ruminating on its back, and she put out the joint, letting
its fragrance linger in the air one last time in the sanctity of the
intoxicant and, of course, now lingering with it was the gigantic
Secret . . . And what detectivy thing was she supposed to do with
this? Did she have any choice but to c o n f r o n t h i m –
and then run back to Ljubljana! and hide under a silk blanket!
run back to the flat where she now lived alone, although her

mother had furnished it with plenty of down and feathers and enough cotton for her to be completely and forever safe inside it! – was there any other choice but to confront him (her belly button sucked inward and her bowels were being pulled in every painful direction), any other possible choice if she so deeeearly wanted (crap, she was starting to feel queasy again), if she so deeeearly wanted to piece together her brother's Story – since Dražen was Dražen first with other people, and it was with other people, maybe with one other person, maaaybe with Kristija – nnnooo, stop, she'd gone waaaay too far, why oh whyyy was she always smoking, *whyyyy*, when that fucking weed had long ago stopped settling her nerves? So it must have been *with some person*, then ergo fucking therefore, that Dražen died.

Her legs she laced gracelessly between the bars of the balcony railing and placed her hands between her thighs, hands that in times of crisis always wanted to roll *just one more*, even if it meant that her moral crisis would then become physical sickness. Some birds (already migrating?) coursed across the sky, travelling, hey, north-east, towards Ljubljana (smart little animals), while below the balcony – what floor was she on? third? second? not too far from the ground; Dražen and her father would have survived (Dražen, indeed, would right now be sneering in her ear about that Englishwoman coming back from beach, hidden under a straw hat and revoltingly pale), she, however, at that moment at least, just like her father, was not entirely sure she would have wanted to survive, oh dear – and below the balcony (come on, Dunja, focus) among the many others, a car with Ljubljana plates had just parked and a young couple was stepping out of it, worldly types (heh-heh, as if a holiday in Portorož had anything to do with the world), but they both had terribly contemporary coiffures and a style of dress worthy of the streets of London or Berlin, and as they were unloading their shopping bags and shoulder bags and other bulkier luggage, even (hah!) a jittery little dog, the woman, in a surprised but flinty voice, asked the man, 'Y e a h , b u t h o w d o y o u t h i n k y o u ' r e a c t u a l l y g o n n a p u l l t h i s o f f ? I t d o e s n ' t s o u n d s o e a s y - p e a s y .'

The blond head slammed the car door shut and then, all at once, like petrol catching fire, became a face: this *Ankica* or *Hanica* or even fucking *Inja* was *looking directly* at Dunja. She was *intentionally looking up* – at *her* – fuuuuuck – and Dunja dashed back into the room, her lips sciatically clenched and her stomach on the verge, and collapsed on the bed as if into her grave – fuuuuuuuuck – yes, exactly, how would she a c t u a l l y p u l l o f f a meeting with Kristijan?

She was drenched in a menopausal hot flush, so she first rolled in the sheets, then dried herself on them and finally wrapped herself in them; it would help – oh yes, she thought, and covered her face with them too – it would help if only she could weep everything out, a few tears each for every improbable and impossible thing, such as: *Hey there, Kristijan, I found out you're gay – don't be afraid, I'm totally OK with it but I doubt Katarina will be – in short, just how is this connected to the two deaths in my family?* Or: *Oh, Kristijan, I found out you've been hiding something important from everyone, and, well, a person hiding one important thing is probably hiding something else important. Get my drift?* Or: *Hey, Kristijan, do you mind if we have a little talk about your sexual orientation and all the other things you've probably been lying about?* Or: *Hey, how's it going? What a nice day! By the way, I happen to know you're gay, so could you please tell me if you were so madly in love with Dražen that – now, how should I put this? – you fucking murdered him in a jealous rage?* All she asked was a few damn tears but no, no matter how hard she tried, they just wouldn't come. That fucking weed had dried her up completely and instead of tears, instead of an eruption, there was only drilling – no, worse – fucking *fracking*—

J u s t w h o d o y o u t h i n k y o u a r e , D u n j a ? And w h a t d o y o u , a w r i t e r (h a h a h a !), t h i n k y o u w i l l e v e r f u c k i n g s o l v e ?

Won't you at least – hah! – AS A START (do you even hear him, Dunja? Do you even recognise his voice? This is Reason talking to you) muster a bit of fucking courage, some much-needed courage, scaredy-cat Duni, and invite Peter, absorbed though he is in his whisky and rum, to have a fucking juice or a soft drink with you so the old drunk can give you some sober advice: *Don't lower yourself, child, to walk in these gumshoes; they can't take you anywhere, not forwards, not backwards.* But you can't be bothered, can you? *Who is he to tell me what to walk in?* No, you're gonna soar above the living fire of tragedy like a fucking dragon, aren't you? Unstoppable, mighty and – shit! – almost indestructible. You're gonna fly – hahaha – above the trees of ash, the charred stones and the flames, oh, the flames as high as ever, and solve, truly *solve*, what Peter and Simon were unable to solve in nine fucking months? Peter and Simon at least brought *something* to term, and they had the full knowledge and resources of the State behind them, Dunja – the fucking *State!* – and not merely their imagination, *Dunjica darling.* So, magnificent drag-oness, you're gonna hunt down and visit everyone Peter and Simon hunted down and visited, everyone who's still alive, that is, and force them to talk? You're gonna spew out your fire on them and, *voilà, each and every one of them* will start babbling out their true intentions? And *each and every one of them*, of course, will be the still-missing piece in the mosaic. So let's you and I go through them all rationally, in order: Kristijan's brother and parents; Mirela's father and mother; those plastered girls from Dražen's school, Klavdija and the others, whose names you don't remember, but Peter will tell you their names, so you don't have to worry, and, hmm, there are sure to be one or two others we don't know about yet, Dunči dear, but that's how it goes in a, you know, *criminal investigation*; it's organised like a ladder, but at a certain point – which no one can foresee – it becomes a rhizome, you know, like a ginger root, growing in all directions at once, you know, but like I said, don't worry about a thing – as an *artiste* you should have no trouble picking out all the damn threads and weaving them together. After all, we've both decided that you are *ultra-competent, ultra-prepared, ultra-astute, ultra-talented, ultra-mega-agile and not the least bit fragile*, which means that, *ulti*mately, you will be the one who pulls the fucking rabbit out of the fucking hat, the rabbit that almost died, which is to say, you will be the one who sniffs out – no, *IDs* – let's use the right jargon – that *mysterious figure*, and after far too many years closes – OK, say it your way – closes, *as if filling a deep hole*, this damn, fucking, unresolved case! You, Dunja! Ha! No one but you! Ha! Ha! You and you alone! Only you, only the Great Detective! Fuck those two fucking detectives, it's *only youuu*, Dunja! Ha! Ha! Ha! Ha!

The one and only youuu-oo-oo-oo-oo . . .

Dunja was sobbing – sweeeet mercy! – she was finally, only, crying. For Dražen, for her father, for her mother, for Katy, for Cvetka and Duška, for Kristijan (yes, even for him), for Mirela, that poor wretch of a witch, for Peter, for Simon and for herself – yes, for herself too. Tears were dripping, dripping, dripping, down onto the cotton sheets until her mouth and forehead and nose, aaaaaaaah, finally relaxed and the cement crumbled from her windpipe and the fingers between her thighs at last grew still, aaaaaaaah, and she had cried herself out.

She crawled slowly – first head, then neck, chest, belly, thighs, and finally knees – out of the sticky cocoon of sheets. She had been in this pupal form a thousand times before, and had crawled out of it a thousand times, but, obviously, never as a butterfly. Only as a maggot, an incompetent, unprepared, unastute, untalented, unagile and, especially, ultra-fragile *maggot*. And every time after being born this way (she ran her fingers through her hair, wiped the sleep sand, no, the *weep sand*, from her eyes, and rubbed her temples), every time, life was the same for the maggot. She wanted to eat something and shuffled to the edge of the bed, only there was no food in the hotel room; the food was on the ground floor – an unwelcoming, too draughty, too human territory. So if eating was not an option, then the maggot – she chuckled: my God, how many interior landscapes had she explored that night – the maggot wanted at least to walk around a little, but the arthritis did not permit it; of course, she managed admirably to stand up from the mattress, but a moment later she was pitifully, exhaustedly, waddling. To the shower, *yesss, to the shhhower*, and the maggot – she could not stop her prattling: the *poor little grub* felt strangely relieved – the maggot might just get there! She removed her short dress, a dress she wore only at home, and – oh for God's sake, really? Right now? In this

brief interval of tranquil privacy, these few minutes, maybe an
hour, when nothing truly horrible, nothing at all, had any hold
on Dunja, in this maybe-an-hour, not before or later, when her
anxiety would be much closer to peaking, but dear God, *right now*
that damn *iPhone* had to start ringing so insistently?

And in that damn Desigual bag, too, whose every thread
so selfishly caught at anything. So she basically had to dig the
phone out, which was displaying, fortunately, not the name of
the care home, and, unfortunately, not Vesna's or Ana's names,
but a number she didn't recognise – 090 399 399 – always a
creepy nine-petalled blossom.

She pressed the green. 'Yes?' she said, but quickly corrected herself. 'Hello?'

'Dunja, is that youuu?' The question was an awkward
wheeze.

'Mirela?' She couldn't believe it. 'How did you get—'

'The office phone keeps a record of all the numbers, you
know; it's important to have all the numbers recorded because
sometimes you need to call someone back, and sometimes this
scares people.'

Dunja herself, now *called* and not *caller*, was a little scared.

'You know, I was thinking it might be nice if we could get
together again. I was so happy you found me, I really was – so
very happy you found me.'

Doubly happy (all Dunja wanted was to slide onto the
floor, she was so unbearably tired), doubly happy then, although
she could swear (let soberness correct her later) that *happy* was
hardly the right description for how Mirela had been acting.
And now to have to see her again? *Her?* To spend more time
with *her?* To chat with her, on and on, *interrogate* her, on and
on, and keep finding out more and more? Fuck. She focused her
eyes on the television set – hahaha – the whole thing was just
a trashy TV serial. But fuck. She supposed she would have to
do it, do it all, for Dražen's sake, for the sake of her father and
mother, for the sake of Duška and Katarina, even for fucking
Kristijan's sake, which meant, essentially, she would have to do
it for, what? For her own sake? She supposed she would have to

suffer a little, such was the universe, even though she was only a maggot, and barely that, and already so unbeeearably tiiiiired. If only she could think about it later, when she'd had a teensy bit, please, just a teensy bit, of sleep!

'So what do you say? Would you like to get together?' There was a scratching of nails, as if Mirela was gripping the phone more tightly.

For Dražen's sake (she at last sat down beside the television set), for the sake of her father and mother, for the sake of Duška and Katarina, even for the sake of fucking Kristijan, which meant, essentially, for what? For her own sake? Yes, fucking 'Yes.'

'Oh, splendid, that's splendid!' Now the happiness was heard distinctly, and even more distinct was the bubble of the first tears. 'That means a lot to me, really, a lot, it means so very much to me.'

'OK, sure, fine.' Dunja was still coming to terms with the idea. 'So when?'

'It means so much to me that you sought me out, that my connection with Dražen is so . . .' It sounded as if the first tear was falling. 'I could hardly believe it, you telephoning me after all these years.'

She spoke as if Dunja had *ever* phoned her before, but – haha – the little grub let it pass (we said she was tired) and there was nothing to be gained from scrutinising Mirela's degree of coherence. 'So, Mirela, when shall we meet? I'll be here at least another ten days.'

'Oh yes, of course.' It sounded as if she'd wiped her eyes. 'The weekend's best. Yes, the weekend. So we'll have plenty of time.'

Oh God, they'd have plenty of time (now it was Dunja wiping her face) but maybe time was all the maggot needed. 'OK, well, let's say Sunday. But where?'

'Why, at my place, Dunja! At my place. Nowhere else.' Strangely, even for Mirela, there were new tears starting. 'Come at eleven. It won't be the right time for cocktails, but I'll do whatever you want.'

'Coffee will be fine.' Unless, haha! (she was already moving the phone away from her ear) – unless it had been sitting forever on a shelf. 'OK, Sunday morning at eleven. See you then.'

'Yes, great, that's great. See y—' Dunja pressed the red, with just a teeeensy bit of guilt, and shoved the device deep in the bowels of the Desigual – let that overpriced sack suck the phone in, let it devour it – then continued where she had left off: Hello, bathroom! The phone call had – hallelujah! thank you, Mirela! – sobered her up a little. Her legs could walk again, nice and steady, even if it hurt like hell, and what her eyes saw, well, it was no longer a montage of mostly feelings but again, at last, objects and things, and what her ears heard, well, her hearing had not really improved, it was still rather watery, but in a nice way, not like in some Dario Argento nightmare. She stepped in front of her image, which is to say, in front of the mirror, which showed her only down to the shoulders, down to her pointy collarbones, and, in the mirror – wow, a surprise: nothing white, pink or red, nothing slimy, swollen, ridgy (eww, gross) or menacing, nothing, in other words, maggotty, nothing that anyone would rather not see (or try to, eww, crush). Simply a washed face. Simply the features of a face. Eyes wide open and clear. The pride of a nose, the slits of a nose. A mouth, well, not exactly smiling but also not icy. But also there were no – come on, don't be ridiculous – no colourful patterns on her skin, no long antennae sprouting from her head, no wings attached to her shoulders, nor were there any other insectoid appendages on her body; in her eyes, however, oh, in her eyes, there was again that desire, no, that striving, to become *a free, fairy-tale creature.*

9

Mafia? Uh-huh, absolutely. But which sort? Cocaine? Yeah, definitely. Amphetamines? Sure, maybe that too, although she doubted there was much money in pills, much *real* money. Not enough for *real* property, *real* cars, *real* clothes and shoes, *real* watches, *real* influence and *real* status; not enough for a *real* 'legitimate' business and *real* money laundering in a *real* day-and-night bar, café and/or restaurant, where bank cards are not accepted and where the menu of five varieties of cappuccino and seven different kinds of ice cream sundae far exceeds demand. It could even be (Dunja was squeaking on the plastic chair, tucked away among the lush rhododendrons), could even be *white slavery* (a term both racist *and* sexist), with 'packages' of Bulgarian/Romanian women distributed throughout the Italian provinces, except that (being all alone in the place, she gave the chair another squeak so the staff would at least be aware of her), except that, well, people in that line of work, every last one of them, are bereft of the social graces and, what's worse, of any sense of humour – indeed, in none of the aforementioned branches does anyone have any taste at all – so they could hardly have come up with those alliterated names for their coffees and sundaes and never in a million years would they have decided on that orange-and-pink neon name *From Hocus to Pocus*. Given the little glass tables and baby palm trees and, what, progressive house?, the last thing Dunja would have imagined was a connection to the arms trade, to handguns, semi- and fully automatics, Kalashnikovs, mortars, flamethrowers, corpsethrowers, fucking submachine guns and tanks, since, sorry, but *that* business was either eerily bleak, local and poor (all darkness and toothless men and car parks and car boots) or eerily rich and arrivistic — it was too international, and definitely too bleak/wealthy for a run-of-the-mill Portorož café. Yes — she went back to her original idea — it must be cocaine, cocaine with a pinch of some cheaper narcotic: that was the *ousia* of this 24/7 deadness.

And so was Kristijan a *druglord* here? Hey, look, after harbouring one secret, which had exploded like an oil tank, why not another? He certainly looked the type as he climbed the steps to the day-and-night terrace, or, more precisely, looked more like a mob boss than . . . well, let's put it this way (and pardon the preconceptions, but a person's orientation is important in life) — he looked more *godfather* than *fairy godfather*. Not only was he grim — seriously, dangerously grim — and not only did he walk like he was trampling something down, like he was a fucking bulldozer, and not only did he seem to hold his slightly flexed arms (the price of lifting weights) next to his body like two oversized tote bags, but his godfatherhood was gleaming particularly from his hair, which he had slicked back into cement, from his ponytail, which he tied severely above the nape of his neck, from his aggressively pink Cavalli polo shirt and from his wide, black, indisputably leather belt with its heavy buckle, which defied the main purpose of this fashion accessory by dragging his light-blue jeans down, down, down (but hey, it was Cavalli, which his shoes probably weren't); but that *capo* vibe emanated most of all from his thick silver bracelet, a bracelet as thick as (Dunja smiled) her own fucking leg.

But as soon as Kristijan sat down — and he sat down like Brando, too — she swallowed her smile. This thuggish style, this ugly demeanour — were not they his heaviest, most effective, most compelling, most costly, most notable, most fucking lethal, *most-most-most whatever* artillery? A fucking cannon whose thunder raises into the air all the sand in the desert, truly all of it, so

nothing can be clearly seen any more. A fucking aeroplane dropping bombs like eggs, thickly, in clusters, so that all the fucking
land below is levelled. Fuck! she thought. It's sad, it's really
sad, and agonising too, but sorrow and compassion, sure, that's
what she should have been feeling but didn't. Didn't feel any of
that. In her stomach and in her heart she was blocked, or more
precisely, both those salvatory valves had been dialled back to
1. Detective Maggot wanted, there and then, to gnaw her way
through, just to gnaw and gnaw and gnaw and chew everything
thoroughly, until what finally dropped out of Kristijan's damn
mouth bore at least some fucking resemblance to the TRUTH.

'So' – his knees spread apart but his lips hardened – 'you
wanted to see me. Why *again*?'

His gaze narrowed too and, yes, Dunja had to admit that
for a few moments this method of his was working. For those
few moments *she* was the one resitting the exam, standing
before the tribunal, on the hot seat in the interrogation room;
for those few moments, every breath, in and out, was a kind of
explanation; during those few moments, her palms were sweating and her eyes were restless, but – hah! – by the seventh or
eighth moment Dunja was no longer a puny grub but a battle commander: her voice, hands and face instantly fell in line
like a company of foot soldiers. Being in command, after all,
does not mean overmastering others in the decision making,
but rather, before anything else, overmastering the poor wretch
that is yourself. It means standing up to that self, to that inner
groan (she smiled wryly at her quip) which says *Please, just leave
me alone.*

'I think,' she began, the smile fading to seriousness, 'or
rather, I suspect' (the Great Detective has returned!) 'you hav-
en't told me quite everything.'

'Everythi—' He was interrupted by a man in a uniform:
a white T-shirt and white trousers bearing the café's logo.
The waiter took their order the way a novice picker plucks an
olive, a single olive, a holy olive, a fruit that must be handled
with special care, and Dunja, at his *thank you for your choices*
(Dunja's double espresso and Kristijan's cappuccino) felt a chill

of embarrassment for the boy. Perhaps he did not know who he was working for. Or perhaps he *did* know. But our Dunjica doubted he was merely being extraordinarily polite.

'OK, now where did we leave off?' Kristijan said as he opened his hands and froze them halfway into the gesture. Halfway between reality and memory. Halfway from *OK, Dunja, now where did we leave off?* after her mother brought a tray with juice and three glasses into the room just as she was moving her queen from e1 to a5, *which is a bad idea, because now the queen is threatened*; halfway from *OK, where did we leave off?*, whenever Dražen got *carried away again with something about Michael*; halfway from *Now then, where'd we leave off?*, when Dunja had distracted them on the beach in Koper; halfway from *OK, Dunja, where were we?*, when she was bored with chess, when she didn't want to defeat the white king, when she didn't want to capture his queen or his pawns but only to capture Kristijan's kingly heart. As if they were starting a game, Dunja shifted anxiously to the edge of her chair and realised that Heraclitus had in fact been slipshod in his thinking. Had been horribly romantic. Because a river is always the same: the faster and stronger it flows, the more it's the fucking same, the more it's nothing but fucking water. And us? We change nothing but our outward forms (she set her elbows on her knees); the idea, however, yes, well, the idea always eludes any change.

'We left off with me suspecting, or, well, having the feeling, that you haven't told me everything.'

'*The feeling*, you say,' and the white pawn moves perfunctorily to d-fucking-4. 'I don't know how I'm supposed to respond to your *feeling*, Dunja.' He runs his hand over his brow, the top of his head, his hair.

'You could, for instance, explain to me how I might have got this feeling.' Black pawn to f5. Hey, the Great Detective noted with surprise, that's the fucking Dutch Defence!

'Dunja,' – a second pawn to c3: nothing special, right? Dunja almost didn't notice it – 'I completely understand. If I were in your position, I'd suspect everyone around me. So I completely understand that after all these years you want some answers. Believe me, I want them too.' Reconsidering, he touched the knobbed head of the white piece and pushed it one square forward, to c4, right next to d4. Dunja understood that he was, however hesitantly, building a barricade. She understood (but they had only just begun!) that he was counting either on Dunja, impatient and obstinate, just giving up, or on him defeating her ONE-TWO-THREE. She understood that his eyes were not the least bit restless, that this was his show, it was his fucking show, which had every time hidden the fact that he was smiling inside, with a great big smile. She understood that, fuck, compared to him, she had only meagre skills, but, hey, this was no time for another fucking breakdown: black knight to f6.

'Kristijan,' the little horse whinnied (their coffees arrived and they rattled out *thanks, thanks*), 'you probably heard me telling Katy the other day about my visit to Mirela.' She d r e w   o u t   the name, she   s a n g   it – of course she did, o b v i o u s l y.

'No, actually I didn't.' And a white horse jumps to c3. 'I was in the shower.'

'Anyway, the point is: I tracked down Mirela and learned quite a few things about her, or rather, about the relationships between the three of you.' That cautious sipping of espresso you hear is a pawn sliding to e6, away from the head that wears the crown.

'That's still not the point, Dunja.' White knight to h3 – or rather, no, a quick hop to f3. 'But still, Dunja, it's very brave of you, it really is, to trace these difficult, fucked-up, painful tracks.' And suddenly there appeared above the little white horse a compassionate and, hmm, uncalculated smile. And again, above his brow, the top of his head and his hair, that beautiful hand – some urgent rethinking? Preparations?

'Brave? I suppose that's true. Thanks.' A black pawn now hovered in the air, high over the mental chessboard, but (still mere Dunja, still a mere foot soldier) with no fucking perspective. The gentlest of breezes wafted through the artificial scarlet flowers, and in the re-dimensioned café it was still just the two of them. Still, *still, sti, st, ssssss*... OK, here goes: d5. 'Sad to say, but I didn't remember Mirela at all. I'm not really sure why; I guess because, you know, she hadn't visited our home as often as, well, you had *suggested*.'

'I didn't *suggest* anything.' A quick white pawn to e3. 'She and Dražen used to hang out together, but, you know, I didn't keep a precise record of every time they met up. I didn't exactly *memorise* that.'

'Well, you see,' – an even quicker black pawn to c6 – 'memory is the essential issue here. If, in fact, I *had* remembered Mirela from before, I would have had completely different questions for you on Sunday. Because you know, Kristijan, I remember you and Dražen very well, extremely well.'

He at last dipped his spoon into the settled foam of the cappuccino, stirred it brown but refrained from tasting it. His beautiful hands slid to his thighs, stroking them a few times, and Dunja predicted – no, Dunja *remembered* – that this gesture would be followed by the bishop's first move. His big, ostentatious unveiling – to d-(ohoho)-3.

'I remember Dražen too. *Dorro*. How could I not? How could I ever forget him?' Exhaling, he hung his head above the gathering crowd on the middle squares, then, with a sigh, raised it again and – poof, boom! – G-A-Z-E-D into her eyes. 'And Dunja, I also remember *you* very well, very *dorro*. I remember how you were in love with me, how you'd always watch me like crazy. But look, and I'm being honest here so don't be offended, but when you accuse me of lying I can't decide if maybe you're trying to get revenge on me or if you just want some time with me alone. To get to know me again or something. If that's what it is, then you should know, I do understand that – in a way, despite everything, there's a connection between us.'

There was not a single wrinkle on his face, but in his eyes, a thousand hints – after two hundred smiles, three hundred laughs, two hundred tears, one hundred blushes and two hundred stampings of feet, hints, hints and fucking more hints (she drank the damn coffee: what was it, Illy? *What the fuck else?*), he still thought he was good, thought he was the fucking best at this game; he was still confident he could bring her down with cheap tricks. Well, fuck your damn provocations (it was bitter on her tongue), fuck you, fuck you, fuck you, the black bishop cries, hurrying to – hah! – d-fucking-6.

'Come on, now,' – she rotated her bishop to face his, to have a good view across the pawns – 'let's not make this about me, OK? What I was trying to say was that after I met Mirela and learned *all about* the relationships between you, it somehow seemed to me – hmm, how should I put it? – not particularly logical that you and Dražen would have been in love with her.' The black bishop winks at the white pawn in his sights, and the little fellow feels a chill. 'Yes, it didn't seem *logical*. That's the word.'

White castles.

Fine, sure – heh-heh: black castles too.

'Logical? Well, then, I guess you've never been' – *whee-hee-hee!* The white horse jumps to the bright e2 square – 'a stupid teenager?'

'Being stupid is one thing, but' – the second black horse, finally out of the stables, wants to go to a6, since he's no hoofed coward – 'i m p o s s i b l e, is something else altogether, I think.' Thick sheaves of light were getting loose beneath the green umbrella (it was advertising, what, Heineken? or, shit, Laško) and running wild over tables, glasses, faces and, oh dear, now Dunja's arguments, too, were getting loose, metaphorically speaking – they had been spending far too much time with her emotions, fraternising with them, leaning on them, getting drunk with them like sluts. One stealthy ray fell on the tip of Dunja's nose and spread its warmth like sand across her cheeks and – hey! *Come on, Dunja, it's as plain as day*: black knight to d7, directly in front of the motionless queen. 'The two of you used to make fun of her – *behind her back*, Kristijan, and if I understood anything about you and Dražen, it was at least this: when it came to making fun of people, when it came to your *insults*, you were always very serious. This was something I could really *depend* on back then.'

The white horse (from surprise or panic?) gallops from f3 to g5: 'You've gotta be joking, Dunja. What am I supposed to make out of everything you've been imagining?'

The black bishop, yum yum, eats the pawn on h2, and
Dunja thinks, *This is my first fucking CHECK*. 'You could make a
lot out of it – in a sense, too much maybe.'

'What are you suggesting, Dunja?' The white king raised
the cold coffee to his lips and, dodging the shot, stepped to h1.
'If you're suggesting *I* had anything to do with Dražen's death,
well, then, shit—'

'Then *what*?' Dunja's knight, f6 to g4, moves ever closer, oh
yes, to the royal doors. 'Then fucking *what*, Kristijan?'

'Then I . . .' – white pawn at f2 moves two spaces ahead –
'Come on, Dunja, I had nothing to do with it!'

'I have suspicions' – the queenly black crinoline rustles
one square to the left – 'but I don't know for sure.'

'Dunja!' the white pawn, stepping to g3, cries out – so
loud the waiter swooped over from behind the spacious counter,
but *it's nothing, nothing*, both players smiled to him at once, *nothing, nothing, no need to worry*. The boy stood there a moment; for
a moment it seemed as if he even intuited the dynamics between
his customers, but, Dunja corrected herself, he was too wooden
for something like that.

'It's simple, Kristijan,' she said in a whisper, clenching her
teeth, clenching her anger and also, fuck, clenching her damn
tear ducts. 'If you don't want my speculations to go too far, if
you don't want me to *do* anything about them, then you'd better
fucking start telling me what the fuck was going on back then.
It's not about you or me any more, it's about my fucking brother
and my fucking father. Don't you think it's time to put an end to
this charade? They might be fucking dead, but don't you think
they deserve that? Don't you fucking think anything?'

Threats and extortion? Yes, absolutely. The underhanded
methods of a *queen*. So of course, the black lady, elegant and
self-assured, with only an amulet in her gloved hand, praying
that her threats will work, glides elegantly and assuredly to,
ta-dah, h5.

'Yes, of course they do, Dunja, of course they deserve
that.' The white king, now on g2, was also whispering, but the
cadence of his voice remained, well, the cadence of screaming.

Just then, the light-to-shadow ratio beneath the umbrella shifted suddenly in favour of the afternoon light – of that cursed floodlight, which until then had not revealed a damn thing to her, which had been so fastidious about illuminating lines and colours, modulating the degrees of sharpness, making sure, yes, making damn sure she didn't see anything more in front of her than a fucking *persona* and not, God help us, Kristijan the fucking *person*. The dry-to-damp ratio beneath Dunja's arms was, accordingly, in favour of that annoying dampness, which now suddenly decided to spread also to her palms and neck and knees and, no point denying it, even to her hypothalamus or hippocampus or *hypo-hippo*-something, or maybe not *hip-* or *hyp-* at all – in any case, to wherever her fucking *ideas* and fucking *solutions* came from. The slow accumulation of moisture into droplets, that slow drip-drip-drip through – what, the brain stem? – dripping and trickling to the very core of her consciousness and then evaporating again, evaporating into a fucking cloud – it was making her furious, as if she were about to have a fucking childish tantrum – she could not come up with a single *solution*, not a single *idea*. How the fuck was she supposed to continue? But hadn't (she took a sip of water) the little maggot decided to take a risk with this fucked-up game? And wasn't taking a risk (wow, the water was absorbing the droplets before they could evaporate) the same as – hah! – scratching what truly itches you? Didn't it mean skipping the prelude/prologue, the sudden shifts, the complications, the endless descriptions and fucking metaphors, the extended dialogues, the needless outrage and anger, the pain and suffering and little crises, the painting of atmosphere, the creaking of sounds and the rustling of figures – fuck, didn't it mean skipping/omitting anything that might mitigate certain *possibilities and conditions*, the possibilities and conditions for a denouement in which, while there might well be victims, *she* would most certainly not be among them? Interesting, right? the little grub thought as she sipped the water; interesting, interesting and, surprise! The black bishop steps onto the exposed first square of the g-file. 'I was talking to Duška the other day, or rather, she was talking to me.'

Kristijan's pupils, no longer pinpoints and always a bit lazy in too-bright light, now instantly became (as befitted the setting!) *cocainishly* wide. And no less cocainish was the pulse pounding in his neck and temples and forehead and, Dunja wagered, dispatching its wild, vexatious offspring to his bowels, but unfortunately, Kristijan's sharpness and speed were also cocainish – the first hit, as everyone knows, is pure sweetness – so his Lipizzaner now galloped off after Dunja's bishop, who, as you'll remember, was on square g1.

'Ah, yes, our Dušica.' Even his tone was cocainish, calm, controlled. 'I truly love that child, but I expect it'll take some time,' – the Lipizzaner nabbed the bishop – 'a fair bit of time, for her to find herself. She's confused, although she acts like she's not, but you know how it is, teenagers have a talent for making you think they're on top of the world. I was the same way.'

That was bait, thought Dunja, the kind of bait Kristijan had always set before her: a valuable chess piece wandering off to somewhere she couldn't help herself, *I just had to take it* – and (unbelievable!) it worked, so here you go, the black queen saunters down the edge of the board to h2 and, *tum-ta-ta-dum*, CHECK.

'I agree with you about teenagers, of course, but Duška, confused or not, is very perceptive. She reads people better than many adults, Kristijan – better than her mother, for instance. And Duška, although she's basically glad to have you in her life, well, she made a point of telling me that you're strange.'

'She said that about you too.' The king takes a short diagonal step to f3.

'I believe you, and I'm not at all surprised.' Black pawn sacrificed to white, white pawn sacrificed to black knight, black knight sacrificed in turn to white pawn, white pawn sacrificed to the second black knight, and oh, what a festival there is on e5 – now what was she going to say?

'So why are you even bringing this up, Dunja?' the white king, stepping to f4, anticipates her.

But in fact, kingy-boy only *thought* he had anticipated her, because, you lying kingy-boy, take this: CHECK by the damn horse – a damn clever, well-calculated fucking check: 'Yes, I'm aware that I seem *strange* to her; I give that impression to a lot of people. But probably she does *not* think I'm *queer*.'

So, finally –

F I N A L L Y –

there it was. What she had been waiting for. It fell fell FELL. That cocainish mask fell directly into the last fucking phase, the phase of paranoia, the phase of bewilderment, the phase of disgrace, the phase of loss, the phase of that bitter *Give me another*, which is, at least in semi-rational people, concurrent with *On second thought, maybe I shouldn't*, into the phase of restless hands and shaky wrists, trembling jaw and sweat beading on the lip, wobbly knees and drooping shoulders, into the phase of *Why did you have to say that*, the phase of *Will somebody drive me home*, the phase when you need to hide, to wrap yourself in something warm, to eat something, drink something (haha) non-alcoholic, when you need to but just can't can't can't fall asleep, to sleep through the phase that always comes next – the minor but, hey, never-to-be-forgotten, *life-stroke*.

'Wh-whaah?' kingy-boy exhaled, barely audible, as he retreated.

'It doesn't bother me at all, I have no problem with it. How could anyone? So you don't need to worry,' Dunja hastened to stress, as the Great Detective/Chess Player (of course) moved her pawn resolutely to f4. 'The only problem is that this changes everything.'

'Fabrications don't change a thing, Dunja.' With a short, fearful step, white pawn takes black pawn.

'It's not that I don't understand you, Kristijan,' – she lifted the black bishop above his bright square – 'but surely you must be tired, dreadfully tired; I'm tired myself from this one fucking game' – and deposited him on the bright g4 square: check. 'I'm giving you a chance to rest, to *finally* rest. I can't imagine what struggles you've been through; I wouldn't ever want to go through them myself.'

'Dunja,' – he hurled his doomed crown at the bishop – 'Dun—'

'Yeah, Kristijan, I get it. But please, let it end now. Just tell me . . .' One last time the black knight leaps, one last time a white pawn attacks *aaaand* a black pawn advances *aaaand* Dunja has her first, her first hard-earned, no, *hard-fought* and not merely given

c h e c k m a t e. Her first bitter, *too* bitter, checkmate.

He hung his head the way a snowdrop hangs its fragile blossom in spring. And his body too, his chest and arms, shoulders and throat, were suddenly fragile, crumbling, sinking into themselves and then down to the ground, to the subterranean source, no, even deeper, to the *burnt-out* core of the earth and the empty core of the world. She thought he might actually be crying, but this impression of course went too far; he wasn't some gay teenager from the movies and she wasn't his tyrannical father, although at that moment, regardless of the circumstances, she was, in fact, the next-worse thing to tyranny. She too hung her head, although through her crown she could see the eyes of the man in front of her squeezing shut. Could see him clasping his hands together. That his knuckles were grey. That relief and despair, both at the same time, were coursing through him. That he had no response available, since he had never rehearsed his truth. He had always only rehearsed the poison. She saw how frightening it was – it was *the most frightening fucking thing!* – to be without words. How frightening it was – *the most frightening fucking thing!* – when the story in which you have invested everything begins to fucking shake. And then, no matter how hard you try, collapses. And in the end, no matter how much you have defended it and protected it, it fucking explodes. Not like a water glass, not into mere shards, but like a building, into heavy, unwieldy, dusty blocks of concrete.

'Can we order something else to drink?' He straightened his neck and looked to the side, looked basically into the sun, which had reached the peak of its daily strength.

'Sure, Kristijan, of course.' Dunja obligingly waved to the uniform and, so it wouldn't notice the changes in their

microclimate, transmitted the order – *Two lemonades! No sugar!* –
high across the tables. The way you might toss a stick to distract
your dog from a second dog approaching on the left.

They waited in silence for the drinks. A fraught silence?
Umm, no. A pure silence.

'First of all, Dunja, please, don't tell Katarina about this.
If she . . .' – he wrapped his hand around the glass, from which
came the fragrant smell of lemon – 'if she's going to find out,
it will be from me.'

'I already told you: don't worry.' She copied him; she was
his sour mirror image. 'That doesn't interest me and I'd rather
not talk about it. Of course, I want only the best for Katy, but—'

'Sorry, I did understand you. I just need to pull myself
together.'

He took a sip of the lemonade. And another. And a third.
He drank the whole thing and then for a while played with
the straw, using it to fish the pulp, the bits of lemon, from the
bottom of the glass, and Dunja felt her throat tighten: she too,
not only him, now, when it was becoming ominously *real*, when
the spectre of it was dissolving into tissue, into living tissue,
she too was resisting this new story, was afraid of it. So how
dare anybody claim (she massaged her neck, trying to undo the
knot) that anybody ever knows what they really want!

'So maybe, OK, well, maybe I could start with our fight. I
mean the fight between Dražen and me.'

'Sure, maybe, Kristijan. Start with that.'

✳

A Ringing in the Head – the title of a lame film and middling novel
but perhaps appropriate here? After their conversation, Dunja's
head was precisely that: *ringing*, and she wasn't entirely sure how
she had managed to cross the road through such dense traffic or
what exactly had led her to that newsstand hidden among the
shrubbery where for the first time in maybe fifteen years she had

bought actual *cigarettes*. A pack of fucking Marlboro reds AND
a pack of red Gauloises. With one pack in her left hand and the
other in her right she had then charged off, umm, *somewhere* as
the sun lengthened her shadow to near titanic proportions and
the low-hanging Desigual bag thumped against her arse and,
hey, she had thought, sensibly enough, if she was hell-bent on
smoking, it would be smart to drink something too, but at the
first shop she came to, *of all fucking places* an airless kebab joint,
where she had to wait in queue with some horrible Germans, she
bought water AND a yogurt, which she hadn't even wanted, and
then charged on and on, farther and farther, until, with her rear
end aching from the rhythmic thumping, she stopped in front
of the Portorož marina:

So was Dražen gay too?

She stowed the Gauloises in her bag and unwrapped the
Marleys as she walked. The plastic wrapper (oops!) fluttered
out of her hands, but, upon seeing a super-tanned and, in an
environmentally conscious way, super-fit Dutch family on one
of the yachts she decided to pick the wrapper up and toss it in
the nearest bin. Never before had she walked and smoked at
the same time – *Nicht laufen und rauchen*, the Germans say, but
to hell with that, maybe this was the only way she could put her
fucking thoughts in order.

The boys had not fallen out over Mirela (the Marley burned
a little at first, it had a bite). They had fallen out because (but
with the next inhalation she was enjoying it) Kristijan kissed
him. Or *tried* to. They were sitting the way they often sat, with
the necessary amount of space between them (now the smoke
was blowing back into her face) and were sitting *where* they
often sat: on the wild beach, where it curved into a view of
the vast salt pans, and were sitting (she coughed) as always, in
the still-starless dusk, a dusk assaulted by thousands of human
lights, from hotels, street lamps, casinos, bars and beaches,
although these were shining in and from the distance. So what
were they talking about? *Umm, you know, Dunja, I honestly don't*

remember – they must have been exchanging opinions and jokes, taunts too, and various problems (she took an audible drag on the cigarette), they must have been talking about lots of things, but, *Dunja, that wasn't really important*, since all at once there fell between them, all at once there blew between them – *It came on the wind, I'd swear it was carried by the wind* – a warm and full and thick – *incredibly thick, Dunja* – silence. *At the same time, Dunja, at exactly the same time*, or maybe that's just how it seemed to him now, they both took off their shoes and slid in their socks down the craggy rock, as if they wanted to make a hole in it where raindrops would collect during a storm, would collect into a puddle, and crabs would fall into it and be so surprised they dropped their prey. *At the same time, Dunja, at exactly the same time*, or maybe that's just how it seemed to him now (she dragged the cigarette along the graffiti-covered wall of a closed restaurant, which made a black line through the *FIA* in *KOPER MAFIA*), they both stretched out their legs: Kristijan's feet reached just a bit lower, and Dražen's feet fell outward, with his toes not far from Kristijan's ankle – *but his feet didn't just fall like that, Dunja, Dražen* placed *them like that*, and they both – *We must have, Dunja* – felt the heat of the incipient touch; they both – *We must have been, Dunja* – were extremely aware of the circle, however tiny, in which the pressure of the touch would burn them – for Kristijan this was a circle on the bone of his outer ankle, for Dražen, a circle on the tips of his second and middle toes – and they both *must have felt this* because *at the same time, really, at exactly the same time*, which is probably *not* just how it seemed to him now (she stuck a second cigarette between her lips), the two circles pressed against each other, *Dunja, they really did, they pressed together*, so that they both, one through the sock, the other through the jeans, almost caught fire. *The touch was undeniable, Dunja*, the touch was visible (she took a puff) and they were both gazing at it *tensely, intently, fearfully, Dunja*, the way any of us would gaze, if we could, at the promise of an important new change in our life – we would cross our fingers to make it happen, dig our nails into the fig to make it pop, hope that our present circumstances would collapse as soon and as gently as possible – they were gazing, then, at two points touching, merging into one, and they both silently rubbed their hands in their laps and *at the same time, I swear, at exactly the same time, we lifted our hands to our hair, Dunja* – Kristijan was the original and Dražen was the mirror, or no, Dražen was the original and Kristijan was the mirror – and their elbows pointily, pointedly, grazed each other, *Well, I'd say they bumped each other, Dunja*, and each to the other, mirror to mirror, they apologised for the bump, but even before the word *sorr*— was out of their mouths they broke into nervous laughter. Dražen's laughter (she blew the white smoke into the nautical grey) did not want to subside, its rises and falls, its thrusts and retreats sounded painful – *It was forced laughter, Dunja, hundredpercent* – and at that very moment – *Oh, Dunja, I don't want to sound dramatic, but at that moment something finally* woke up *inside me* – Dražen's meaningfully insincere laughter was like a lubricant that carried Kristijan's desire, his suppressed and disgraced, overlooked and a hundred times effaced desire, to the edge of the possible, so that all at once he put his arms around Dražen, his right arm around Dražen's waist, his left hand locked behind Dražen's small, delicate ear, and pulled him, *not roughly, Dunja, not at all roughly*, pulled him to himself – he had said *pulled him* onto *me* – Dražen's torso onto *his* torso, Dražen's arms onto *his* arms, Dražen's face onto *his* face and most of all, most noisily and forcefully, Dražen's lips onto *his* lips, Dražen's pink, moist, full, heart-shaped lips onto his own thin and dry and incredibly parched lips, and (she puffed out the smoke) he could have told her that he was overcome with joy, with joy that was shame that was a mistake that was joy; he could have told her that for the first time ever his very being was set on fire in all dimensions but just as it was reaching full blaze it went out (the way Dunja's cigarette, tsssss, was going out in that fucking puddle, that little puddle of not-yet-evaporated seawater), but Kristijan was not dramatic, Kristijan just stammered out *Then D-dražen g-got r-rough, and he p-pushed m-me away from him really h-hard*, so that at first Kristijan was afraid of him, and then *he hit me, Dunja*, with his open hand, a hand that not long before had been so enticing; *he slapped my face and screamed that he wasn't, that he would never be, Dunja,* and then ran off, ran so far it was like he had never been close and, *Dunja,* he vanished into the trees and bushes, vanished even before the sting on Kristijan's face had died down, even before the skin had truly evened out, even before the print of that open, not-long-before-enticing hand had settled into the subcutaneous tissue and from there, like a spear, pierced directly into his vocal cords and – yes, nothing made sense, it was all pain – and at the same time directly into his gut, so that Kristijan had to press his knees against his chest like an infant, because if he hadn't, well, *Dunja, then I don't know,*

Dunja,

then

I really

don't know.

A week later (the Gauloise was burning her) *we talked after school, Dunja, not like friends, Dunja, but coldly, and decided what and how* they would tell their classmates and parents and brother and sister about their rift, if they were forced into an explanation. *It was Dražen's idea* and (she coughed directly into the back of the head of a man walking past) he had to admit it was good – *it held water, Dunja* – sure, like a damn grate, since it soon drained out, as if down a greasy gutter, straight to Mirela, who strutted strutted strutted and swaggered swaggered swaggered, Mirela, who took up residence in their lie as if it were a fucking palace and then swanked it up for anyone who cared to listen – and back then everyone cared to listen, obviously, since people (as the Great Writer once wrote) are like bison and elephants, they flock to the river to drink when it's the fullest, when it's almost overflowing, and they all drink at the same time; since people can hardly wait to be thrown a bone, thrown five bones, fifty bones, a ton of bones, and it doesn't matter if the bones are tiny, like knucklebones, or big unwieldy thighbones, so long as they can comment, while gnawing, comment loudly on the origin and structure of the bones, on their colour, odour and texture, so long as they can click their tongues, smack their lips, pick their crooked or straight or long or short teeth, greedily

wipe their mouths on their sleeves, mouths drooling with white-
and-red fat and oozing with that other viscous substance found
in bones (Dunja, not being a biologist, could hardly be expected
to know all this stuff) – in other words, people can hardly wait
for the thing they need most, Dunja concluded (God, she was
already on her sixth crappy cigarette), which is the feeling that
they are changing reality simply by gnawing on it a long time,
zealously gnawing with fucking devotion, until they have well
and truly gnawed it bare. So they can then somehow vote on it.
So they can then somehow—

—well, you get what she means, right? She went back to
the pack of Marlboros, rummaged one out and went back to
Mirela, too, who with no real invitation but just by osmosis
had eagerly participated in Kristijan and Dražen's narrative,
supplementing it with her own piquant details, *for instance, she
told people, Dunja, that we had argued a few times in her presence,
threatening each other in front of her, Dunja, and had nearly come to
blows* and *that we had begged her – but Dunja, she was crazy – that
we had begged her to choose between us, to choose one or the other*, but
what worried the boys most was the thought that she might
spread it around that she was *in an actual relationship* with one
of them, *or whatever it's called when you're a teenager and imagine
all sorts of nonsense*, but, *fortunately, Dunja*, it never got as far
as that, *at least not while Dražen was alive*; Mirela's insane ideas
didn't really, *well, take off, you might say*, until later, *until after
he left us*. No doubt – Dunja stopped walking for a moment,
holding the cigarette at her hip. God, where the hell was she?
To her left, the wide, sparkling sea, and to her right, a greyish,
squarish building, incised in the sky's warm hue, with great big
garage doors and great big dusty windows – no doubt Mirela
had dumped all these lies on Peter and Simon too, *who did not
for a second* dream, *Dunja*, who could not have *imagined*, that
they were in the middle of a stupid teenage play in which he
and Mirela – fucking Kristijan and fucking Mirela – were acting
out parts from an air-tight script with no actual author – fuck,
she realised as she toddled to the corner of the warehouse, it
was a script from *fucking hell*! He didn't know about Mirela,

but Kristijan could not *ease up* on it: he never revealed, *not to anyone*, the true content of the plot *because, Dunja, since, Dunja, because, Dunja, since* he was afraid, he was fucking afraid, *not for myself, believe me, Dunja, but for Dražen*, believe me, believe me, Dunja – that tired, worn-out, d e s p i c a b l e, heartless refrain – *because, Dunja, since, Dunja, because, Dunja, since he must have been the same as me*; Kristijan *felt* this, he felt it in his gut and in his chest – everyone always feels it in their gut and in their chest, gut and chest, the fucking centres of the world – felt it sometimes as a stab, sometimes as a lurch, sometimes as a horrid explosion of tiny, razor-edged, pointy little creatures pushing their way over to Dražen's tiny, razor-edged, fuckingly pointy little creature with a gagged mouth and blindfolded eyes, to that little creature nesting even deeper in his chest/gut, even deeper in his fear/pride, even deeper, *Dunja*, even deeper, even lower, even low— . . . So Kristijan felt all this and said nothing, nothing at all, he outright lied *to protect us*, to protect them *both* – protect himself from the humiliation that would have shredded, would have shattered, *I'd say, would have taken my life from me, because you have no idea, Dunja, no idea, how much my father, my cousin, my uncle despised THOSE PANSIES POOFTERS QUEERS*, and protect Dražen from the humiliation that would have *defiled, yes, defiled, smeared, blackened* his fucking memory. It was important to *preserve his memory, Dunja*, to preserve it free of *repugnant details*, since that was only way *you and your family, Dražen's family, Dunja*, could keep the tragedy i n t a c t. Since that was the only way they, Dražen's family, could have grieved without people whhhisssspering behind their backs, without the gravity of the event becoming distorted, blunted, peeled away by, *yes, Dunja, even by my* hateful clan.

Around the corner she saw another three or four piers, where people were disembarking from yachts and sailboats and hydrofoils, seemingly without a care in the world, and in honour of the discrepancy between those white-haired strangers and herself she decided to light the fucking joint she had prepared that morning, to light it like a damn weapon, to do away with, to shoot down, no, not *shoot down* anything, but rather to *catch* her brittle balance. She decided to, and was about to, but didn't. Feeling woozy, she sat on the edge of the first bench she came to, one left over, she assumed, from when that garage/warehouse was still a sort of work site, and lit only a cigarette – she was close enough to the evening-time marina to read the unimaginative names of the luxury vessels – *Susanna, Lady in White, Beautiful Galley* – yet far enough away that the upper-crust revelry did not make her thoroughly loathe, well, the upper fucking crust.

Close enough to the marina, far enough from the marina – a metaphor she would never have used in her novel, not in a million years, but even so, at its worthless core it most likely held a fucking big reminder: she was close enough to Dražen to say that Kristijan was lying, and far enough from Dražen to say that Kristijan was right. Vis-à-vis her brother – no – vis-à-vis her brother's sexuality (him being dead, was this word unbearable or outrageous?) she was – (she waved the cigarette in front of her nose and then, like a sleep-deprived bookie in an old film, rested her smoking hand on her thigh) – vis-à-vis her brother's sexuality, then, she was in fact *nowhere at all*, and in fact – no, more than in fact, in fucking *actual* fact – she didn't give a shit about it! Because it didn't change a thing! Because she was close to him, because she was far from him, blah-blah-blah, vis-à-vis her brother, she would, did still, and would *always*, love him

l o v e h i m

L O V E H I M!

She held her chin high in the air and brought the cigarette to her mouth in a wide arc, just as she had seen both men and women from School Street do in that small enclave of bars which had once, too long ago, been the greenest heart of the neighbourhood, and turned her eyes away from – what was that boat's name? *Our Little Princess? My Little Princess?* Or just *Little Princess?* – in any case from all that stupid littleness and (as a character in her novel would never do, not in a million years) gazed up at the sky. Not to marvel at it, at this ironically, achingly pink sky, a sky without a single blue stain, but to ask it, to ask that farther (father?) sky, which couldn't care less about her own pathetic pain, to ask it, well, a little question:

Hey there, ironically, achingly pink sky, sky without a single blue stain, so who should I believe now? Kristijan, who seemingly fell apart a little in front of me so he could seemingly finally tell me that Mirela had ensconced herself in a borrowed fabrication? Or Mirela, who flew into a rage in front of me, adamant that her love for Dražen was no mere infatuation? So who should I believe, sky, which doesn't give a fuck about me. Because, sky which doesn't give a fuck, I seem to be walking on the thinnest possible ice, through which I see all the benumbed (or are they life-loving?) plants – because I seem to be walking on the slippery slope of faith.

And in fact, she slipped her body lower, arched her back and at once (ow!) found herself at odds with her lumbar region. She suspected she had made her plea to the sky, the sky that didn't give a fuck about her, out loud, since there was a man staring at her, a shady type, the kind who most *definitely* used an alias (and probably not *Teddy Bear*), and who most *definitely* was headed behind the garage/warehouse in order to purchase from, or maybe sell to, somebody, hmm, well, *something*, and certainly *not* a fucking nut roll. She suspected he was actually—

—whoa, was that Katarina over there? *That* being a woman in a terribly close-fitting, terribly short black dress with shoulder straps sprinkled with little crystals which shone in the sun like a disco ball, even though it couldn't be much past, what, six? – a dress from which her breasts were, hmm, delectably protruding and in which her bum was evenly distributed, its convexity softened by an inch or two. On her head she wore, oh my, a very contemporary, very colourful bohemianesque ribbon/hairband tied at the top in a bow, which was totally not her typical style (although it probably was Duška's style) and, at the nape of her neck, an extremely tight chignon, which Dunja could imagine her wearing only at a funeral since (if this even was Katy, right? Boobs and bum and a sexy swing of the hips don't tell you everything!) since it was at a funeral (it must have been her father's, back when Katarina had enchantingly long, thick hair, her own natural hair) that she had last seen her coiffed like that.

And *over there?* Let's not forget *over there*, no more than an athletic sprint away: the woman, possibly-probably-maybe Katy, turned sharply from the pier closest to Dunja, on which the Great Detective had picked out all the key figures (she was, as we said, *close enough, far enough*), onto the path along the canal, which, if the G.D.'s memory served, would take her at least out of the marina, and as she was turning, her upper body slightly pivoted, as if to acknowledge someone or at the last moment glance back at something. She may even have *said* something. She had definitely not shouted (the G.D. ground the cigarette with her heel) because if she had, the air being so still, the G.D. would have heard her.

So what now? Again, the same damn problem Dunja was always facing, although this time it was addressed directly to the G.D., who – fuckingshit! – rose up off the bench as if she had not spent the past quarter of the day playing mental chess, the past quarter of the day withering inside, the past quarter of the day moaning, the past quarter of the day fuming, as if her arthritis were basically an uplifting breeze, as if no earthquake, no fire, no flood and no ice had the w h o l e fucking day drained the blood from her face, as if nothing had happened at all – and she even ran a little towards that notorious canal, so she could still maybe catch maybe-Katy or maybe-her-silhouette, which was climbing the footbridge to Lucija. She stopped for a moment, somewhat agitated, and deftly, *G.D.-ishly*, plunged her hand into the Desigual – hahaha, now what was that she'd been theorising earlier about people and bones? about gnawing and passions? – and pulled out her iPhone, happy that it recognised her, and, with *G.D.-ish* calm, started tapping and swiping the screen:
→ *CALLS*
→ *RECENTS*
→ *CONTACTS*
→ *ahhh, here she is, KATY KAT;*
then a final, sweaty tap, accompanied by the inward screech *What the fuck are you doing?* (from G.D. to Dunja), and after just

a few rings Katy Kat, who had disappeared *beyond the horizon*, picked up: 'Dunja dear! Hey, I was just thinking about you!'

'Ohhh, uhhh . . .' – Dunja was still wrestling with the Great Detective for words – 'ehhh . . .' She transferred the phone to her left hand and raised it to her left ear; she needed her right arm to anchor her unbelievable acceleration (oh, she needed to watch her breathing, her breathing!) as she came to the bridge and then crossed it, looking left and right and—

'Dunja, can you hear me?'

—next to the restaurant across from the Mercator supermarket she spied the woman in the terribly close-fitting black dress with the terribly bohemianesque hair ribbon and the terribly tight chignon, who was pressing a phone to her head and spinning her hand as if she were twirling a chain—

'Duni?' The woman stopped and perplexedly – BINGO! – *glanced at the device*—

—and the G.D./Dunja vented a silent sigh and grinned. 'I can se— *hear* you, Katy! Sorry. This iPhone isn't worth what I paid for it.' She stepped behind the nearest larch tree and peeked out at the pavement where Katy was standing. 'Well, anyway. I was thinking about you too. What are you up to?'

'We-e-ell . . .' – and Katy, in the terribly close-fitting black dress with the terribly bohemianesque hair ribbon and the terribly tight chignon, suddenly, in a single motion, pulled apart that same chignon and ruffled those few straggly hairs – 'let's see now, I was in the supermarket but those Italian *turisti* create crowds like you can't believe, and everything was taking so long that I left.'

Really? Why, you don't say, Katy Kat? She still knew how to lie brilliantly, like an autocrat.

'You, um . . .' Dunja/the G.D. clenched her little fist as best she could, and at last found the magic words. 'I wanted to invite you to go to the beach with me tomorrow. That's why I'm calling. I haven't been in a hundred years, Katy, not in a hundred years!'

'I can believe that.' Now, in the distance, she also removed Duška's boho hairband, but did not stick it in her handbag

because – curious, right? – she didn't have one with her.
'Suuure, of course let's do it, what a *dorro* idea. You know, I
thought you were upset with me the other day!'

'Upset? No, not at all,' she swore, relaxing her fist – it was
almost the honest truth. 'Don't be silly, Katy,' *because we've been
through worse, Katy, you know we have.* 'Just tell me when would
be good for you.'

'Yeahhh . . .' her friend murmured beneath the overpass,
its walls no doubt lined with posters for concerts by tribute
bands. 'Do you still object to strong sun? I mean, would you
prefer morning or evening?'

The G.D., of course, would have voted for morning, but
Dunja was suddenly picturing a nice, big, well-stuffed joint. So:
'Let's make it afternoon. Say, five o'clock?'

'Five it is! Lucija or Portorož?'

''Rož.'

'Oh wow, cool!' She disappeared into the tunnel. 'I wasn't
expecting you to say that. So Kanel Beach then. Remember it?'

Of course she remembered. That was where Katy always,
without fail, would ask her to be her cover – for the motorbike
and the lipstick and Jan and Željko etc. etc. etc. – where she
would ask her, in other words, to *lie* for her.

And what had Dunja done back then when Katarina made
such requests? Why, as you know, she complied. Of course she
did.

10

The *spiaggia*: a largish patch of sand/concrete, bordered by bars and trampolines and a beach volleyball court and bumper cars and, umm, maybe a little train for the kids; a patch of sand/concrete dotted with stands for popcorn and ice cream and alcoholic beverages – a Smile Beer perhaps? Or a Corona? – and umbrellas too; a patch of sand/concrete where people dig holes, play catch, shout, play cards and, as Dunja just implied, drink; a patch that extends into the shallow, eww, too shallow, water, where, as the tourist catalogues proclaim, 'you can sample' waterskiing and sailboarding, surfing, rowing and sailing (what had they called it? *Sailing with your little pioneers?*); and especially, a patch of sand/concrete where the reigning activity today (yesterday too) is (and was), well, sex – all in contrast to a *beach*, which is a patch of sand or rock or grass, where in, let's say, *relative* quiet, you could unroll your ArmaFlex mat and (so Dunja dreamed) do un-catalogical things. Like pick at your toenails, pluck the occasional unwanted hair, doze a little or read. Obviously, Dunja-the-child had wanted to go the *beach* and, no less obviously, Katy had always pushed for the *spiaggia*, and, even more obviously, Dunja, before her bestie said even a word, had almost always complied, not from any Dunjaesque submissiveness, but because giving in to her *paid off.* On the *beach*, where the two girls went a total of maybe three times, Katy Kat

had never given Dunjica the peace she needed for tending to
her little blue toenail, skimming stones, dozing a bit or read-
ing – not at all, nothing of the sort – Katy was always like a
little puppy, endlessly yapping, constantly swearing, standing
up, sitting down, standing up, even pulling pranks on her –
sprinkling water on her legs, on her face and one time even on
her BOOK – she would so shamelessly suck up every ounce
of Dunja's attention that Dunja, even back then, would return
from the *beach* exhausted as a granny, no, worse, as a *factory
worker*, her head completely buzzing, and not giving a damn
about *niente* any more. But on the *spiaggia*, oh, on the

s

p

i

a

g

g

i

a,

Dunjica had had all the fucking peace in the world! On the
spiaggia, oh, on the *spiaggia*, she had slept as much as she liked
and read the most books, too – Do you want Agatha or Enid
or is your heart set on comics? Do you want Emil and his gang
of sleuths or D'Artagnan and his musketeers? – because on the
spiaggia, oh, on the *spiaggia*, Dunja had been for Katy (pardon
the expression) *surplus to requirements*. On the *spiaggia* there had
been puh-*lenty* of other people, which is to say, puh-lenty of
boys and men, bestowing attention on Katy automatically, and
doing so in numbers that, to put it diplomatically, were impres-
sive – certainly, every second male, whether her own age or
an elderly invalid, whether single or married, whether with or
without a queue of children, or their mums, snaking behind or
in front of him – and at a rhythm that continued relentlessly for
hours and hours, in a form that oscillated between high and low
and with content that naturally suffered from the same. Katy, on
the *spiaggia*, had been far too busy for Dunja, as she was com-
pelled and determined to absorb democratically, like a sponge,

like a first-rate dishcloth, all that the boys and men were exud-
ing at her, over her, for her, and to respond to these exudations
non-selectively, indeed, appreciatively – to giggle and laugh at
them, wink and chat, stand up and sit down and sit down and
stand up, to attractively arch her back and lie down, to play with
her sunglasses, to bend over and search through her bag, where
she was *sure* she had some *peaches and apples*, to sprinkle sand on
her legs, pour water on her neck, untie, retie, tie up her bikini,
reach beneath the wet textile, adjust her ponytail and comb her
hair, to do this and do that, to herself, for herself, to them, for
them, to delight them, to give them unfaaaathomable pleasure
and also, always, to be a little afraid of them.

The same, therefore, applied in Anno Domini 2019: Dunja
sitting Indian-style (a position in which her arthritis was more
or less OK), engrossed in a book, a pretentious novel by a young
female author written in a remarkable style but (God forgive
her) lacking any real substance; Katarina, for an hour, or probably longer, going crazy, yes, totally crazy, from working the public – it was as if she did not really notice Dunja until the audit—,
or, umm, *immediate vicinity* died down a little, emptied out.

'Wow, Dunja, you're so white – you never used to be so
white. Don't you ever go out in the sun up there in Ljubljana?'

*She looked like a clown girl whom no one had laughed at for a
long time, but only pitied.* She finished the sentence and lifted her
head astonished, as if a group of young carollers were ringing
her doorbell in mid-August.

'So you're saying I'm yogurt?' she answered with a sour
smile. 'No, I suppose I don't get much sun any more. Living
in the city, I guess I just lost the habit.' *Lost the habit* means, if
we're being precise, that she had actually *forbidden* herself such
pleasures. She was, indeed, *shielding* herself from them. Because
enjoying the sun is, first of all, freedom and freedom is untroubledness and untroubledness is safety and safety is home and
home is Lucija and Lucija is the sea and the shore and the beach
and the *spiaggia* and the sea–shore–beach–*spiaggia* are days and
years and days and years are her childhood and her childhood is
her memories and her memories are steam and mist and steam

and mist are a ghost and the ghost is her Dražen and Dražen
is her father and her father is her father is Dražen is her father
is the night, first two nights then a thousand, and the night is
in the flood tide and in the flood tide waits the ebb tide and in
the ebb tide is dry land and in the dry land is fucking sod, is a
grave, and in the grave is a letter and in the letter are words and
in the words is a voice and in the voice is glass and the glass
is in shards and in the shards is a home and in the home is her
mother and in her mother is darkness and in the darkness . . . in
the darkness? in the d a r k n e s s ? is . . . ? (Somehow s o m e -
h o w always everything.)

'Umm . . .' — she was suddenly light-headed — 'but it
feels nice. Today it feels really nice. And it would be great if
it became a habit again, you know.' She closed the clown-girl
book but didn't set it down. She needed to cling to something.
To hold on to something. Everyone needs something to cling
to, to hold on to.

'Did you even put on sun cream? If you did, I didn't see
you. It can't be good for you not to use sun cream.'

Had she been healthy, she thought, instead of literature
she could have held on tight to good, caring people as well,
but, yeah, she just didn't. Instead, she merely pulled out the sun
cream, factor *four*, from the Desigual.

'I meant to, you know,' she said and shyly held the luxurious tube in front of Katy's nose. 'But, um, I got a little
distracted. It shouldn't make any difference; it's evening now
anyway.'

'A *little*?' Katarina laughed from her heart. 'I'll say you got
a *little* distracted.' She pushed herself off the beach towel cat-
style, her tail/bum lifted high in the air, at which her male public began reassembling and/or repositioning themselves; then,
even more cat-style (*cat-stylishly?*), she sat behind her friend and
wrapped her left arm around her so firmly, with such unexpected
strength, that Dunja simply melted onto her shoulder, despite
being at least a head taller than Katy, despite being (as you
have had the opportunity to learn) dreadfully stiff, and there on
her shoulder, on Katy's, ah, so soft, so absorbent, margariney,

silky shoulder – fuuuck – there, there was still home. If only a second one.

'You're funny, my Dunjica, you're still funny.' And she *kissed* her, kissed her on the parting in her hair, and Dunjica, for the first time *ever*, completely without shame, *for the very first time*, as if this position were somehow hers by rights, sweetly closed her eyes in unreserved surrender. *I am happy that I'm here* – she could have said this to Katy then, and would have added, *I love you, despite everything I somehow still love you, thank you, Katy, really, thank you*, and she herself might then have *cradled* her friend in her arms – could have, would have, might have – but she either missed the opportunity or for some reason or another did not truly seize it, not then nor a minute nor an hour nor a month later.

'I'm happy you're here, I really am. So happy you're here,' Katarina said as she opened Dunja's cosy nook and – clearly, intentionally, *deliberately* – withdrew. Her eyes, and with them her stomach and even her heart, slipped away from Dunja to their new nearest neighbours, three men of triathletic, which is to say triangular, build, who had no doubt arrived primarily to display their unsurpassable, unsurfuckable, swimming abilities and, secondarily, well, to see Katarina, who was already stretching her adorable legs, leaning back on her arms, sucking in her belly, and thrusting out her breasts all the way to Piran. Dunja's cheek and neck and waist and scalp were still vibrating with her friend's peaceful warmth, which made those areas feel strangely itchy, and no doubt red as well, and suddenly – again *for the first time ever* (even if such adverbials are always contrivances, stylised yet lovely little literary lies) – she was overcome with the need to alleviate that itching and that redness, and to alleviate them specifically with Katy's body, with Katy's arms and her fat little fingers, but, in fact, Katy's renewed attention would in itself have been enough; her renewed attention would in itself have filled her with meaning; it would have scratched that fucking itch, it would have calmed her. And when, sitting next to her mothe—, I mean, next to *Katarina*, behind Katarina's back, she found herself lingering like some fucking (steam or mist or) ghost, when with her open woun—, I mean, when she could do nothing but observe the long and subtle interaction taking place among the *beach towels* – the tango, the salsa, the foxtrot of desire! – when she could feel the tension and eroticism turning into something material, when the tension and eroticism, like a swarm of bees, like a swarm of fucking wasps, started sting-ing and stabbing her, too, but then dispersed like a swarm of fucking cockroaches or grasshoppers, which is to say, when one of the men, with great self-assurance, his chest thrust out, like hers, all the way to fucking Piran, said fucking *hi* to Katarina and fucking introduced himself – it was again some Jan, again some Željko, maybe a Žan? – well, that's when Dunja felt herself shaking, probably between her shoulder blades, maybe in her lower back, but almost *certainly* behind her forehead, and there it was: she could barely hold back the hail of angry tears. But as for the rain, oh yes, even so, she had to rain.

'You know I saw you yesterday, Katy.'

Her friend's eyes were still on Jan-Željko-Žan and her lips (Dunja saw them in profile) were oh so pouty and warm that her response, 'I'm Katarina,' came out clear and crisp, ripen-ing into an apple that Jan, Željko or Žan would simply have to bloodthirstily – umm, but an apple doesn't bleed – umm, OK, so then – *ravenously* bite into.

'Katy, did you hear me?' Dunjica now even touched her, pinched her shoulder.

'Aaa!' Her mothe—, fuck, I mean, *Katarina* turned around annoyed and asked in a whisper, 'Dunja, what's going on?'

'I said that I saw you yesterday,' the little gir—, no (but this really has to stop!), *Dunja* said sternly.

'OK . . .' Katarina's eyes again went somewhere else. She seemed to be looking, seeing, solely with her peripheral vision, more aware of the male trio and what they were doing than the pallid woman sitting directly in front of her. 'Just what exactly are you trying to say?'

Dunja felt a little queasy – since, you must remember, she *somehow, all the same,* did *still love* her friend. Since she did not want in any way to upset her. Since she did not want to cause her embarrassment or worry, about anything. Since she had decided – and decided entirely out of concern for her friend's stability and peace! – to wisely, oh so wisely, say nothing about what she had learned from Kristijan barely twenty-four hours earlier. Since she did not have the heart to push Katy closer to that open fire where she and Duška were sure to get seriously burned – Duška, especially, would get burned, oh yes, for she would lose her one and only worthy approximation of a father, who might then be followed by yet another quick succession of Jans, Željkos and Žans, from low to lower to lowest – since she did not have the heart, ergo, to boil that soup to magma and then, of course, naturally, obviously, head back to Ljubljana. Since she did not have the heart to boil that soup to magma for the very woman who, when it really counted, had always been her mothe— (*shit!*), been her *refuge*. Since she really did not care what Katy had done yesterday or the day before, or the day before that, since she had no desire to cook, or cook up, anything from it, at least nothing truly poisonous. Since it was all becoming clear to her anyway and she had no desire to drag her friend before some fucking tribunal. Since she, Dunja that is, was hardly the person to assess the situation or pass judgement! Since since since she still loved Katy, since since since, but – OOPS, oh dear,

but,

with the word *say* still echoing softly in the air, Katy, with a *laugh* – with a patronising, belittling, fucking *arrogant* laugh – turned her back on Dunja. You understand? She literally *turned her back* on her. And aimed her most beautiful smile and most beautiful words, her smooth words, her empty words – *So where are you boys staying? Are you here on holiday?* – at Aljaž-Boris-Rok – at which Dunja, well, Dunja, you might say, w e n t f u c k i n g   n u t s.

'Kaaa-tyyy,' she began, pounding her back, syllable by syllable, *toof toof toof toof*, 'when-we-were-tal-king-on-the-phone-yes-ter-day-I-saw-you-leav-ing-the-ma-ri-na-but-you-told-me-you-were-com-ing-back-from-the-su-per-mar-ket.' The hammering on Katarina's skin was by now making itself known, but

little-girl-Dunja, child-Dunja, could not stop. The syllables just
fell from her mouth the way a good Communist might sing 'The
Internationale'. 'I-saw-you-on-the-pier-and-you-were-in-a-ver-y-
at-trac-tive-out-fit.'

Katy had probably never before looked at Dunja with
such anger; her look was almost threatening. (Dunja had probably never before given her a reason to look at her like this.
She had probably never before – hmm, let's choose something
mild – been such a *pest*.) She really had never known Katy like
this, which is why she had never learned, never actually *seen*,
how unbelievably ugly, how repulsive Katy could appear: the
way her eyelids drooped, as those of Slovenian actresses do,
the way her petite nose and forehead and chin gathered into
a snout, the way her face, all at once, turned pale and the way
this pallor accentuated the plasticness, fakeness and heavi-
ness of her make-up, the way her ears, meanwhile, turned greyish, the way her forehead and neck looked raw and stretched,
like Mickey Rourke's or maybe the classic example, Pamela
Anderson's, the way she seemed to be (oh good grief!) hissing
from every orifice in her head, even (good grief!) from her ears
and her eyes! And, finally, the way she sounded, too, when
words like *bitch*, *scum*, *stronza* and even *fucking whore* just had
to be stuck in her throat, the way she sounded (oh God!) like
an old used-up saw.

'Dunja! What are you telling me? What is it you want?
What are you trying to accomplish here?'

That, of course, little-girl-Dunjica did not know, and she
instantly regretted having provoked Katy, but – and what a lot
of fucking buts there were, as if they could replace the force of
gravity! – *but* simply retreating from the quarrel, retreating now,
when there were four pairs of fucking cattle eyes staring at her,
retreating now when she had nowhere left to go to escape the
verdict *That woman's mad, and jealous as all hell*, not to her hotel,
not to the sea, not to the fucking public toilets; retreating, in
other words, now when the kamikazette had already jumped,
when she was already falling, I mean, flying, in the wind – this,
we know, was simply not an option.

'I'd like to know why you felt it necessary to lie to me,' she said in a softer voice. 'I'd like to know why you felt it necessary to hide anything from me. I'm just curious about where you were.' Although, fuuuck, she really, really wasn't.

Katy shifted to, umm, the hero's position: she sat back on her heels and at the same time shrieked: 'Why do you even care? Do you think you're my fucking mother?'

'No, I am nobody's mother. As you are well aware, YOU ARE THE ONLY MOTHER HERE, KATY!' Dunja – *what the fuck, Dunja? Disgusting moraliser! Depraved aesthete!* – and so her hammer swung over the head of h e r f r i e n d and pounded her into the sand like a fucking cork, and that instant, *that very instant*, her friend started gasping for air and her admirers – oh, her admirers! – scattered like fucking animals at the pop of a firecracker, scurrying from their soft mats to their hotels, to the sea, to the fucking public toilets, leaving behind, of course, rumpled towels and a whirling wind and a ton of whirling, riotous void, as Katy's ugliness slooowly receded, the snout reverting to her – adorable! – *human* features, her forehead and neck again soft and oh so charming, and amid the layers of powder and rouge, like a river in a malleable limestone-white valley, the tears came, a hundred gentle, but heavy, tears.

Even so, when the powder had all melted away, even so, there was a whisper: 'You b-bitch.'

Huff. Sniffle.

'Wh-what a bitch.'

Sniffle. Huff. Directly into her forearm.

'What a *stronza* you are, D-dunja.'

Huff. Sniffle. Ssssssssniffle. Into her fingers, into her hands.

'What the fuck is wrong with you, Dunja? Did I do something to you? Did I?'

She just shrugged and stared at Katarina's round knees, her terribly calm knees, although above them, yes, above them was a tempest. And as she stared at those round and, fuck, incredibly calm knees, she drew a line in the sand with her index finger. And then another line. And a third. She saw she had a triangle and, automatically, drew a circle on top of it and, below that, two new lines, now parallel. To the little body she then added two little arms and a bit of curly hair on the head and immediately, after drawing a few last, longest, curliest hairs, she angrily – *Dunja, fuck, you are so stupid, you really are not normal –* brushed sand over the little girl.

'Katy . . .' she muttered, turning over the little pile of sand, looking for the tiniest, most invisible '*I'm sorry.* I was just worried that . . .' – then she spread out the pile and smoothed it down – 'I was worried that, oh, how should I put it? Katy—'

'Oh God, don't start babbling again! OK, Dunja? That's what I want to say, OK? Because I know you think I'm not capable of understanding anything else.'

'Katy,' – her hands were now shaping another stupid pile – 'you know I don't think that.'

Katy pulled her towel into her lap as if it were a veil – not a bridal veil, a mourner's – and quickly, apathetically, used it to dab her sunken, quivering chin and swelling eyes; then she half-folded, half-rolled it up.

'Please, Katy,' – she felt a stinging pain beneath her fingernails – 'don't do this. Please don't do this.'

Don't do this: Katy had pulled her big sparkly bag over towards her and was now loading it with, not just the towel, but all the other aids she had brought to that fucking *spiaggia*: not only the sun cream but also a brush, a one-piece swimsuit (magnetic magenta!), cigarettes, a lighter, sunglasses, a fashion magazine (summer 2016), a tunic and a sarong and, oh look, two more bikinis, one *brasileiro*, the other *bandeau* (neither of which, to the misfortune of the three-headed octopus, had she yet had a chance to, um, *wear* that day), and, last of all, two little bags, one of which, to judge by the rustle in it, contained a fluttery little substitute dress (since you never know where the evening's energy will take you), while the other, to judge by its clinking sound, contained mascara, lipstick, tweezers, nail files, a pair of little scissors, nail polish and, of course, eyeshadow. She took her time packing, a lot of time, too much fucking time, with too much fucking calm. Dunja's 'Katy, please, don't' – 'No, Katy, please' – 'C'mon, Katy, don't be angry' were losing their conviction – what had started as remorseful continued as humble and, oh yes, as wounded and sad, and there, somehow quite incidentally (that's how it happens with Dunja), mutated into full-on disappointment, acquiring more or less autonomous contours, completely separate from the input data of the recent, still fresh-as-a-fucking-kaiser-roll experience and the, hmm, equally crunchy fucking thoughts that had ensued; it acquired, then, the contours of patronisation? haughty disgust? fucking compassion or, worse, *pity?* – in short, all the possible contours of *distance*, which, Dunja thought when Katy stood up and was looming above her, had to be, fucking ergo, just had to be, the fucking diametrical, most fuckingly diametrical, opposite of love.

'OK then bye,' Katarina said, her lips clenched, and, stumbling a bit, marched off, flip-flops in hand, away from little-girl Dunja. Yes, I'm sure you noticed, noticed certainly before Dunja did, that Katy had *not* got dressed, that she had put on neither shorts nor tank top, that she, in fact, had put on nothing for the walk *home*. Instead, turning onto the little stone path that cut through the *spiaggia*, she hurried on to its even more populated, even more boisterous (even more boys-are-us!), even more germy and virusy core, straight to the *centre of the action*, which is where she had wanted to be *in the first place* but there was no way, *not a chance*, she could ever have persuaded Dunja to go there. Dunja, meanwhile, hunched among her belongings as if (sorry, but it's true) they were rotting carrion, watched with watery sunken eyes, watched a long, long time, as her friend – her *friend?* – h e r f r i e n d walked away, but she didn't see her sit down, make herself comfortable and randomly, *spontaneously*, as Katy was famous for doing, start chatting, start exchanging glances with someone, start mindlessly flirting with someone – no, she only saw Katy walking away, walking away without even once turning around and looking for her tearfully in the crowd; she only saw her *abandoning* her, and fuck, fuck, fuck, *this*, more than any of the sitting down, chatting, flirting, chatting, exchanging glances, *this* is what hurt *most of all*; *this* is what she *had never been able to get used to*, although the truth is: she could have . . . What is it people like to say? You need ten thousand hours to become an expert at something? To master a skill? Fine. Well, Dunja had certainly put in more hours than that: all those hours in the fucking past twenty years – hours, however, that had never properly sunk in, at least not into any fucking fertile ground. But as we said, the truth is: she could have got used to the *reagents* of abandonment and parting, which meant she could in fact have abstained from the *reaction*, and really and truly kept her fucking cool – just as she could have done earlier, when she *pounced* on Katy – but the truth is: she *could have* and *didn't*. The truth is. She could. Have. Screaming and in desperation! Simply. Run. After her.

11

Same evening, one hour later, version no. 6: 'Katy, forgive me.'
Seen 8:56 p.m.

Same evening, three hours later, simple and from the first version: 'Katarina, forgive me.'
Seen 11:01 p.m.

Night, the night from Saturday to Sunday, three times *Select all* followed by *Delete*, and then at two a.m., again, *Send*: 'Katy, can we at least talk on the phone before I go? Or better, see each other? I expect I'll be leaving on Tuesday. Well, I'm supposed to but I'm not sure, at reception they said I could basically extend my stay. Whatever. I really am sorry. I was unfair to you. Very.'

Seen? At nine in the morning, when she lumbered into the hotel's breakfast room and, hollow inside from having been too nervous the night before to eat dinner, was absorbed in the abundance on offer – eggs (scrambled whipped hard-boiled) and bacon and white little bananas and white little sweet rolls and *even whiter* little crescent rolls and cherry tomatoes and grappolo tomatoes and Istrian cucumbers and Natura flakes (oat rye buckwheat) and hazelnuts and walnuts and figs and plums and, oh wow, fresh-made vegetable juice! and cheeses (oh my, a whole *palace* of cheeses) and crêpes and three hundred thousand kinds of tea and plant-based milk – well, as she

was loading up her plate, there was still only the grey word
delivered beneath her last-sent text. Carrying a mound of food
in one hand and a too-hot cup in the other, she balanced her
way to a table by the window and knew that for breakfast she
would be eating all the emotions of the day just past, the day
beginning and the day still to come, just as she had done in her
fucking 'golden' teenage years, when she would take food from
the fridge and shelves in an exemplary manner, prepare it in an
exemplary way, eat it with exemplary decorum for one or two
or at most three days and then, without warning, an attack: a
wad of animal hunger, of lust, beneath her tongue, the insistent
sobbing of one and only one idea in her brain – to seal every
crack in her body with cake, pastry, biscuits, to fill the void
between the disgusting flesh of her organs and her blunt, cold
skeleton – there would be diabolical, yes, d i a b o l i c a l, anxiety and agitation in her nerve plexuses, while in her limbs, only
bickering, followed by gobbling up, shovelling in, gorging and
wolfing, almost choking; in her tear glands, pressure and burning; in her salivary glands, hah, definitely anything but fucking
graciousness; but in her consciousness, nothing less than, yes,
a fucking orgasm, which, just like the 'real' one, would then
lapse into numbness.

She deposited the mound of food and the already cooling cup on the table, again checked her messages – still nothing but fucking *delivered* – consoled herself audibly – 'It'll be
fine, it'll be fine, you'll be OK, Dunja' (what a weirdo) – and
silently decided to consume this bit of breakfast/drug and later,
at Mirela's – *ugh, what could be waiting for her there?* – ugh, at
Mirela's, n o t   t o u c h   a n y   f o o d, not a morsel of that
stupid brunch. And this too: nothing but water, yes, she would
drink nothing but water.

The ensuing ritual was, of course, brief. When she stood
up, she realised that, although it had only just ended, she no
longer remembered it – what did she even eat and how much? –
she had not been at all present in the enjoyment of the food:
throughout her gobbling, shovelling, gorging and wolfing,
her eyes had in fact been on the iPhone and not on the, umm,

allegedly grainy texture of the breakfast biscuits. That the quantities were surely enormous she judged only from the bulge of her belly, which was protruding more distinctly, oh, much more distinctly, and more ponderously, oh much more ponderously, than her other, well, relatively speaking, *curves*. She descended the hotel steps feeling (as noted) drugged and with an abundantly heavy (heh-heh) conscience. A most welcome heavy conscience, for it had, you know, almost entirely replaced the stupid emotional nexus that was plaguing her.

She should at least walk off the calories (well, if she wanted to walk them *all* off, she'd probably end up in fucking Alaska) and this *had been* her grand plan all the way to the hotel exit, but, well, the morning's worsening heat, which like a jealous, or rather, *insane* lover unexpectedly seized her by the neck just beyond the glass doors, promised no release; it was only whispering, *Oh, Dunjica, shuuuush, shuuuush,*

puuuuublic

puuuuuuublic

traaans

pooooooort.

She heeded the whisper but also did something against the calories: she walked to the *next* bus stop, which was set a little into the bushes among some young larch trees – true to the catalogical keyword 'excellent location', the first stop was literally twenty steps from her hotel. And was terribly crowded too, with pensioners, pensioners, pensioners, and terribly exposed to the sun and horribly exposed to the exhaust fumes and somebody had obviously thrown up in it during the night. But OK, people (plural) had been throwing up behind the next bus stop too – the night there had been particularly, *ick*, toxic and sour and, *eww*, there were caustic odours coming in hordes from the dried puddles, and there was nowhere to escape from them and, ohhh, her breathing was getting shallow and her breakfast, another puddle, a burbling one, was lurching annoyingly in her stomach and – there you go – the only solution that presented itself to her was reorientation, that is, a new *focus*, one that she might come to regret, a focus that meant typing and deleting

and arranging and barbering an apology, even if beneath the
previous one there was only still that same fucking *delivered*.
And so: 'Katarina, forgive me, I get why you're angry, I really
do, the thing yesterday was no way for me to act, I was stupid
& horrible but want to make it all up to you, really. You probably don't think I'm worth your trust but let me prove that's not
true, that I'm still the same Duni & you can rely on me. Call me
when you can, pls, it would mean a lot to me. See? I'm thinking
about you.'

Aaaand *delivered delivered fucking delivered*, that imper-
ishable millennial refrain, but, fortunately, a little bus soon
swallowed her up in a sort of thunderous blast of air, casting
her into the throng, of course, of the very pensioners she had
hoped to avoid and some others who, from the look of them,
had been just as carelessly sucked dry, most likely employees
at some supermarket chain – Mercator, Tuš, Lidl or Spar –
who, whenever she saw them, made her wonder what the fuck
kept them going. Kept them standing. Kept them awake. In that
god-awful job. What the fuck could even be leading them on?
Did their 'safe' 'family' 'haven' truly make up for the bleakness
they experienced day after fucking day: the beeping of scanners,
light so constant and strong it hurt the eyes, air conditioning set
either too high or too low, the drudgery of stocking and clearing
shelves, the constant asking *Do you have our loyalty card? Our discount coupon? Oh, you don't? You don't? You can download it on your
phone, you know*. Or were the 'safe' 'family' 'haven' and 'quality'
'leisure' 'time' merely mythic narratives conceived by fucking
corporate hegemons to keep their employees from thinking
too much, from rebelling – in fact, to keep *us all* from thinking
too much and rebelling? Was it possible thaaa— oo-oopsy, the
b-b-bus driver braked hard as they were descending the hill
to Piran and a man from Mercator? Lidl? Tuš? maybe Spar?
angrily, vehemently, almost violently pushed at her from behind
and then groaned when her bones pinched back at him – ooof,
so then, was it possible thaaa— damn, she had lost her train
of thought, well, it wasn't like it was of any importance to anyone . . . For her, the only important thing was that she was on

her way to visit that exasperating, most bizarre woman Mirela, while, for the people from Mercator or Tuš or Lidl, it was that they had not yet gone nuts. That they were still able to get off at Tartini Square and continue on to somewhere or to someone. But destination isn't everything, Dunja reminded herself as she hurried off, stumbling beneath the statue of that second-tier musician; there is, people say, a certain charm to be found in/ on the journey.

She had a difficult climb ahead of her from the centre of Piran, and her belly was still a balloon of acid, and the most revolting belch (*pffft*) was forming in her throat, so she stopped for a moment before the ascent, checked her phone (nothing, not even the latest from *The Guardian*) and automatically, almost against her will, surveyed the clean, white, attractively paved square (more precisely, an ellipse), which was scattered with stands selling artisanal bric-a-brac – lotions and creams, bead-work, floral arrangements, wooden items, olive oil (oh my, an entire civilisation of virgin oil) – around which apathetic vultures – I mean apathetic but noisy families – were circling. She looked at all this *against her will* because all of it – the stands and the bric-a-brac and the stupid baubles and the families – all of it quickly, so very quickly, evaporated, receded, into a kind of who-gives-a-shit, a kind of *background*, and what she r e a l l y saw when she t r u l y looked at that fucking damn square/ ellipse, at its fucking t r u e reality, was only

DRAŽEN,

Dražen in a black hoodie,

Dražen staggering,

Dražen mumbling, babbling

when he runs into those girls,

Dražen

shifting his weight from foot to foot,

trying, trying to get away from them,

Dražen,

who owed them no explanation,

and then, suddenly,

sud

den
ly,
(*Dunja, like I was swinging a katana*)
DRAŽEN
climbing onto Tartini's statue,
grabbing his bow and violin –
Who are you playing for, you baroque fool?
Dražen
attacking the *fool* with his fists,
attacking the *fool* with his elbows,
Dražen
bleeding,
Dražen
howling, *Fucking blind man!*,
screaming, *They call you a WITNESS?*
To me you're a nothing but a DEAF MUTE,
Dražen,
his fists and elbows
pounding and pounding,
FUUUUUCK,
POUNDING at the metal,
BEATING it into a different shape,
the shape of his own eternal *self*,
his *self* in a black hoodie,
his *self* with his fists
(*Like a fucking Partisan, Dunja,*
don't you think?)
his fists raised to the pointless
the point less
sky,
his *self* with that gaping mouth,
his *self* with
– what was it her mother didn't tell her? –
his *self* with
– come on, what didn't she say? –
his *self* with
– with what? –

his *self* withhhhh
– yes! –
his *self* withhhhh
thhhhose gaaaaaping,
waaaasssshhhhed-out
abysssssssezzzzzz
for eyes.

∗

She stared at Michael's lyrics above the door and belched –
Jesus, what a belch! – like she'd never done before and her only
relief would be to vomit, or no, to well and truly *puke*, and it
was to puking that she directed her acidic prayer – *Make a
change, make a change, make a change* – repeating it over and
over as she pressed her, oooof, prrreeessssed her hand to her
stomach and leaned her head forwards – textbook position,
which should have worked but didn't, fucking didn't: her stomach, though fully bloated, would not surrender; it sent up only
– what was that anyway? Toxic fumes? Only *air*? On the verge
of tears, she shut her eyes tight and counted *one, two, three*,
added *four, five, six*, breathed *seven, eight, nine*, breathed deeper,
inhaled *ten*, held *eleven*, exhaled *twel—*, OK, exhaled *thir—*, yes!
– come on, stay calm – inhaled and exhaled twice more and
then, *fucking yes*, she stopped the bulldozer even if she sensed
that its stubborn, heavy tracks were not yet dismantled: there
was surely still enough down there for them to have one more
fucking dance.

But whatevs, she righted herself and, 'good as new', took a
deep breath: even this semi-victory over her body would suffice,
at least for now. She was about to press the doorbell (decorated,
of course, with Mirela's favourite image) when the door itself
swung loudly open in front of her.

Loudly meaning: 'Oh *my*, Dunja! You look awful! Are you
OK? Because you really don't look OK.'

'Hicc—' Dunja accidentally let slip, and Mirela (good God, how dare she!) grabbed her by the hand, pulled her closer and wh-wh-wheezed into her neck to come inside at once, yes, do come in, oh yes, she was so happy to see her anyway!

Happy *anyway*? Fuck, Dunja thought, Mirela's superspindle was already spinning, and, fuck ugh, Dunja, not gently (what? She was fucking nauseous!) but in fact firmly, pushed her away and to the sound of, fuck ugh, her hostess's offended 'Oh myyyy, you are reeeally *not* OK' shoved straight past her, fuck fuck ugh, into the house. She could feel Mirela watching her dejectedly from the doorway as her bristling back slowly receded and could also, of course, hear, now for the third, the fucking third, time, that revolting falsetto warble 'Oh myyyy, she reeeally is *not* OK. Today she's so *aaangryyy!*' Ugggh fucking ugggh. Once inside the Jacksonian basilica, she plucked her iPhone from the Desigual. Although she had absolutely no *organic appetite* for this visit, the Great Detective was obliged to go through with it; it was her absolute *organic duty*. So then: one last, straightforward *bu-urp*, another *rub-rub* of her balloon-belly and a quick look at the grey notifications under the blue boxes, which informed her that her damn texts had been read – read at eleven-oh-three. (And this too: she turned up the volume and, for the very first time, put the phone on *vibrate*; she did not want to miss anything from dear Katarina.)

How long had it been since she was here? A week? Ten days? The basilica had in the meantime undergone a teensy makeover. The now-empty walls were freshly painted – oh my God, in bougainvillea purple! – and the posters and drawings and pictures and cards were lying on a thick pink mat surrounded by little plush soldiers. The gigantic *This Is It* poster was unfurled across the table and cascading over its edges; it was weighted down with candlesticks and toys. The sofa (definitely leather, she remembered), which like the other furniture had been moved away from the wall, was now draped in a new, awful, polyester cover, probably once a flag, on which were three huge pillows – the motif was predictable: golden-gloved Michael with a, hmm, perversely playful smile across his face.

Dunja guessed the flag and pillows had been purchased from a collector, the nearest being, hmm, in Trieste probably? On either side of the sofa stood the famous stands full of CDs, DVDs and (you remember, don't you?) *twinned* albums. The arrangement reminded her of a spaceship – a vessel for people whom something in reality has, well, really and for all time offended: you just sit down and blast off, or lie back and blast off, out of and away from the world, from the narrow, suffocating, grey and oppressive fucking adult world. Maybe, she thought as she and her gurgling stomach headed to the captain's bridge, maybe she too needed a sofa like this, not to take her to Galaxy M.J., but a soft, absorbent sofa to take her somewhere closer, to some place where . . . where things would be easy. Ordinary. Where everything would be *OK*.

'Do you like it? Do you like the coooolour? I hope you like the coooolour.' Mirela, who had sneaked up on the G.D. from behind just as she was sitting down in Spaceship M.J., seized her by the forearm (could she please fucking stop doing that?) and yanked her up so abruptly that Dunja felt an immediate stab in her lower back.

'Do be careful, Mirela! That really hurt!' She wrenched, yes, *wrenched* herself from her grip, and Mirela jumped back in alarm and started stroking Dunja's hand, a hand Dunja had definitely *not* offered her.

'Oh, I'm sorry, so sooorry!' Her play-acting was poor, very poor, since she then picked up right where she had left off. 'But do you *like* it? Do you like the *coooolour*?' She was looking at Dunja very intently, as if to see if Dunja recognised, if she remembered, this particular hue, but despite the evidence, the G.D. thought it unlikely that Dražen would have told anyone, let alone Mirela, what his favourite colour was – or, indeed, anything about himself that *reeked of queers*. While such obvious evidence, thought the G.D., who only now managed to slip back into Michael's glove, might well find a place in some revised storyline, in fucking *literature*, she would not let its shiny face intrude on her *investigation*. In any case, and this was important, she knew her own brother well enough to kno— Ohhh, fuck.

Shit. Did she? Did she really? Where did she even get that idea?
On what basis was Dunja, having matured into the grand G.D.,
making this assumption? Was it on the basis that she had not
known who it was that *her own brother* had locked himself in the
bedroom with (if he had even done that) or for whose benefit
he had been so chummily mumbling into the phone? On the
basis that she had never had even a fucking clue where or for
whom or why her own brother would be wandering the streets
of Piran in the middle of the night like a damn lackey? Had she
made this assumption possibly because she had gone to the
beach with her brother a few times and a few times to the damn
cinema? Had she made this assumption possibly on the basis of
what a girl, a very young girl, had once shared with her brother?
(The little they had shared, just a little too little.) So then, how
did Dunja – sorry, by now nothing less than the G.D.! – OK,
so how did the *G.D.* arrive at her indignant calculation? Hmm?
And what a fucking amateur a person must be to allow herself
such indignation?

'Personally, I'm not particularly fond of the colour.' She
decided to be prudent. 'But Dražen loved it. It was his favourite.'

'Yeees, I knooow!' Mirela exhaled and Dunja had the
impression that she would have liked to have twirled at the same
time, done a little twirl on her heel – you know, like a child in
an animated film when she first sees a lavishly decorated tree
on Christmas eve. But Mirela curbed the impulse – it was only
her torso she pivoted – and then stood looking down on Dunja
as if, well, riveted.

'I gather that's why you chose it? The colour, I mean?' *I
gather you are (were) totally crazy (for him).* 'How did you even
know about it?'

'Oh, Dunja, when I heard your voice, when I saw you,
when after aaall theeese yeeeears . . .' She sailed to the middle
of the room and the G.D. had the feeling, from Mirela's precise
facial expressions and elevated gestures, that she was watching a TED Talk performance or, perhaps a more appropriate
comparison, a school nativity play, with a very promising and
ambitious girl in the lead. 'When I saw you, Dunja, I knew it was

an opportunity – you have no idea what an opportunity, after aaall theeese yeeeears, a real opportunity!'

Ohhhh, yoooooy, aaaarrrgh – the rustling in Dunja's head (and we won't even mention her stomach) brought grumpy/tired/ desperate furrows to her brow, but the *Grand* Detective beat back all resistance (*I just wanna go home!*) with a pickaxe: 'Sure, Mirela, but please, finish your thought. An opportunity for . . . ?'

'Aren't you hungry? Wouldn't you like to eat? You look pale – maybe you're hungry?' The performer, at variance with her role, twice cleared her throat and possibly (the G.D. was not entirely sure) blushed a little. 'I'll bring the food in now, don't worry. Oh, Dunja, I'm so happy to see you!'

'Uhh, uhh, uhh,' – the G.D., tensing like a meerkat, pressed her elbows to her knees and, ouuuch, stretched her lower back – 'uhh, I'm not hungry, Mirela. Really, that's the last thing on my mind. But please, tell me what you meant just now by *a real opportunity.*'

'Oh, Dunja, forget it, just forget it.' Mirela flapped her little hand and turned towards the kitchen. 'Sometimes things get ahead of me. I guess I meant I was happy, Dunja, to have the chance, well, that we'd have the chance to get to know each other better.'

Then she really did twirl on her heel and her face now seemed to be, oof, not merely blushing but, despite her make-up, *burning*. Still flapping her hand, she added that, in light of this o p p o r t u n i t y, she had 'cooked quite a bit, Dunja, and even did some baking. I know I said *brunch*, but, well, it looks like it'll be a full meal – you know, *lunch* – and I do hope you're hungry because, like I said, you certainly look pale and hungry to me.'

She twirled onward, opened the kitchen door and, *swoooosh, tap-tap-tap, clop-clop-clop*, into the living room ran the whole feline procession, seemingly already fed. The little pred- ators laid siege to her in unison, and she did her best to fend them off – vocally only with Darling (*Go away, ick, shoo*) since she knew the poor creature's name; the others she tried flick- ing away, not with her hands of course (that would never have

occurred to her) but with her sandaled, rheumatic feet. With no
fucking success. With Darling, the biggest, taking the lead, the
cats out of curiosity (*Whatcha got there? What's that little wiggly
thing?*) only came closer, and the smallest of the four started
sniffing Dunja's toes (*ick, ack, ewww*), and when she felt the wetness (*ick, ack, ewww*), the u t t e r l y d i s g u s t i n g wetness
of the cat's nose, which had to be coating her skin in micro-
spores, all the frustration of that superstrenuous Sunday – the
overeating, the texting, the suffocating bus ride, the near-vom-
iting, and that awful Mirela – now collected in her tear ducts
and who could say, who could really say, what prevented her
at that moment from not just *flicking* the kitties away, no, but
actually *kicking* them, and kicking them hard, the way she had
once seen Dražen, on one of their rare family outings (where
had they gone? Gorenjska? Maybe Dolenjska?) kick at a toad-
stool, a fly agaric, and heard him, as he did it, swear under his
breath that the poisonous fucker was getting what it deserved
(*Now it's dead, it can't kill, can't torment, any more, Dunja*), who
could really say why, at that very moment, instead of following
her brother's example she merely clenched her fists, lifted her
legs onto Michael's sofa and pressed her feet – no, *kicked* them
– against her body. (Meanwhile, in the commotion, the damn
Desigual slipped to the floor. But did Dunja bother to pick it
up? Did she try to protect her iPhone and sunglasses? To check
if her monologue had become a dialogue? Umm, no. Not moving was a sweeter idea.)

Her pacifism eventually did achieve something: three of
the predators wandered off, one after the other; Dražen, however – I mean *Darling*! – hopped onto the sofa – was he autistic
or something? Well, at least he didn't touch her; he just snug-
gled beneath the soft armrest, curled into a pretzel and at once
dozed off. Now she too, carefully, taking every precaution not
to wake him, with her knees still tucked beneath her chin, snug-
gled into the other armrest, on the right. Cats – and this you
must understand – did not normally disgust her *so* very much,
not so much that she was actually afraid of them, and she had on
many occasions rather easily let her guard down with them, for

instance, with her friend Ana's Norwegian Forest. But Mirela's quartet, oh God, Mirela's quartet! They exuded a kind of – how to put it? – sinister – no, more than that . . . Mirela's quartet exuded an uncanny, an *unhomely*, yes, an *un-home-ly* threat!

Darling curled into a pretzel, Dunja/the G.D. curled into a bread roll: despite her knotted stomach, there was, all the same, something comical about this, and she tried – take note! – *tried* to at least smile at her predicament, if not, as it deserved, to *laugh out loud* at it. And just then (of course), when she was grimacing like a baby but finally, perhaps for the first time that day, able to relax like an adult – placing her feet on the ground and unclenching her arms – well, just then, with a theatrical 'Ooooh! Aaaah! Look what I have for you!', her hostess, whom she would sooner describe as a flatworm or parasite, returned. She wedged the door open with a piece of wood, allowing the kitchen's sickly yellow to gape into the living room (from where she was sitting, Dunja – let's hope she'll soon be the G.D. again – could see only its bumpy walls) and carried to the table, not all at once of course, three very *bougie* goldish platters laden with – y o u   c a n ' t   b e   s e r i o u s – figs, various cheeses, scones, raspberries, strawberries, blueberries, orange sponge with (visibly melting) whipped cream, potatoes roasted and boiled, rice, salad and – r e a l l y   y o u   c a n ' t   b e – fucking *squid*, certainly grilled, their little molluscous bodies singed red, their tentacles burnt nearly to black. She did not have the will to explain just how very much squid *repulsed* her or how very much she suffered because, as a devout heterosexual, she associated them with vaginas, or how vividly she pictured them (alive of course) as swimming, pulsating genitalia, and last but not least, how *repulsed* she was, too, by everyone who nevertheless went on chewing and nibbling their fucking calamari while contentedly smacking their lips, and also, of course, by everyone who tried to make her eat those fluttering labia.

'Come, Dunja, come to the table! My daddy always said that calamari is the very best source of protein!' The hostess/parasite quickly bent down in front of her, swooped Dunja's Desigual onto her wrist and – careful! – did *not* grab hold of her guest this time, for just as Mirela was extending her tiny hand, the G.D. resolutely (*painfully*) stood up.

'Come, Dunja, come!' she repeated as she hung the bag on the back of a chair (at the head of the table, of course) and sat down in the chair next to it – a somewhat official arrangement, as if they were planning to address, well, a crisis.

'You mentioned your father. Is he still alive?'

'What?' She cast a sharp glance across the *This Is It* poster at the G.D., and the G.D., hoping the flatworm might correctly interpret at least one pitiful gesture, nudged her plate away. 'What, whaaat?' Mirela repeated, fussing with the – oh my, they were *gold* utensils. 'No, no, no, no, we're not talking about that, nothing about that.'

Umm, dead then. So all her men are dead, Dunja thought and almost expressed her condolences, but Mirela had hurried on; she was already loading the hot foods, a whole serving spoon each, onto Dunja's plate in a way that resembled an obtrusively concerned grandmother. And was sort of likeable. Which is why Dunja, despite knowing that she would not be eating anything, made no objection to the plate-loading.

'Er, please, Mirela . . .' – at the sight of her hostess digging that big spoon into the molluscs like a damn shovel, her stomach did a flip – 'not that, please, none for me, really.'

'No?' Holding the shovel briefly above the table – Dunja easily imagined the slimy little bodies falling off and bouncing straight at her – she stared in disbelief at her guest, who understood that Mirela's 'no' was anything but a question – it was a statement, maybe an imperious imperative – since the shovel, determined as a razor, stopped directly in front of her, with sea juices landing on the tubers below.

'Well, bon appétit, Dunja! Bon appétit! I hope you like it!'

Abandon all hope ye who enter here, our G.D. surprisingly decided, and without a word, albeit with a look of reproach on her face – *reproach* to no purpose, since even if she had still been staring at Dunja and not already diving into the dead molluscs, even if Dunja's facial expression had been equipped with a fucking *caption*, Mirela would hardly have noticed, let alone

understood it – well, in any case, the G.D. irritably but word-
lessly pushed her chair away from *la table vivante* and crossed
her legs and arms in protest. She could feel the rumble of her
intestines beneath her hands, the hard work of her exhausted
peristalsis.

As the peristalsis goes, so goes the detective (haha), but
nonetheless: 'You know, Mirela, I've learned that you haven't
been entirely candid with me. Well, that you haven't been candid at all.'

'Kristijan!' She did not even *try* to put her knife and fork
down quietly, did not even *try* to finish chewing those horrible
little legs, did not even *try* to play the innocent. 'Kristijan! You
talked to him again, Dunja! Oh why have you been talking to
him, Dunja? I thought we agreed, Dunja, that you wouldn't talk
to him any more.'

'Agreed? We certainly made no such agreement.' She knotted her arms even tighter, in anger, and Mirela did the same,
except that what suddenly came over *her* was not anger but agony.

'Mirela . . .' – the G.D. moved her right hand lower, to her
abdomen (for courage? to pinch herself? to calm herself?) –
'Mirela, Kristijan told me . . .' – *told*? more like *confessed*, but
that detail was confidential – 'that he and Dražen did *not* fall out
over you, that he, Kristijan, could never even . . .' (um, careful,
G.D.!) 'had never even been in love with you—'

'Ach! That scumbag!' Mirela screamed, and two little, oh
fucking God, *squids* – despite being dead, they were no less
surprised than Dunja – tumbled from her plate. 'You see how
he lies! What did he tell you the first time, huh? What did he
tell you? He makes stuff up, Dunja, he just makes stuff up and
you fall for it! Oh, how you fall for it! Me, I keep saying one and
the same thing over and over, and I always will, but he invents
things . . . he makes stuff up . . . oh, that dog! . . . that pig! . . .
always adapting his story . . .' etc. etc. From one sentence to the
next – no, from one word to the next – in her movements, her
posture, her eyes, she kept stoking a bigger, ever more incan-
descent misery – her nervous hands, fluttering like finches over
her food, her crushed shoulders and neck and, needless to say,

the start of heavy, bitter tears – and at the peak of this misery, she stood up – of course she did – and started pacing back and forth next to the table, and then, covered in a sticky, glistening cold sweat, again crowed out the same refrain with which her *dramatis persona* had opened the drama: 'That scumbag, that scumbag, that scumbag! You see how he makes stuff up, and you, Dunja, you fall for it! Oh God, oh God!'

And yet – the Great Detective thought with a shock, frozen in her chair like some Lorelei on her rock – and yet, putting Mirela's theatrics aside, her point could not be entirely denied. Had Dunja (since the G.D. never would have) *in actual fact* been taken in by Kristijan? Had she in actual fact overlooked or, more precisely, *disregarded* his manipulative nature the moment he presented to her – the moment he conveniently *placed before her* like some personal ID, like a fucking passport – his a l l e g e d *inner struggle*? Had he – even worse! – been able to dupe her because she had believed him to be entirely sincere that day? Because she had associated sincerity exclusively with the revelation of torment and pain – after all, it doesn't require inner strength to tell somebody you're doing great, that you're OK – and then had further endowed this with a kind of goodness, a fucking nobility of character? Was her myopia the offspring of her own personal (but also a somehow more *general*) naivety, a naivety that pays obeisance to the least bit of candour? What the fuck! – she would have liked to shift in the chair but just then her sciatica joined forces with an intestinal cramp – What the fuuuck! she wanted to shout, maybe she had quit right when she should have begun! Right when she should have bound Kristijan's inner wounds into a fucking motive! Right when she should have laid into him, laid into him out of frustration, laid into him out of fury, and turned those damn fucking r u d i m e n t s into fucking correlations, into fucking causes and reasons, into a fucking story! A story that in all probability would have prised out, would have w r e n c h e d   o u t, her very soul, but it would have been – she could feel the pressure mounting in her tear ducts – it would have been, well . . . would have been . . . come on, fuck, what would it have been? Compensation, maybe? Oh, Dunja/G.D., do neither of you understand that the promise of compensation is the biggest piece of crap left over from Christian eschatology: it's nothing but ordinary fucking bullshit!

'And now you say nothing?' Mirela wheezed. 'Don't say nothing, Dunja. You know what is true, you must feel that Kristijan has misled you, Dunja. He misled you, but I have been nothing but good to you, I try only to be good, Dunja, only good good goo—'

'I get it, Mirela. Come on, calm down now.' She was telling her to do something she herself was at that moment incapable of doing – in her arms and legs a small earthquake was happening, and in her stomach, a fucking bonfire. 'From what you are telling me, I can only understand you to mean that Kristijan was the one who . . . that it was he who . . .' – she raised her hand to her throat, not to act out some grisly fucking murder, but to help her gulp down the lump that was forming there – 'that it was he who, well . . . oh you know.'

'Oh no, no, not that, Dunja, that's *not* what I mean, oh no, no, I don't mean that specifically, nothing of the sort, no, no, Dunja, not at all, never, I'm a good person, I only wanted to make it clear to you that he's been making things up about the three of us!'

'But if he's been lying about you . . .' – the G.D., shaking, decided, fuck it, she would lay into this utter madwoman just as she should have done two days earlier with Kristijan and his adolescent love affair – 'then he must have been doing this to deflect' – holy shit, she could not believe this was true – 'to deflect all suspicion from himself and place it directly on you.'

'Oh God, let's just eat! Please, I beg you, let's eat, you must be hungry, this whole thing must be so terribly upsetting and painful for you, and I'm sorry, Dunja, that it's so upsetting and painful for you, and I'll put everything right, only first, please, eat, Dunja, eat as much as you like!' She was leaning on her chair and rocking back and forth, and side to side too, and the G.D. – no, *Dunja*! – felt somewhat suffocated by the scene in front of her, by its rigid symbolism: Dunja too, these past few days, had been sadly rocking, rocking, only rocking o n a

s i n g l e   f u c k i n g   s p o t, rocking back and forth, and side
to side too, like a fucking wind-up toy, yes, nothing but a *toy*, a
doll probably, which somebody – who? Kristijan? no! – which
everybody was constantly borrowing, each in their own fucking
way, for their own fucking purposes and objectives, their own
completely banal and utterly cruel purposes and objectives, a
fucking wind-up toy that could barely still keep going (being
only a fucking toy), that could barely still keep fucking enter-
taining them, with its faulty mechanism, broken ceramic arm,
snapped-off ceramic skirt (a damn tutu!) and fucking chipped
base – a fucking wind-up toy that any moment now might fuck
shit fuck rock straight into fucking madness, fuck shit fuck—

'Shit, Mirela! How can I make myself clear to you? I am
not going to eat! I don't give a fuck about the food! I'm asking you about important things here, things that are vital to
me – get it? – *vi-tal-ly im-por-tant to me*! Fuck! I have lost two of
the people I loved most in the world and you keep harping on
about some fucking lunch! So fucking pull yourself together
and fucking *talk to me*! That is how you help me! Pull yourself
together! Find some fucking courage! If only somebody would
finally TALK TO ME!'

That Mirela would stop rocking, rocking, on the chair,
back and forth and side to side too – *this* Dunja had expected;
but that she would then cry out in a frightened, desperate
voice, 'Tea! I'll make you some *tea*!' and f l e e i n t o t h e
d a m n k i t c h e n – fuck! aargh! – this she had *not* expected.
A tooooyyyyy! A fucking wind-up toy! Clearly, she should just
leave, slam the door and never come back, but out of – hah! –
wanton, arrogant, bloody-minded stubbornness she refused to
do that. She grabbed her Desigual, collapsed onto the sofa and,
completely wound up, to the bitter max, she first checked the
iPhone (fucking *seen*), then, for a few seconds, shut her eyes,
but behind her eyelids . . . yes, even behind her eyelids (well,
what did she expect?) there was not much peace to be found—

—her mother, her mami, is nagging her father because he didn't
blow his top at Dražen when he really should have done, when

he caught him *that very evening* opening their *sacred drawer*, the
drawer where they, members of a foolish generation and the ene-
mies of banks, stored their hard-earned cash, and her father is
explaining simple-heartedly that Dražen had *only taken the coins,
and the boy couldn't do much with, what, a hundred dinars or so, it
wouldn't get him very far, haha,* and she, little Dunja, curled up
on the sofa, is observing them with her eyes closed and cooking
up a plan for her first grand larceny, her first suspicious sneak-
ing around and keeping a lookout, her nimble, silent creeping
and not the least bit creaking, oh none at all, from that very
same drawer, and not the least bit rustling, oh none at all from
those smoothed-out banknotes, or, well, only from two of them,
and her careful, oh very careful, but resolute rolling of these
banknotes into her pocket and her cunning concealment of the
curled cash beneath the shell of her plastic turtle, the queen
of her one and only shelf, and then later (exactly when, she
couldn't know), after her parents discovered the teensy loss, her
heaping the blame on her thief of a brother, oh the scoundrel, as
she batted her little-girl eyelashes and wrung her delicate white
hands and lowered her flashing almond eyes – *Oh, Mami, you
know I would never steal ANYTHING! I'm not like that! Oh Daddy,
Daddy, you do believe me, don't you? I would NEVER go through your
things or open any—*

—OK, Dunja, OK, having once been nearly a brigand, be
enough of one now – she opened her eyes and saw the stand
with the albums – at least enough to . . . Yeah, she thought as
she shifted to the edge of the soft sofa, that never-realised leap
into larceny was quite inspiring; it was inspiring to see, to merely
have a glimpse at, how determined, how resourceful – she ran
her fingers over the softened edges of the album covers – how
fucking *forceful* little Dunjica might have grown up to be, how
she might – from the tight-packed row she pulled out a random
Jackson: *Dangerous*, hah!, a most appropriate extraction! – how
she might have stood up to her parents, to her brother especially,
and forged her character through fucking ordinary *adversity* and
not through some *apocalypse*, which ripped open, no, burnt to

ashes, her fucking heart, how she might – she was already exam-
ining the second *Dangerous* LP: apart from the Batman sticker, no
major differences, at least none she could see – how she might,
therefore, as a teenager have graduated from the gentle, gracious
I'd like to have this and – she swapped the second *Dangerous* for
the first *Bad* (oh! she'd been here once already, or thought she
had) – and simply advanced to, well, the level of *I'm gonna take
it* – ahh, here we go, and pulled the second *Bad* straight into
her lap; so what if she had been here before, since everything
is always merely repeating, always turning tiresomely like the
earth with every new season – because, after all – she opened the
album – being brave is not always the sssame as being original;
bbbravery is a ssssort of remnnnant, a sssort of sssurrrplusss,
a kkkind of tessst, and alsssoo, yesss, a cirrrcusss and an ulcccerrr and an ulcccerrr and an uuulcccerrr – she was gulping
down the saliva flooding her mouth – bbbraverrry is a kkkind
of dddeluuusion, a legggionn of ettterrrnal jjjiiittterrs – gulping
down the tide flooding Dražen, Daddy, trying to dry them off,
to save them, the little sister little sister little daughtter little
dddaughttter trying to sssave them—

In memory of my Dražen
27–28 June 1991
Friday–Saturday

Your own
MIRELA
    MIRELA
       MI RE LA
          MIIIIIIIIIIIIIII
           SHE WAS THAT FIGURE, IT WAS *HER*
           THIS WAS THAT GIFT, IT WAS *HER* GIFT
              not heavy
              but BIG
        This was *her* gift in that plastic—

'—bags, Dunja.' *HER HER HER IT WAS HER* saying as she
entered the room,

I only have ttteabags, Dunja; I'm sorry I'm sorry I'm so so rrry
I wasn't v errry d d dorro *not so* do orroo *not so* dorro *prrepppaa*
aaaaaaaaaaaaaaaaaaaaaaaaaaaaaaaaaaaaa-
aaaaaaaaaaaarrrrr

✳

Porcelain. Shards of porcelain. All around *HER HER HER IT IS HER* shards of porcelain.

'Do what you must, Dunja, do what you must.' Mirela weeps this, wheezes this out, her head bowed low.

Is it the little girl weeping this? The teenager? The woman? Weeping, weeping this in a cold fever.

The water for the tea on the floor does not reflect. Water cannot reflect when it is cloudy. When it is pale.

And Dunja is a heap, Dunja is a ditch. Dunja is a contradiction. Cloudy, pale waste water in a ditch.

She touches a neck, touches a nape. Touches temples, eyes, ears, forehead, mouth and nose, a chin, soon collarbones and beneath them breasts, a *heart*.

Her tongue is thick and swollen. It is wide and spread out, it pours across her teeth, gets stuck in the gaps between them.

And now it is dry, it is dry, it hurts, it hurts because it is dry.

(She has dried only her own flesh, but – the tide? Did she wipe up the tide?)

What she breathes in is a breath
is fever is fire is god-awful pain
is a fucking right cross
is her father's is Dražen's
lethal exhaust
is STEAM is MIST or is maybe a GHOST.

But her breath is enough. Enough for her to crawl into a sitting position that is not, will not be, can never be upright.

(What is it she suddenly hears and smells? Is the ceiling cracking?)

'Do what you must, Dunja, just do it, do what you must, Dunja, I didn't, I didn't mean to.' *She it is she* in shards rocking back and forth among the shards.

Do what she must, do what she had to, do do do do what she never wanted to do.

'Miwewa, buh why?'

She it is she pressing against the shards, grabbing hold of them, squeezing them, loudly moaning and in the cloudy water gleams a girl teenager woman – gleams a chimera.

'An accident, Dunja, it was an accident, I didn't mean to I didn't I didn't I didn't mean to.' Clenching squeezing. Bleeding.

'Mirela, b-b-but wwwhy?'

(She runs her hand through her hair and removes a piece of plaster. A little piece of plaster that must have come down from the ceiling. A little piece of plaster that turns to dust.)

Shards next to *her it is her*, who is kneeling in shards, bright red shards – red confetti, red comets, *red glitter, Dunja, I put on red glitter. I'd never worn glitter before, but for him I was wearing it, I was wearing it for him, and I climbed through the window, Dunja, I climbed out and I cut myself, climbed out, I cut myself a little, and I ran, I ran down down, dooown to Piran, Dunja, to where we were meeting, and he was drunk, Dunja,*

(She runs her hand through her hair and removes a new piece of plaster, a little piece of plaster that couldn't wait to come down from the ceiling and . . . dust, dust, quicklime breath.)

Dražen was already rather drunk, and we went up to the church, and there was nobody at the church, it was a little past midnight but there was nobody there, and we sat on the wall and he was mumbling to me, Dunja, he started mumbling, 'Mirela, I'm sorry I said those things about you, I said terrible things about you, and today, today once and for all, I'd like to make it up to you,' and he wanted, he wanted to move closer to me,

(Dust, dust, magnesium breath and new new new little pieces are coming off and sprinkling down like snowflakes, yes, like snowflakes, like little grenades exploding on the floor and on Dunja too.)

and he moved really close to me, all the time mumbling, 'Look, look what I bought you,' and pulled from his pocket, Dunja, he could barely pull it out, a little bell, but in the darkness I couldn't see the picture printed on it and he said, 'Trust me, it's Michael's glove,' and in the same breath asked, Dunja, he asked right away, what I was carrying in my bag,

(Little bits of plaster keep falling and falling and lying dustily on the floor in a white-white blanket, a soft-soft blanket, which the dead and the living and the living and the dead are happy to be covered in.)

asked me what I was carrying in my bag and I handed it to him, joyfully, Dunja, because I knew he'd be thrilled with it, I handed it to him and, yes, he could have shouted with joy, could have shouted into the darkness, howled at the moon, howled at the moonlight, but he didn't. He started laughing, he was laughing, drunk, playful, playful and drunk, and he gave me a peck on the ear, 'Oh my, what a good girl you are, Mirela, such a very good girl, Mirela,' and I wanted to ask him what he meant but I was afraid, Dunja, I was afraid he didn't really like me so very much,

(And a chunk, yes, a *big chunk* of white ceiling breaks off and crashes precisely, precisely, between them, breaks off with such force it creates a gust, which Dunja inhales, shutting her eyes tight, as tight as she can.)

I was afraid he didn't like me, I wanted to be his whole world and even more, like he was to me, but he showed me, he wanted to show me, playful and drunk as he was, that my fears were groundless, Dunja, that they were entirely, completely groundless, and he hugged me by the waist and came at me, he was so playful and drunk with passion and he came at me, Dunja, kissing my lips, my face, and his breath wasn't like honey and it wasn't a dream, it wasn't at all what I'd imagined, what I'd so long been dreaming about, it was only wine, only booze,

(A second chunk of ceiling breaks off and the force of it creates not a gust but a breeze, a breath, which Dunja inhales and inhales, hoping it will suffocate her.)

only wine, merely booze, but I accepted it, Dunja, and embraced him, embraced him gladly, I loved embracing him, and I answered his kisses with intoxicated, Dunja, but in a totally different way intoxicated, devoted kisses, and, Dunja, it was then, Dunja, it was then that he slipped his hand beneath my top, and his touch was not what I'd imagined and what I'd been dreaming about, his touch, Dunja, it was not warmth but brazenness, the boldness of a blade, and it hurt me, Dunja,

(Oh may it choke her.)

and it hurt me so much I pushed his hand away, but he cursed and shoved it beneath my bra and grabbed my breast, Dunja, and it was horribly painful and I asked him to stop, to let go, but he, Dunja, he was so playful, Dunja, he was drunk and didn't hear me, he just went on, grabbing my breast, grabbing it hard, really hard, and he said it was like a mushroom, like a sponge, like a sea slug, like a sea slut, haha,

(If only it would choke her.)

and I kept asking him to stop, to let go of me, but he was playful, Dunja, he was drunk and didn't hear me and just went on, and he grabbed my thigh and started digging, 'Little sponge, sea slug, sea slut, hahahaha,' started pushing his hand beneath my knickers,

(If only it would suffocate her.)

I know it's just the booze, but I'm asking him to stop, to let go of me, I tell him that we're in love and that we have time for all these beautiful things, these beautiful things, although, Dunja, when he pokes his fingers inside me I go cold,

(If only it would deafen her.)

these beautiful things, although, Dunja, I'm begging him, 'Don't go inside me,' these beautiful things, but I'm asking him, pleading, begging him to stop,

(If only it would suffocate deafen suffocate deafen deafen suffocate deafen suffocate her.)

these beautiful things, but, Dunja, he's intoxicated, he's drunk, he still can't hear me, these beautiful things, and I take his hand, the hand which is digging between my thighs, and I don't move it, these beautiful things, and I take his hand, the hand which is possessing me, and, Dunja, I don't move it, not even an inch away, these wonderful things, and again I'm asking pleading begging asking pleading begging him, trying to get him off me, moving away, sliding away carefully along the wall, these beautiful wonderful things, at first only a little bit of space between us, beautiful things, but soon more distance between us, beautiful things, and he calls me a sea slut, a worthless whore, beautiful things, and again he comes at me, beautiful things, but I'm fighting back as hard as I can, I push him off me as hard as I can, yes, he's intoxicated, Dunja, just terribly drunk, terribly incredibly happy and playful, and he loses his balance and—

'Lies!' Dunja cries, coughing up all the dust – 'Nothing but lies, fucking lies, f u c k i n g   l i e s!' – and is bulging out her heavy eyes like she's pushing the white-white dusty blanket away from the door, a blanket the dead, only the dead, are glad to be covered by – and she springs to her feet but loses her balance on the dusty floor and falls, but picks herself up again – in the chimera's dust, the c h i m e r a's dust – and the landscape in front of her is suddenly changed, it's brown and red and swaying like algae, but popping and scratching and cutting – are those shards? in the chimera's shards, the c h i m e r a's shards – crunching and piercing and breaking too, but Dunja shuffles along, shuffles up to *her*, the c h i - m e r a, who is kneeling, to the three-bodied monster, whose hands are bleeding, and she reaches for *her her it is fucking her*, reaches furiously, and lifts *her it is fucking her* – are c h i m e - r a s so light? – into the air in a whirl of plaster and shards, of dust too, grabs her, the girl-teenager-woman, grabs her by the shoulders and shakes her and shakes her – *What did you just say, what lies were you telling me?* – shakes her – *intoxicated, playful* – shakes her – *Look at me, lying bitch, look at me, you slug you sponge you slut* – shakes her – *Look at me, sea slut sponge, and repeat that lie if you dare* – shakes her – *Look at me, c h i m e r a, and lie to me just once more, I dare you* – shakes her and shakes her and the girl-teenager-woman *asks pleads begs her to stop* but Dunja keeps shaking and shaking her – *That is not the story, those are not the reasons, this is Dražen, my brother, you bitch slug slut, repeat it* – shakes her so hard her face spills out and she can hardly see her – *You little slut slug sponge, repeat it* – shakes her so hard her gestures spill out and she can hardly see herself – *You slut slug sponge, repeat it if you dare* – shakes her so hard her words spill out and she can hardly hear her – *D-d-dunja, l-le-g-gooo* – chokes her — *can't b-b-breeeathhe* — chokes her — *You slut slug sponge, repeat it, that is not the story, these are not the reasons* — chokes her — *This is Dražen, m y f u c k i n g   b r o t h e r, my family* — in her fingers, a persistent throbbing — *This cannot be the story, this is not the fucking story, it's only your lies* — beneath her nails, a wild, wiiiild throbbing — *Do you think for a moment I believe you, poor, innocent, oh so innocent Mirela* — in her fingers, cascades, cascaaaades of blood, beneath her nails, a tiny scream — *L-le-g-go-a-me, D-d-dunja, caaa b-b-breeeathhe* — in her wrists, thunder, in her elbows, thunder, in her shoulders, thunder, in her chest, creeeeak creeeeakkk — *Do you think for a moment I don't remember, slut slug sponge Mirelllaaaa* — in her chest, creeeeak creeeeakkk — *Think I don't, huh? Think I don't, Mirela?* — beneath her fingers, a tiny breath — *I caaa, D-d-dunnn, I caaa breeee* — in her fingertips, a silky throbbing — *This is not the story, this cannot be the story, the fucking story, this is Dražen, my brother, my fucking brother, this is my father, my fucking mother, this is me, this is fucking ME* — in her fingers, beneath her nails, a little slit — *It's fucking m e, it's fucking ME* — beneath her fingertips, a reddish chill — *Le-g-g-gooo-a-me, Dunnja, le-g-g-gooo* — beneath her fingers, beneath her nails, Dražen's intoxicated playful happy drunk violent cold much-too-cold blank face, beneath her fingertips, a brother's fury anger and rage, beneath them, a brother's burbling, a brother's excuses, a brother's *you all owe me something*, a brother's thrill, beneath them *OH GOD, OH GOD, MIRELA, NOT ME TOO—*

—at which point she abruptly jumps back, letting her hands slide down Mirela's arms and over her waist, but she does not yet bring them back to herself, oh no, those beasts she does not yet bring back to herself; she looks at them first, looks at them as if they were not hers — the left wider than the right, the more quickly to kill you with; the right with longer fingers, the more easily to choke you with — and then looks at *her, yes, it is her*, but *she* is flushed and numb and her eyes are shut, so she can no longer, *because this is the story, this is the fucking story*, can no longer ask her whether *my Dražen, my brother*, when he was out of breath that night, when he was o u t o f b r e a t h, *when he was* d o n e w i t h y o u, also looked in bewilderment at his wrists and fingers and knuckles? Did *Draži, my Draži*, horrified and frightened and split in two, also, like her, look at his – h a n d s?

Ebb Tide

'So where did you vanish to last time, Duni? Do you know how worried I was?'

She had a new hairstyle. An elegant pageboy, parted on the side. It suited her. Now in more-discreet make-up, her face was displayed in a newly dyed, bright frame – an Istrian stained-glass window.

'I'm sorry, Katy.' She sank into her jacket's high collar. 'I really am, but it was all just too much for me.'

'First you bombard me with text messages, then you vanish! You should have told me, Dunči. You know I'd understand.'

'I kn-n-now.' Her teeth were chattering. They were sitting outside – of course they were, two smokers – and the late-November air was damp, which Dunja had unfortunately forgotten. But the evergreen trees had not forsaken her, how they looked at this time of year: a little compressed, *depressed* – or on the contrary, at rest? – under the weight of the grey-and-brown clouds, which, lined up like freight wagons, had to transport, above the region and *out of* it, tons and tons of run-offs – suppressed, unexpressed, unfinished, never done, done in error, overdue, gone awry, gone too soon, dead – to ensure that nobody, absolutely nobody, ever mixes the past into the present, to guarantee that in the spring, when the clouds again unveil the sky, each of us will feel the many, so very many, unlimited, unmeasurable, unfathomable, unbearable, un, un, un – all the radiant *possibilities*.

'So you what?' – her lips were now clenching not an Eve but a Glamour cigarette – 'Just upped and left?'

'Yes.'

The very next day, the very next sleepless day, she had packed her things, got on the bus, and left. The sky had been clear and blue, vast, with nothing at all to intercept at least something – s o m e t h i n g – of her waste water.

'Oh, Dunja, you're so strange. But I understand you, I do understand you.' She placed her right hand, her smoking hand, for just a moment above her heart, beneath her collarbone, which is undoubtedly where she kept her empathetic self. 'I hope you won't be angry with me, but later that week I telephoned Mirela . . .'

'Mirela?' And she too, a mirror, pressed her smoking hand to a spot above her heart, under her collarbone, where she undoubtedly kept her . . . burnt-to-ashes, desolated landscape, a black, the very *blackest*, swamp. A landscape she had not yet been able to endow with a comprehensive, entire, fully healed narrative. A landscape strewn with nothing but the charred branches of bushes and trees, a landscape strewn only with victims, only victims, only v i c t i m s, an abscess of victims.

'Yes. Mirela. I'm sorry, but she too was really worried. She said you had seen each other but that you had left her right after lunch, that you had been there for the last time – that's what she said: for the last time – and then she just went on and on about how much she liked you and that you're beautiful, beautiful like a fairy, and Dunja, I could barely get a word in edgewise. That woman! She's a real pain in the ar—'

'Umm, yeah. I know,' Dunja interrupted her friend and flicked ash from her landsca—, no, from her *cigarette*, onto the saucer. 'I know she's not the greatest, but let's not talk about her now, Katy. It's you I came to see today. I wanted to see you again. I want to apologise to you, Katy. I acted like a child, ugh, a horrible, jealous child. And I am horribly ashamed of myself.'

'You mean that thing in the summer? Oh, Dunč, what happened back then . . . Dunči, don't worry about it.' She brushed the air with her French nails. 'So long as *we're* OK.'

It seemed as if she was about to flick the Glamourous ash onto the ground but then, changing her mind mid-motion, she leaned forwards, still holding the stub comically far from her head.

'But Dunja, the thing you saw that day at the marina, well, that thing . . .' – she spoke in a whisper, but was rattling off the words – 'can we keep it between ourselves?'

'Between ourselves,' Dunja agreed, gingerly shifting in the chair, and felt through her jeans the plastic chill of the chair's edge, which her backside had not yet warmed. 'Brrr, it's really cold. Sure, Katy, don't worry. It'll stay between us, since – you remember don't you? – *we keep all sins between ourselves.*'

'*Sins*, Duni? What on earth are you talking about?'

About the pledge they made as children, which Katy obviously did *not* remember, which is why she too, only more nervously, now shifted in her chair, pursed her lips and crossed her hands stiffly over her knees, just as she always used to do when she was about to serve up some nimble excuse or lie for Dunja to swallow. That Thursday (or was it Friday?) she would have been (Dunja could read it in her restless eyes) *on a yacht* either *taking care of some elderly people* or *having a job interview, which I didn't tell you about because I didn't want to jinx it* or doing *something* – *something* connected with Duška, maybe talking to the father of a child who'd received a bump on the head from her daughter . . . either this or that, the endless back-and-forth, no, the eternal return, of Katarina's fictions. But before Katy could pick one, Dunja slammed the door, lowered the lock, chopped down a pine tree and whatever else was needed to dam the shallow stream and forestall the loss of damn time: 'Katy, please, I'm not judging you. We really don't have to go there.'

'You're not *judging* me?' the other murmured. 'But I was only—'

'Katy, it doesn't matter any more. Just leave it. Please.'

Her friend's hands wandered into her pockets, while her face drooped a little but then turned playful: the simple joy of alliance, the holy innocence of *feeling accepted*, yes, of being *eternally yours, your eternally affectionate Katarina.*

'But tell me, Duni,' – she cleared her throat – 'so you didn't discover anything new? You won't be writing anything?'

'I did. Something.' Her nervousness, which was hypothermia, and her hypothermia, which was nervousness, she hid by lighting her third Marlboro. 'But it basically added up to nothing. To basically nothing at all.'

Dunja, you see, understood – umm, no, at the time, Dunja only *sensed* – that nothing, zero, is the only real, the only p o s - s i b l e sum of love plus horror. Of adoration plus anger. Admiration plus contempt. Empathy plus enmity. Peace plus disquiet. The only possible intersection of *beloved brother* and *my brother the perpetrator*, the only r e a l crossroads of *Mirela Dolorosa* and *Mirela the murderess*, the only p o s s i b l e intersection of all elements, concepts and roles, the great equilibrium, as great as God. *Nothing* – Dunja sensed this at the time and felt a chill – was the most accurate description of . . . my, your, their, our . . . ambivalence towards the world. And just how, Dunja wondered as she angrily blew smoke into the air, just how would such a story, such a fucking story, unfold? As life, right? Not as some crime novel, social novel, psychological novel – not as any fucking novel.

'Oh, I'm so sorry, Dunč,' Katarina said, and took her hand in hers, 'but at least we got to see each other again.'

'Yes, something did work out.' She kept her hand in Katarina's for just a moment and then, since it felt awkward, removed it.

Katarina glanced at her mobile and announced, with some hesitation, that she had not been able to help herself and had mentioned their 'date' to Kristijan and Duška.

'Kristijan?' Dunja pulled on the Marley.

'He's got her interested in chess now, you know. She's obsessed with it. It's all she talks about, but I don't understand the first thing. Well, she'll tell you all about it. They'll be here in a minute.'

'Kristijan?'

'Yes. My fiancé, Dunja. What did you think? Despite that other thing' – she patted her hair – 'he's still my partner, you know. Regardless.'

'Oh, I understand,' Dunja hastened to swear. 'I do understand.' But all she really understood was that each of us in our own way is waiting for an endlessly open spring sky.

About the author

Ana Schnabl (b. 1985) is a Slovenian writer and editor. She writes for several Slovenian media outlets and is a monthly columnist for the *Guardian*. Her collection of short stories *Razvezani* (Beletrina, 2017) met with critical acclaim and won the Best Debut Award at the Slovenian Book Fair, followed by the Edo Budiša Award in Croatia; the collection has been translated into German and Serbian. Three years later Schnabl published her first novel, *Masterpiece* (*Mojstrovina*, Beletrina, 2020). She toured Europe with the English, German and Serbian translations of the book, which included a residency at the Museumsquartier in Vienna, the Literarisches Colloquium Berlin, and the first European Writers' Festival in London. The novel was given favourable reviews and mentions in numerous Austrian, German and English media, and was longlisted for the Dublin Literary Award. Her second novel *Flood Tide* (*Plima*, Beletrina, 2022) was nominated for the Slovenian Kresnik Award. Her third novel *September* (Beletrina, 2024) won the Kresnik Award in 2025.

About the translator
Rawley Grau has been translating literary works from Slovenian for over twenty years, including by such first-rate novelists as Dušan Šarotar, Mojca Kumerdej, Sebastijan Pregelj, Gabriela Babnik and Vlado Žabot. Six of his translations have been longlisted for the Dublin Literary Award, while his translations of Šarotar's *Panorama* and *Billiards at the Hotel Dobray* were shortlisted for the Oxford-Weidenfeld Translation Prize. He has also translated poetry by Miljana Cunta, Miklavž Komelj, Janez Ramoveš and Tomaž Šalamun, among others. In 2021, he received the prestigious Lavrin Diploma from the Association of Slovenian Literary Translators. Translations from other languages include *A Science Not for the Earth: Selected Poems and Letters* by the Russian poet Yevgeny Baratynsky, which received the AATSEEL prize for best scholarly translation, and, co-translated with Christina E. Kramer, *The Long Coming of the Fire: Selected Poems* by the modernist poet Aco Šopov, which won the 2025 International Dragi Award for best translation from Macedonian. Originally from Baltimore, Maryland, he has lived in Ljubljana since the early 2000s.

Other books out with Divided

In Thrall by Jane DeLynn
A dazzling classic of lesbian adolescence.
—Brigid O'Dea, *The Irish Times*

Darryl by Jackie Ess
Jackie Ess's vicious wit and humane soul refuse to settle for
anything less than an enhanced interrogation of human frailty,
here through the psychosexual evisceration of an ordinary,
relatable guy. —Harry Josephine Giles

How to Leave the World by Marouane Bakhti
Translated by Lara Vergnaud
Visceral scenes and fragments of shame, desire and displacement crystallise as sentences that are felt before they are
understood. —Bhanu Kapil

I have brought you a severed hand by Ghayath Almadhoun
Translated by Catherine Cobham
Many poets attempt to traverse the gulf between the experience
of tragedy and the ability to relay its magnitude to anyone else.
But few living have done it with such flourish, such sustained
passion and formal precision. —Kaveh Akbar

Bourgeois Coldness by Henrike Kohpeiß
Translated by Grace Nissan
Elegant and erudite in equal measure, this book will stand as
a landmark diagnosis of the practices of denial in our time.
—Andreas Malm

Disorganisation & Sex by Jamieson Webster
Being dragged into the orbit of Webster's mind is like entering
the Magic Mountain: you go in as a visitor, and stay as a patient.
—Tom McCarthy

Night Philosophy by Fanny Howe
The most important thing for you to understand is that Fanny
Howe is a rebel, down to the cellular level. She walks with the
prophets and with the unborn. There is no writer like her.
—Ariana Reines